INTO THE
RIVER

INTO THE RIVER

TED DAWE

Copyright © 2012 by Ted Dawe
Interior design and formatting by E.M. Tippetts Book Designs

ISBN 978-1-943818-19-8
eISBN 978-1-943818-20-4
Library of Congress Control Number: 2015956269

First hardcover edition June 2016 by Polis Books, LLC
First published by Random House New Zealand Ltd in 2014
Published by arrangement with Random House New Zealand
1201 Hudson Street, #211S
Hoboken, NJ 07030
www.PolisBooks.com

POLIS BOOKS

ALSO BY
TED DAWE

Thunder Road
K Road
And Did Those Feet
Captain Sailor Bird and Other Stories

To my father and mother,
Bruce and Jean Dawe.

"... and my ashes delivered to Otaki. Please tip them into the Waitohu; go to the yellow bridge (it's white now!) Down the road from Peter's house. Easy access I think. Then my ghostly remains will glide down through Ringawhati Bush and so to Otaki beach, scene of much fun in the past..."

(Extract from the will of Jean Dawe)

ONE

There was a tap on the window.

Te Arepa sat up.

It was Wiremu!

He had forgotten. After thinking about nothing else for days, he had forgotten.

And he had slept in, he could tell from the light.

"Wait there! I'll be right down."

He pulled on his shorts and checked shirt then made for the back door. The house was quiet: Ra had taken his sister Rawinia to visit his mother at the hospital. It took most of the day, this trip, especially if they went to Aunty's to see Aroha on the way back. Te Arepa would go next time and Rawinia would get minded. That was their system. The hospital was strict: only two visitors per patient, no exceptions.

He went out the back and let Wiremu in.

"Take your shoes off, man."

Their joke. Neither of them wore shoes.

"Hungry?"

Wiremu nodded. He was always hungry.

Te Arepa cut four big slabs off the loaf on the bench.

"Vegemite or just butter?"

"Vegemite, and thick too."

The two boys sat in the kitchen, their mouths too stuffed to talk for the moment. Te Arepa put his line on the table. Forty feet of green fishing string wrapped round the stub of a broomstick, with a big hook and an old cog for a sinker. Wiremu reached across and felt the tip of the hook: it was sharp all right.

"Where's Ra?"

"Visiting my ma."

"When's she coming home?"

Te Arepa shrugged.

Te Arepa got up and walked to the fridge. He didn't want Wiremu to see his face. After the slow study of the fridge's contents he pulled a chunk of meat off the side of last night's mutton roast, wrapped it in a piece of newspaper and put it in his pocket.

"Let's go." Te Arepa's voice was a little higher than he expected.

When they reached the bridge over the Pokaiwhenua they climbed up onto the concrete barricade. From here they had a clear view upriver. It was grey overhead and the water looked dark and dangerous. There was a series of willow-fringed pools where the stream changed direction. Each one of these contained a taniwha[1]. Everyone knew that. This meant that they couldn't swim here unless the day was bright. "It's just not worth the risk." Wiremu's catchcry.

They eased themselves off the barrier and then stepped over the remains of the little fence that kept any wandering cattle from taking a detour. After clambering down they worked their way up the river until they were well away from the road. At each place where the water spilled over boulders they both climbed in and began turning over the larger rocks. It wasn't long before Wiremu yelled "Bootlace!" and Te Arepa saw a thin eel about as long as his foot racing over the shallow rocks. The trick was to flick it onto the bank and hit it with rocks.

---

1 river monster

The tiny eel kept changing its mind: at first trying to hide under a boulder and then heading downstream after all, with the boys stumbling after it over the sliding rocks. With only a metre to go before it reached the safety of the deep pool, Wiremu managed to get a hand under its slimy body and flick it high in the air. They watched it bounce once on the bank and then fall back into the deep water.

"Good one, Wiremu, I had it, man!"

"You bumped me, man. Anyway, it was mine, eh? You get your own one."

After a while they came to the barbed wire fence where the Pakeha Goldsmith's farm started. They weren't allowed to go any farther. The word was he shot at people on his land. Hemi Davis said his brother had been shot at, and all he was doing was just leaning on the fence. It was some time later that Manu Wihongi told them that Hemi's brother had been stealing a farm bike at the time. Manu knew these things: his mother answered the phones at the police station.

The water upstream was slower and deeper. The sort of place where the big ones lived. About a hundred metres in was a stand of bush where the bank reared up high and the stream snaked in a series of deep pools.

This was the place. This was where the big ones lurked. No bootlaces here. They'd all get eaten. You wouldn't want to swim here either. Who knew what was lurking in the reeds under the banks? The big ones could live for fifty or sixty years: this was where they grew old and clever.

The boys crouched by the fence. Goldsmith's farmhouse, although two hundred metres away, was in clear view. They would be spotted as soon as they put their foot up onto the first wire. Without saying a word, Wiremu flattened out and slid underneath. Te Arepa followed. They slithered, eel-like, close to the water. It was slow. They must not raise their heads: Goldsmith would get a clear shot. They wouldn't have a chance.

Halfway to the trees there was a place where the cattle had come down to drink. The ground was cut up and there was no way to stop the stinking mud clinging to them. In some places their fists sank deep into the hissing mud before it became solid enough to push forward. Every now and then Wiremu rolled over to check that Te Arepa was keeping up. With about forty feet to go they were tired. Tired and foul with mud. It took all their willpower not to get up and run the remaining distance. But they didn't. They had come too far for that.

When Wiremu finally reached the fenced-off bush he wriggled under the last wire and sat up, panting. Te Arepa lay still in the mud looking at the older boy enviously. The last ten feet yawned before him.

"Come on! Come on Reps, nearly there!"

And so he was. Moments later he was through and sitting in the dense bush, next to his friend. They both looked back at how far they had come. It was an achievement. Not everyone could have done that. This must surely be the beginning of something special.

The bush had been fenced off and left for years. It towered above them, the broad leaves only letting through chinks of light. There was no wind here, and the only sound was the murmur of the water and the warble and cackle of some distant tui². Neither boy spoke now, aware of something powerful here, a presence that needed to be respected. The forest floor was damp and soft under their feet. No stones: just dead leaves and rotting branches. The trees were huge and it was impossible to see any distance ahead through the tangle of creepers and spindly koromiko. Te Arepa could see the tension on Wiremu's face: it was as if he was holding his breath. They both knew they were in a danger zone.

When they emerged in front of the clay cliffs, the sun came out and poured down into the rocky clearing. The water was deep here and took on the rich translucence of pounamu³. Wiremu climbed breathless onto a car-sized grey boulder. He pulled Te Arepa up after him. Together they sat, lost in the beauty of the scene. High on one

2   native bird with musical call
3   jade or greenstone

of the ancient matai[4], Te Arepa could see a bees' nest. The constant swarming traffic lit up in the sunlight reminded him of a firework called Golden Rain.

After a while they lay back, closing their eyes, and let the tension of the long crawl seep from their bodies.

"Eee, you're paru[5], man!" said Te Arepa, his voice breaking the spell.

"You're paru yourself, man!"

And it was true. In the hot sun their mud-caked clothes and bodies had begun to stink.

Wiremu suggested that they wash their clothes in the river and drape them over the rocks to dry. They climbed out along a log which hung some way over the depths of the pool. From this place they waited for the other to go first, the faint fear of taniwha clouding their thoughts. Wiremu slowly leaned forward, grinning at Te Arepa, then, just when he reached the point of no return, he grabbed the other's shirt and they both crashed into the water. It was deep and they had to splutter their way back to where they could stand up. They rubbed their arms and legs vigorously, the brown mud bleeding out into the current. It seemed to Te Arepa that it was wrong to muddy the crystal clarity of the pool. The thought perched in his mind for a moment, like a fantail on a twig, then was gone.

Next they took their clothes off, slowly, item by item, and rubbed them back and forth in their hands in the shallow water. When each garment was clean it was thrown up high on the bank. This done, the boys climbed out and stretched their clothes carefully over the warm boulders to dry. Wiremu bolted back and plunged far from the bank into the centre of the pool. When he eventually surfaced, he was gasping for air.

"Come in, Reps! It's really deep!"

He tipped forward like a duck, and there was a flash of bum as

4　native tree
5　stinky

he dived for the bottom. When Te Arepa could bear it no longer, he dived as far as he could from the rocky bank. They met down on the riverbed where they fought their buoyancy by holding onto heavy rocks. Wiremu's hair floated above his head, waving slowly like a dark flag and small bubbles leaked from his nose. High above them, the surface was a green glow. Both boys fought to stay down longer than the other, until Te Arepa pointed at Wiremu's cock, his face trying to indicate something wrong. After a few moments of Wiremu's watery incomprehension, they exploded into bubbles of laughter and made for the surface.

When they reached the shallow water Te Arepa pointed again.

"Hey look! What's happened to that? Got shrunk in the water?"

Wiremu pointed back. "Look! Same! Eel bitten it off?"

They both seemed to shrink even further at the thought.

"Let's look for some, eh? I bet there's some big old ones here. No one can get at them."

For a while they turned over boulders around the edge of the big pool, but found nothing except a few cockabullies [6] that flashed away as soon as they were exposed. The pool was surprisingly lifeless. After a while, Wiremu said, "There's nothing here, nowhere to hide. Let's search further down."

They found sticks and went down below the pool where there were grassy places along the bank. Places where eels could lurk. They waded slowly down the river, jabbing gingerly at the waving weeds that grew from the bank. Fear as much as concentration kept them quiet. Each jab urged the other on but at the same time Wiremu's suggestion that an eel might bite their cocks off kept Te Arepa's spare hand firmly between his legs.

Then it happened. Te Arepa's stick hit something solid, but not quite.

"Wiremu!" he hissed. "Something slimy and hard."

They watched the spot where Te Arepa's stick disappeared into the fringe of floating grass. Something stirred. A huge grey head peered languidly out from the swirling weeds. It had the vague slowness of a sleeper who had been woken.

They had never seen such an eel, nor even known that eels grew that big. It revealed itself slowly; mouth slightly open showing rough grey lips, little tubes coming from each nostril. Around its pitiless eyes there were deep, white scars. All this was taken in, in a moment, before the boys bounded for the far bank.

By the time they were on dry land the eel was gone again, but somehow it lingered in their terrified heads.

Wiremu struggled to regain his composure then he blurted out, "Big!"

Te Arepa nodded. "That's why there were no little eels back there; this one's eaten them all!"

"Let's go back, I don't like it here," said Wiremu.

They made their way back to the main pool. Te Arepa swam out into the middle but now nothing he said could persuade Wiremu to follow him. He sat on the boulder watching Te Arepa dive for the bottom, float on his back, do everything he could to demonstrate the safety of the pool, but Wiremu was immoveable. He'd had enough of swimming.

"Come on, man!" called Te Arepa, "He won't come here."

It was no good. Despite all his entreaties, the chicken noises, the clowning, it seemed that Wiremu was stuck on the bank for the day.

"I can see there's only one way I can get you back in the water."

"How's that?"

"I've got to catch the bugger!"

Wiremu made a contemptuous noise and rolled his eyes.

Te Arepa picked up the line and the little package of meat. "That's why we brought this, man. We didn't come to catch bootlaces!"

"That monster … he'd pull you in, he'd eat you up. You'd be the bait, man."

Te Arepa shook his head. "Watch me, Wiremu. Watch the man

who knows."

He carefully unwrapped the line, checking the knots that held on the sinker and the hook. Then he checked the sharpness of the hook with his thumb. It needed a refresh. Down at the edge of the stream he selected a wet stone, as he'd seen his grandfather do. He carefully drew the hook across the surface, gradually producing a shine on all its faces.

"Now it needs one more thing."

"What's that?" replied Wiremu.

"Blood. Our blood. Come on. Give me some!"

"Bullshit! You're not getting my blood. Who told you that anyway?"

"That's old as, man. Te ika o Maui[7], man. Now let's have it."

"You first."

"No worries!"

Te Arepa pricked his thumb with the hook and a dark bead of blood bulged to the surface. He painted all sides of the hook with it.

"Now you!"

"No way, one's enough!"

"It's got to be both of us, otherwise it won't work."

"I'm not gonna jab myself with a hook."

"I'll do it!"

"No way! Give it here then!"

He squeezed a boil on his leg and rubbed pus onto it.

"Yuk! That doesn't count, man."

"Yes it does! Pus is a kind of blood, the doctor told me."

Te Arepa shook his head, he didn't like this bending of the rules, but he baited the hook nevertheless and headed back to where the eel lurked.

This time they waded across earlier so before long they could stand directly over the place where they had seen it.

"Is this the spot?" Wiremu whispered. "I thought it was a bit further down."

7   *the fish of Maui* legendary name for New Zealand

"We keep upstream, so he can smell it. Now we gotta wait." They sat on the bank trying to be patient, waiting for something to happen. Te Arepa claimed that they had to keep very still because Ra said if eels can feel footsteps on the bank then they won't move.

Wiremu jiggled his leg, fidgeted, rolled around, until it was clear he could not remain on the bank a minute longer.

"Let's tie the line to a tree and then head upstream. Have an explore."

It was easy to see that he didn't believe there was any chance of catching the big one.

"He'll snap the string if we do."

"Tie it to that log then. If he bites the bait he can tow it along behind him and we can grab it."

Te Arepa didn't like the idea. You didn't catch eels by wandering off, but the mystery of what lay farther upstream, plus Wiremu's fidgeting, helped persuade him.

They picked their way slowly upstream, glancing back every now and then, only partly conscious of their nakedness. Wiremu led the way. They didn't speak, each lost in his own thoughts. They reached another clearing where suddenly they were bathed in strong sun. Here, any noise they made was buried in the throbbing racket of cicadas.

Te Arepa thought about his ancestors, making their way up this river a hundred years earlier, desperately seeking refuge from a Ngapuhi [8]war party. With a start he remembered the dark old story, about the rivers of blood and the lifetime rahui[9]. The place pulsed with angry ghosts.

Farther up, the bush closed in on the river and the boys, as if sensing the threat, moved together and continued side by side. Neither of them voiced their fear, but Te Arepa noticed Wiremu was continually looking back over his shoulder, and irritatingly, this made him do the same.

---

8 Northern tribe
9 a banning or embargo placed on a river after it has been violated.

Then they came to a place where the land reared up ten metres before them. The river had a cliff on one side and was flat on the other, as if the two banks had been separated by some huge underground push. There was a new noise ahead, a deep noise, more felt than heard. It was growing louder with every step. Another two bends in the river and suddenly there it was: a waterfall, the full force of the river rushing off the cliff top and tumbling into a deep black pool. The two boys stood in the billowing spray, and stared into its swirling surface.

It seemed a special place. Dark and dangerous. A place of death. There was no way of continuing. The cliffs on each side were sheer and made of crumbly yellow clay.

"I'm cold, man," said Wiremu, his arms across his chest.

Te Arepa looked at his own body. It too was covered in goose bumps.

"I wonder how you get up there." He pointed to where the river surged over the cliff.

"Want to go back. This place gives me the creeps."

"There'll be a way up. Let's just go a bit further into the bush, see if we can find it." Te Arepa turned and said proudly, "This is where our people ran from the Ngapuhi, they must have got up somewhere."

"Who cares, let's go back."

But Te Arepa, sensing that he was in charge now, made his way deeper into the bush: Wiremu had no choice but to follow.

Away from the river it was different. The cicada noise dropped to a distant buzz as they broached a stippled world of shadows and thin shafts of light. There was little to slow them now, except fallen branches. It was soft under foot, just mosses and a carpet of damp leaves. Then they found it: a break in the cliff where hundreds of years ago some earthquake or landslide had brought it all down.

"This is the place!" said Te Arepa triumphantly.

Wiremu said nothing for a moment: he was staring off into the bush.

"Yeah, but what's that?"

About a hundred metres farther on a flat shape jutted up from the forest floor. It was hard to see in the gloom, but something about the angles looked wrong, man-made. For a moment they stood where they were, not knowing what to do, torn between going on, going back, or exploring the thing. Without discussion, they cautiously approached.

As they got closer it began to reveal itself. Only the straight ridge gave it away from the natural forms that surrounded it: even this was softened by years of fallen leaves and a thick coat of moss. You could tell that before long it would melt back into the forest.

The boys stalked nearer, low and tense, as if it were some sleeping monster about to jump at them. Circling carefully, they found the front, gaping at them like the mouth of a cave. The interior was so dark that only when they had crept within a few metres could they see that it was full of shadowy forms. They loitered just outside, each waiting for the other to make the first move, both caught in a pulsing silence. The air became colder and the goosebumps stood out on their arms. Te Arepa nodded at the entrance. "You," he whispered.

Wiremu shook his head and looked determined. This whole thing wasn't his idea. Yet the doorway beckoned, as though begging them to come inside, to squeeze within its mossy confines, into the underworld. Te Arepa thought of Hine Nui te Po [10]and glanced about for the massive, crushing thighs. The mesh of stories that held him back was finally burned away; he was maddened and desperate with curiosity.

Leaving Wiremu wide-eyed and frozen, he crept inside.

As his eyes struggled with the darkness, familiar objects took shape. A huge old metal bed, the fireplace, the table, a chair lying on its side, the faded pictures on the wall, something hanging from the roof … and then, some dark bulk at the back that muttered, and struggled to stand up. Te Arepa's mouth opened to scream but no sound came. For a moment his movements were so slow he thought he would never reach the gleaming square of doorway. He had the terrifying thought that he was trapped now, in this dark place with the "thing". But slowly, with feet fighting to gain purchase, he barged out the entrance.

As he burst from the little cabin, he collided with Wiremu, who had just stepped up. A moment later both boys were tumbling and rolling among the leaves and twigs outside. Without a word or sideways look they picked themselves up and charged off through the trees, dodging creepers and leaping over rotting trunks. They ran and ran until their lungs burned and they could go no farther. When Te Arepa dropped to the bed of leaves that littered the forest floor, Wiremu threw himself down beside him, so close he was almost touching.

"What was it?"

"An old, old man, wearing white clothes."

"True?"

"And he was angry. He had this look, eh?"

"What look?"

"Like this." He gave Wiremu a fierce stare

"Eeee, I knew it was dumb to go there. Let's go home now. I've had enough of this. It's boring."

Te Arepa longed to return for one fleeting look. But it was no good. Without Wiremu, he couldn't do it. This would be a mystery that would itch away at him like a mosquito bite on the toe.

Back at the clear pool not a word was exchanged. They both dived deep and surfaced only to dive again, trying for the very bottom. The water was still stingingly cold. Perfect to calm their electric skin. To wash away the fear.

Five minutes later they were out again: it was way too cold. They stretched out on the big rock to dry off before putting their clothes back on. The sun was strong now and beat down on their backs.

"Good chance to tan our white arses," said Wiremu.

"Yours is pretty brown already."

"It's just my colour, eh? You must have some Pakeha [11]in you."

"Yeah, course. Santos, eh. Not a Maori name. That's where I get the

---

white arse from. And the green eyes."

"Is that the Diego guy?"

Te Arepa nodded.

"My grandma says he was a horny dude, a fence jumper. He seems to have got into everyone's whakapapa[12]."

"True. Ra says there was a big shortage of men after the wars, and Diego was a keen fulla[13]. Lady killer."

"He killed ladies?"

"No you dumb Maori, it's just a saying. It's like he was a stud."

"Ahh."

They lay there for a while, thinking it all through, mellowed by the sun's heat beating down and the rock's warmth seeping up. After a while they had to jump back in to cool off. It was a cycle that repeated itself several times before Wiremu finally began to put his clothes on and made to head back.

"Hey! What about the eel?"

Te Arepa had forgotten all about it and hurried into his clothes.

Wiremu got there first and called out. "It's gone! It's gone!"

It was true. The line had gone. Snapped. All that was left was the bit of broom handle and the log that it had been wrapped around.

"Great idea leaving it, Wiremu! Now I've lost Ra's eel line. He's had it for years. He'll be giving me a kick."

He unwound the handle and the remainder of the string and they started back along the river. Something had gone from their adventure. Instead of returning full of the stories of discovery and conquest it was all clouded by the loss of Ra's line. Te Arepa hadn't even asked to borrow it.

They made their way gloomily along the bank, not talking now: somehow there had been enough talk. When they got to the final bend, the riverbed became mud and was covered in weed. They hadn't noticed it on the way in. It swayed gently in the current like long, green

12 family, history
13 'fella'

hair. They were standing on the bank, staring at it without comment, when Wiremu pointed.

"What's that?"

There was one strand longer than the others. The recognition came to them both at the same time.

"The line!"

It seemed to come from the thick grass growing from the bank.

"It might have an eel on the end!" said Wiremu. "It might be the big one. That taniwha[14] eel."

The thought had already occurred to Te Arepa. He was thinking about how he was going to get the end of the line without going in the water. He had had enough brushes with monsters today and just wanted to retrieve Ra's property and go home.

Farther on there was a stand of scrappy manuka[15], some of their long, thin trunks almost silver. Sure enough, there was one that snapped off at ground level, giving Te Arepa nearly four metres of branchless stick. From the bank he could reach the point where the end of the eel line flicked playfully in the current. He could touch it, but not quite lift it clear. With Wiremu holding his left hand, he leaned out over the stream and carefully lifted the line on the stick. When it came to the surface its weight and the current tugged it back down again. After a few more feeble attempts it was clear that this was not going to work. Someone was going to have to wade in. And that was not going to be Wiremu.

Te Arepa rolled up his shorts. Slowly and carefully he stepped down onto the creek bed. It was different here from the smooth, stony bed farther up. His feet sank into the soft floor, creating a little cloud of muddy slipstream. Below the soft surface there were sharp things, leaves or sticks. There was no chance of a quick exit from this place; each footstep took a new level of commitment. The water above his feet was still marvelously clear and much deeper than it looked from

14 monster
15 small native shrub

the bank. Soon it was lapping at his rolled up shorts. For a moment he thought he would get out and try again, bare arsed. It was no good. Once back on the bank he knew he wouldn't get back in, especially if it meant exposing his poor cock to the ferocious jaws of an angry eel.

With another step the water was about his waist and he was able to grab the dangling line and wrap it around his hand. He gave a pull and immediately felt the dead weight of a snag.

What a relief, no eel to contend with.

He had had enough of eels and rivers; in fact he had had enough of the day altogether, and wanted only to go home. He gave another yank, harder and from a different angle. This time his yank was answered. A surge came down the line as the eel broke cover. A sick feeling flooded Te Arepa's gut as he struggled to get free, and struggled to stay up, but it was no good. The line was tightly wound three times around his hand. The boy, line and eel had become one unit. He plunged forward, dragged into the churned-up water.

The realization came to him as he gasped for air. They came to catch an eel, but here he was, caught by an eel himself. At the same moment, Wiremu screamed from the bank. "It's the eel, he's coming for you. He's even bigger than I thought."

Once Te Arepa lost his footing, it was difficult to get up again. The shock of being dragged under was added to by the knowledge that the eel was heading for deeper water. He took a mouthful and came up coughing. Wiremu was yelling something. The eel stopped again and went under the grassy bank on the deep side of the river. While every instinct made him want to escape, to swim towards Wiremu and safety, something inside told him he couldn't. His only chance was to think it through. He remembered Ra saying that once a big eel made the reeds, the only way to get them out was with a spear. Eels wrapped themselves around the reeds and couldn't be moved.

Te Arepa floated across the current until he was hard against the soft reedy bank. It was high above him and offered nothing solid to pull himself out with. He grabbed a handful of toitoi[16] with his left hand. His right hand was stuck out in front of him, taut and puffy in the tangle of string. He tried to pull himself forward into the current: anything to take the tension off. It was no good; every inch he yielded was taken up by the eel. The eel was playing him like a fish!

Wiremu was nowhere to be seen.

He had run off, the bastard! Now what?

The hand holding the toitoi was dribbling blood: he had forgotten that it was cutty grass. But if he let go, and put the bleeding hand in the water all the other eels would smell him. He would be eaten for sure. He had no choice but to hold on.

The current pinned him hard against the bank and somewhere in its mushy side he felt something solid … well, almost solid. His feet clawed at it and finally found purchase under water. He tried to climb up but found he couldn't. The tug of the current and the softness of the mud made sure of that. There was no way his left arm would be strong enough to pull him out. How long could he hold on before he gave up and slid under to drown?

He floated, water lapping around his chin, caught between the unclimbable bank and the relentless tug of the eel. Slowly his thoughts returned to the place they always went when there was nowhere else to go.

He thought of Diego.

Diego, chained in a cabin.

Diego, about to be killed by pirates.

Diego, heading for the gallows in Wellington.

Diego, jumping into what Ra called "the wine dark sea".

Diego, who had lost everything, except for one last instinct.

The desire to live. To stay alive. To be free.

"Libertad!" Diego had yelled as he jumped into the black water. "Libertad!"

"Te Arepa! Up here!"

---

16   tall, sharp-edged grass

It was Wiremu. He had found a way to cross the river and was just above Te Arepa with his shirt off and dangling from his hand.

"Grab this, man! I'll pull you up."

The shirt fluttered tantalizingly close. He knew the moment he let go of the toitoi he would sink. It had to be done quickly: his first chance was his best. Above him Wiremu lay face forward, one arm behind him holding something, and the other extended as far as it could go.

"Ready?" called Te Arepa.

"Go!" was the answer.

Te Arepa snatched the shirt with his free hand, clung to it, then, with all his remaining strength, tied a loop in it with both hands. It stretched and made a few tearing noises. For a moment he was sure it would split in two and that would be the end of it. But it held.

"Try to climb up, man. I can't pull you," Wiremu called.

He dug his toes into the mesh of weeds and this time he was able to climb. The eel kept the line tight, so he had to move upstream at the same time. At last he reached a point where Wiremu could let go of the branch he was anchored to and haul him up by the shirt. A moment later they both lay gasping on the bank.

"Let's get that eel off you, man, and get out of here."

Te Arepa could see now that Wiremu was as scared as he was. But he shook his head. He couldn't let it go. Not now. It had cost him too much.

"What?" Wiremu's face was incredulous. "He nearly drowned ya, we'll never get him out."

"Give us that stick," Te Arepa said, indicating the winding stick that Wiremu had brought along. He handed it over quickly, and Te Arepa struggled to wind a couple of twists onto the stick, just above his hand.

"Now you pull," he ordered, and the other boy pulled on both sides of the stick.

With the tension off, Te Arepa was finally able to free his hand. He ignored the deeply bruised flesh around the base of his thumb. They had a job to do. Something to finish.

Even with both boys pulling hard, there was no movement in the line. It was as though it were attached to the creek bed itself. The line disappeared into a patch of watercress which allowed no glimpse of what was on the end.

"What now?" Wiremu asked.

"Don't know. Something's gotta happen."

And then it did.

The big eel broke cover heading downstream. Both boys let out a yell. They had forgotten how big he was. Nearly as long as they were, and thicker than their thighs.

"He's a monster!"

"He's the taniwha of the river!"

The eel made his leisurely way downstream, the hook projecting from the side of his mouth. The boys trotted along, keeping pace. After fifty metres, the river changed course and crossed a shallow ridge of river boulders.

"We can get him when he crosses the rocks," yelled Wiremu.

As if he heard, the eel immediately made for the bank. It nuzzled its way into the reeds immediately above the rapids.

"Now's our chance," said Te Arepa. "We might be able to drag him over to the rocks."

They let the line go slack and ran to where it was shallow enough to cross. Once they were halfway across, they began to pull together. At first it seemed pointless. Nothing would shift this monster. But then his head appeared and he made a dash straight past them over the rushing rocks.

"Stone him, quick!" screamed Wiremu. "Stone him, man!"

They both dropped the line and picked up the biggest rocks they could find. The eel came so close to Te Arepa's feet that he nearly dropped his boulder. He threw it wildly. Although it seemed to score a direct hit, the eel carried on undaunted.

Wiremu was more considered, and dropped his directly on the

eel's head. The fish knotted itself in a violent spasm. Its silver underside gleamed as it thrashed in the shallow water. The boys sensed the advantage and pelted it with smaller, more accurate rocks.

"Get it in the tail, that's where its second brain is!" yelled Wiremu.

"Bullshit second brain!" grunted Te Arepa as he closed in on it, sensing the kill.

"It's true, my uncle told me."

That's what Wiremu always said when he claimed some unbelievable statement as scientific fact.

The eel had stopped going anywhere and slowly curled in on itself, as if trying to protect its head from the relentless barrage of stones. After a while all its movement slowed to a sleepy shudder.

"That's enough, Wiremu, he's dead now, it's just the nerves."

Te Arepa was anxious not to spoil the animal's terrifying head. That would diminish their mana[17]. Already he was planning a triumphal return. "Let's get him out!"

Confident now, they struggled to drag the heavy, slippery body to the bank. It seemed impossible. Their hands were hopelessly coated with slime.

"If only there was somewhere to grip him, like a gill or something."

"Wrap him in your shirt, Reps, it's torn anyway, it doesn't matter."

Although it was true, Te Arepa noted he always seemed to be the one making the big sacrifice. Wiremu was fussy about his clothes, baggy old hand-me-downs though they were. With the checked shirt tied tightly around the glistening body they were finally able to haul it up to the safety of the bank. They fell beside it, exhausted. For the first time Te Arepa noted the sky was getting dark.

"I wonder what the time is."

"I reckon it must be about … I dunno. We'd better get back."

Wiremu sat up as the eel's tail gave a lazy flick.

"Woah!" They were both startled, but then it stopped again.

"How old do you reckon this taniwha is?"

"He could be hun'reds of years old."

"Not that old, man, he's not a tree."

"No it's true, eels live for hun'reds of years."

"Your uncle?"

Wiremu nodded.

"Well that was before we came along. The greatest eel hunters the world has ever known," said Te Arepa grandly.

Wiremu liked this idea and sat grinning to himself, memorizing the phrase.

Te Arepa looked at his hands, both of them crisscrossed with cuts and beginning to throb.

"You ready, Wiremu?"

"Yeah, but I don't know how we're going to carry him home. Maybe we should leave him here and get someone to give us a hand."

"I'm not going back without him."

"It can't be done, man, he weighs as much as I do and he's sooo slimy."

They stared at its massive length. The twitches had almost completely subsided.

"Wait here." Te Arepa walked along the bank to a stand of manuka. He was able to break one of the skinny trunks off at the base and after some rocking and twisting had it free. They bound the shirted eel to the long pole by winding the line around it. There was something comical about it, like an eel wearing clothes in a cartoon, the ugly head sticking out of the collar. Most of their fishing line was used to secure it. After that it was just a matter of hoisting it onto their shoulders, like native bearers in a Tarzan movie.

Although Te Arepa's idea seemed a good one at first, the eel soon became very heavy. The ground was rough and they needed to put it down and rest every thirty metres or so. The trip back was much longer than the one in. Their legs ached and they rarely spoke. When they reached Goldsmith's paddock neither of them cared enough to crouch, even slightly. They walked on, silently bracing themselves for the shotgun blast that would end their exhausting trek. It would be a relief.

By the time they made it home it was getting dark. How good to see lights on in the kitchen as they marched triumphantly around the back. They lowered the eel onto the square of light cast from the kitchen window.

Ra emerged with a tea towel in his hand. "Now that's an eel to be proud of." He turned and called towards the house. "Rawinia! Come, see what Wiremu and your brother have caught."

Rawinia came rushing out but then drew back.

"Eee! He's an ugly devil." Then she said, "Why's he wearing your shirt, Te Arepa?"

"He got cold on the way back and asked for it … I reckoned it was the good thing to do."

"True?" she asked.

They all laughed.

In the old washhouse Ra slowly untangled the line and then slid the big eel into one of the wooden tubs. He put the plug in and ran water over it.

"Ooh! He's coming back to life," said Rawinia.

It was true the tail made a few languid movements as if waking up.

"No, they often do that, eels, this one's headed for the smoke-house. So boy, where did this one come from? Goldsmith's Bush?"

Wiremu and Te Arepa were startled. They nodded.

"How did you know?" asked Te Arepa, and then added guiltily, "We haven't been there before."

"That's the only place around here where you get eels that big. Further down the Pokaiwhenua they're much smaller."

"Why's that?" asked Wiremu.

"We don't fish there." Then, by way of explanation, "There's a rahui on the river where it goes onto Goldsmith's land." He paused, then said almost reverently, "An old one that's never been lifted."

He saw the boys beginning to look uncomfortable and he laughed.

"Don't worry! You're not going to have a makutu[18] placed on you. You didn't know."

"How come there's a rahui[19] on the river up there but not down at the bridge where I always fish?"

"That's a long story and it's time for Wiremu to be going home."

He turned to Wiremu who was leaning against the wall, eyelids beginning to droop.

"Wiremu, your folks will be wondering what's happened to you. They'll think that you've been eaten by this taniwha."

Then, noticing Wiremu's reluctance, he added, "You run home. Tell Mahu he's got half of a big eel headed his way in a day or two."

That night, as Te Arepa was about to go to bed, Ra called out from the sitting room, where he sat in front of the fire.

"Boy! You asked about that rahui. Come through and I'll tell you."

Te Arepa sat on the floor beside his chair.

"People talk about Goldsmith's Bush, but the bush isn't his, it's iwi[20] land. Our people don't go there much because they have to cross his land to get to it and there have been a few arguments over the years. A bit of bad blood. But that's not the main reason. The main reason dates back to your beloved Diego."

Te Arepa's face lit up: Diego was a name that always caught his attention.

"Just above the waterfall is the ravine where the Ngapuhi visitors finished up. It was the place where Diego taught us the power of secrets.

18   a curse
19   a ban on fishing
20   tribe

How to harness the fear of the unknown. He told us that if everyone kept their silence about this then there would be no utu. That a huge and terrifying monster would protect us."

"What monster?" asked Te Arepa.

"I can't tell you what he looked like but I can tell you where he lived."

"Did he live in a sort of cave house near the waterfall?"

"You went there?" Ra's tone changed to one of alarm.

Te Arepa nodded. "There was something there. We ran."

"So he's still there, eh?" said Ra wistfully. "It's been a few years I can tell you. No boy, that's not our monster, that's another monster. He gave you a scare, eh? What did he look like?"

"I couldn't see him properly. It was too dark in there. I heard a noise and saw these two eyes gleaming in the dark ... then we ran for it."

"Do you know what that was?" asked Ra.

Te Arepa shook his head, eyes wide with suspense.

"It's an old billy goat. He's lived in that house for years now. That house was the place where the tohunga[21] lived. The one left to guard the river, preserve and enforce the rahui. He was so tapu[22] that he couldn't touch food, had to be hand-fed like a puppy. When he died the house was left. Our people won't go in there to this day."

"But I went in there. What's going to happen to me?"

Ra looked at him. "Nothing probably. There's enough Diego in you to give you protection, but your Maori part ..." he stopped then and said no more.

Te Arepa began to feel strange, as though cold water had been poured over him.

"Because you didn't know ... that's not as bad. Had you done it knowingly ..." his words broke off and he thought for a moment. "Had you done it knowingly, it would have been like you were challenging

---

21 Spirit doctor
22 sacred

the spirit world. Not wise, eh?" Ra seemed thoughtful, like there was something else that was troubling him. "Anyway, it's my fault really, I should have told you ... I should have guessed you'd find your way in there one day."

"But that's where the terrifying monster lives, the one that keeps the Ngapuhi away?"

"No, boy. He's much more potent than that. Closer to home." He chuckled and he leaned forward to touch Te Arepa on the forehead with his index finger. "He lives right there. That's where he lives, and once he has been set loose there is nothing in the world that can stop him."

Te Arepa looked disappointed.

"He's just imaginary?"

"There is nothing *just imaginary* about it, boy. The Ngapuhi fear of what happened to their war party was what kept us safe, what saved us, during the dangerous days when Pakeha brought guns to this country. Everyone had their eye on each other's land, everyone seemed to have an old score to settle."

"So what should I do now?"

"You sit quietly. Time for karakia[23], then bed for you."

Ra began his long chant. The familiar tauparapara[24], the lengthy introduction that was like the family signature. Then he went back to the darkness. The darkness before the universe was created. The time when nothing existed. Nothing except the possibility of existence.

Te Arepa leant against the chair. He knew the chant would be long. Exhausting. He knew that the chant was because of him. His fault. That it had to undo the damage that he had caused by going into the old cave of the tohunga. His mind raced with fearful possibilities. A blur of eel, the dank mossy cave of the goat, the deep hidden recesses of the river, Goldsmith's shotgun, and behind them all was his main fear. Death. That it would take his mother. Then Ra, Rawinia and himself.

---

23   prayers
24   introductory remarks before formal Maori oratory

He was awoken by Ra's hand on his shoulder. "You go off to bed now."

Once in his bed, sleep, which had fallen on him so quickly during Ra's karakia, was now elusive. His whole body was awash with unease. He had violated something. Transgressed. There would be consequences. Even Ra couldn't protect him from that. It was many hours before sleep finally found him, and it seemed only moments later that he awoke to the dawn's first bird sounds, panting and drenched with sweat.

Two

"Ra, tell me about the pirate, about Diego."

"Aue! You porangi[25] boy! What about your other tipuna[26]? What about their stories?"

"Tell me about Diego."

Ra chuckled. He knew Te Arepa wouldn't be denied – and it was a tale he loved to tell.

"Diego!

"The man from the sea, our people called him, or sometimes, Tangaroa's offering."

Ra settled back before the fire and Te Arepa nestled on the floor between his legs.

"It had been a time of hardship. The sickness had come and many of our strongest died early on. We had no cure. As if this wasn't enough, or maybe because of this sickness, the northern tribes began to push their dominance.

---

25 Mad, crazy
26 ancestors

"These raids, once rare and timid, now became more frequent and daring. The Ngapuhi had been given guns and now, in their greedy eyes, the rest of Te ika o Maui was theirs for the taking.

"Our iwi had lost many of its best men to the sickness and it was only a matter of time before the Ngapuhi wiped us out completely. All the men killed. All the women carried off. We were a people in decline. The mantle of defeat began to settle upon us. We were ripe for the taking.

"Sometimes, before a great event, there are auguries. The first signs are small. Barely noticeable. A certain kuia[27] had complained that someone had been taking kumara from her storehouse. Now this was a serious accusation, one not made lightly. It pointed to a thief within the whanau[28] itself. The elders wouldn't hear of it. They maintained it was the patupaiarehe[29], the fairy people. But this kuia wouldn't be fobbed off with childish explanations. Her complaints grew louder and more insistent. They were tearing us apart. Ill feeling grew. Something had to be done.

"And this woman was not just any woman. This was Ngahuia, your great-great-grandmother. Her husband had died of the sickness, so she had no man to avenge her. No man to watch out for her. It fell to Ngahuia herself, to lie in wait. But then she was Kahungunu, the daughter of a rangatira[30] ... a real wahinetoa[31] this one, fearless and haughty. As if we didn't have enough problems already."

Ra smiled. He loved stories about this fiery woman.

"All night she waited, armed with a sharpened ko, a digging stick. This was a woman's weapon: she couldn't touch taiaha[32] or patu[33] because they were tapu. Mind you boy, a ko in the hands of Ngahuia

---

27 old woman
28 extended family
29 bush fairies
30 Chief
31 female leader
32 spear
33 hand club

… whew! … not something to be taken lightly."

He held up his stick, as if to strike.

"Days passed, but there was nothing. The thefts, which she claimed had been a nightly event, now stopped. Everyone thought she was making a fool of herself. That she had been greedy. Or that she couldn't count. Maybe even that she had gone mad since her husband died. Of course no one was brave enough to say this to her face. Anyway, after a few nights of wakefulness and bad sleep she was at the point of giving up.

"Then, it happened. In the blackest hour of night there came a terrific crashing and roaring and screaming. In a moment the whole pa was on its feet. The men grabbed their weapons and ran forward. This could mean only one thing: a night raid from the Ngapuhi, the one that would finish us off. But they were wrong.

"Instead all they found was Ngahuia … Ngahuia with her arms and legs wrapped around a man … a Pakeha."

Ra paused, seeming to recall the events of more than a century ago as though they had happened yesterday.

"He was brought back, this Pakeha, back to the wharenui. Everyone was awake now, the whole kainga[34]. Most of them had seen white men before from time to time but never one like this. He had long hair like us, not cut short in the missionary fashion, but long and plaited. In each ear there was a gold ring. And his eyes! His eyes were the colour of pounamu."

Ra seized the moss-green tiki that always hung around his neck and held it out for Te Arepa to look at.

"Yes, Te Arepa, your colour. But this wasn't all. Something else held the eyes of all those present. His legs: they were shackled in iron chains.

"These shocked our people.

"Chains. The Pakeha tools of capture. These chains in the end set him free. Saved him from a sudden death, from ending up in the hangi³⁵ pit the next day maybe.

"Those in the iwi who spoke a little English were brought forward to find out who he was and where he had come from. It was a slow business: he spoke only a little English himself, not much more than our people.

"Once we learned he was not Ngapuhi, the fists were slowly unclenched, the weapons put down. In the course of the next few hours, few days, few weeks, his story came out.

"His name was Diego Santos. Born into a noble family near the Spanish city of Barcelona, he was the youngest son, the potiki³⁶. He had been deprived of his inheritance as he was born to old parents, long after they divided their vineyards between the two elder brothers. When he was seventeen and facing a life without the benefits that were his birthright, he joined a spice ship that was on the way to the Spice Islands."

"Where's that?" Te Arepa asked.

"Indonesia, that part of the world. His ship sailed all over the globe and Diego was on it for seven years. During this time he learned to speak other languages and became rich himself. He had gathered all the trappings of success.

"But this wasn't enough for him. Inside, his heart was burning with revenge. He wanted nothing more than to go back to his homeland: to show his parents what greatness he had made of himself, to show them how much more worthy he was than his brothers.

"For years, as he roamed the world, he had kept this dream foremost in his mind. The power of his whakapapa³⁷, the beauty of his turangawaewae³⁸. In his mind's eye, his old parents were standing in front of the white-walled hacienda. His brothers were there too. Everyone was waiting for him. It was like the Bible. He was the prodigal

---

35 feast from an underground food oven
36 youngest in the family
37 family history
38 a place to stand (somewhere you call 'home')

son, but better. He hadn't squandered a fortune, he had made one.

"When the chance came, he returned to Barcelona. He had never envisaged how much things could change. His parents, who were already old when he left, had both died. His brothers had neglected the family vineyards. The slow accumulation of wealth over many generations, and the honour of the family name, had been eaten away in a few short years.

"Nevertheless, when Diego showed up again he was fêted. His brothers fought over him. Whose house should he stay at? Who was the better host? For his part, he was hungry for their adulation.

"Each brother tried to out-do the other with the richness of their guest's lodgings. Vast bedrooms, scented sheets, feasts every night with Diego at the head of the table. Diego was flattered by their attention as he travelled from one to the other, luxuriating in the attention. He was glad to once again be part of a famous family, this time a celebrated part, not just the potiki. Little did he know that their motives were not brotherly: rather they were after the gold he had laid away during his seven years at sea.

"There was something that they had never considered. Unlike that of his brothers, Diego's wealth had come from sweat and hardship. He was not about to squander it on the schemes they suggested. He had lived where lives were risked and fortunes were made or lost. Where knowledge grew out of pain. Where histories were short and written in blood.

"In Barcelona, it was different. The rules had been drawn up generations ago. The father's role was to ensure that the fortunes stayed where they were. Even today, Te Arepa, Europe is dominated by these old families. They hold onto their land with steel claws. But the older brothers, once freed from their father's control, were not like that. They were greedy and bitter. Their fortunes had come without effort on their part and they wanted more. So they now grew impatient. Diego was not as easy to win over as they had imagined. Their true natures emerged: they stopped competing and joined forces to trick him out of his wealth.

"Diego was told that it had been his dying parents' last wish that the three brothers pooled their resources to rebuild the family name. To restore the fortunes of their once-great family. The brothers showed Diego the title deeds and documents of all they possessed. They didn't tell him that they owed vast amounts of money against these.

"The plan was to combine the titles and give him an equal share. In return, all they wanted from Diego was to use his gold to guarantee a loan which would allow them to replenish their run-down estates. Diego could now be the key to restoring the once-great Santos name, to rejoin the families who ruled Barcelona. These families traced their lineage back to Hamilcar Barca, the great Carthaginian who founded the city before the time of Christ.

"Diego's eyes gleamed. This was a dream even bigger than the one that had carried him around the world. It tied him to his ancestors. And it gave him something more, something that couldn't be ignored, couldn't be bought: mana. The mana that slowly grew from fifty generations living in the same place, growing like a mighty kauri tree amongst the stunted saplings that came and went. At last he knew what he wanted. This plan could satisfy that dull, hungry ache, deep in his gut.

"In due course his name was appended to a multitude of crested documents. Then these were sealed with red wax and imprinted with the brothers' signet rings. The next step was to visit the Jewish money lenders. These were the people who underwrote the enterprises of the high and mighty. The city was abuzz with the name of Santos once more.

"To celebrate their pact, a banquet was organized. The great wood-paneled hall of his parents' home was decked out in finery. This made Diego anxious about their extravagance. The brothers laughed away his fears. Appearances were important in Barcelona. The Santos family was giving notice that they were back: the world should pay attention. The three brothers were about to take their rightful place. This had to be done with confidence and pageantry. Empires were built on little more.

"Diego was flattered that they were making such a fuss of him. It showed him his brothers were sincere in welcoming him back into the family. He knew that at last his destiny had taken a different turn and he could look forward to a life of respect, of stability. Next would come a wife, children, all the trappings of a happy, secure middle-age.

"Diego was seated at the head of the huge table in the mighty feasting hall. All the best families in Barcelona were present. Their titles were long and their histories embedded in the story of the city. It was a circle that he was now part of. One that required more than money as the price of admission. The women were beautiful and the men refined. Their skin was pale and unblemished by the sun. Their clothes were heady confections of silk and damask. Their manner was confident: they had all the easy assurance of people living in a world that had been constructed around their tastes and aspirations. Their conversation was coded and ornate, peppered with Latin, French and English. Diego's final reservations about throwing in his fortunes with his brothers melted away. How he burned to belong in this glittering assembly!

"After the dinner the hall was cleared and musicians were brought in. There was dancing and laughter. Diego watched from the side, afraid of shaming himself through clumsy movement. He glimpsed now all that he needed to learn. All the customs and graces he lacked because of his years at sea.

"At the end of the evening there were toasts and speeches: a chance to show wit and learning. The final toast was to Diego. He was given an ancient chalice filled to the brim with dark red wine. His older brother told the assembly of his accomplishments. His voyages. His heroic return. Diego had never felt prouder. His heart was ready to burst."

Ra leant back in his chair, tired now with retelling the tale. The tale he had been told so many times as a boy. At his feet the two children waited silently for him to resume.

"And that, my mokos[39], is enough. Your grandfather is tired. It takes a lot to pull this big fish out of the dark swirl of my memory. I will tell you more tomorrow, but only if you get ready for bed now."

That was the deal and both sides had to honour it. There was no argument to be had.

The following night, Te Arepa and Rawinia were ready after tea for the old man to continue. He seemed to spend longer than usual fiddling about in the kitchen, and there were numerous trips outside. Each time he re-entered the room he pretended not to know what they wanted. Then, just when they were certain they would have to remind him, he raised a finger and exclaimed, "Oh yes, the story, I had forgotten."

They knew he hadn't.

"Would you believe my mind is completely blank, the story has gone!"

Not true.

"Are you sure that you have done all your chores? I noticed the wood pile in the shed had fallen over yesterday."

They had restacked it, and he knew it.

Finally he stopped teasing them and sat down. It was as if only a breath had passed since his last sentence, not a whole day.

"When Diego awoke he knew something strange and terrible had happened. Gone were the lofty-ceilinged bedroom and the scented sheets. The room stank and swayed and was completely black. His head throbbed and his mouth was dry as dust.

"Where was he?

"What had happened?

"Some time later — was it hours or was it days? — the door opened and a flask of water and a bowl were placed on the floor. Moments later it was abruptly slammed and the darkness closed in again.

"The truth seeped into him slowly, like poison. The ceaseless roll and creak had a more sinister meaning. He was at sea. This was a ship. He was imprisoned in a cell so small he could touch all the walls from where he sat. It must have happened during the celebrations. He had been drugged, smuggled aboard ship. Shanghaied."

"What's that?" asked Rawinia.

"Kidnapped by sailors," said Te Arepa, eager for the story to continue.

"It was a common thing among the rough seaside taverns that lined every port. A drugged drink or a blow to the head was how many sailors got their first berth on a sailing ship."

"That's not fair!" exclaimed Rawinia. "He should call the police!"

She was holding up the story. "There were no police, Winnie. Carry on, Ra, what happened next?"

"Waking up where Diego did, far out to sea, different laws applied. Being a sailor, Diego was better placed than most to adapt to his new situation, but he had become intoxicated with the vision of a new life. This was the plan that had stretched before him like a magnificent dream. It had seemed both remote and tantalizingly within his reach, like little fish in a crystal pool.

"While feasting on this vision, he had lost sight of what was happening immediately around him. After years of trusting no one, of constantly watching his back, he had finally surrendered to the idea of home. To the luxury of trust. To his brothers. He had found what everyone in the world wants: a turangawaewae … a place to stand.

"Now his brothers' betrayal had stripped him of the possibility of rest. He was like the toroa[40] now, the great winged albatross, facing a life of constant flight. There was a sliver of glass embedded in his heart and the only thing that could remove it was utu, revenge. It was all he wanted. Only that would ever allow him to rest.

"When he was finally released from his cell, the only sight of land was a tooth of rock jutting up from the horizon. He didn't need to be told that it was the Rock of Gibraltar. He was on his way to the Dutch East Indies. Diego was a strong swimmer and in his desperation might have been tempted to leap over the side if it were not for one thing: around his ankles were stout shackles joined by a length of heavy chain.

"It was a long, slow journey down the side of Africa and around Cape of Good Hope. The dull routine of ships was a life he knew well enough. But he was just a deckhand now, with no exalted status like in his former life. His lot was the menial duties of the lower order. He kept aloof from the other men, feeding on his anger. He had a mission and nothing would deter him from it.

"At Cape Town the ship stopped only for a day, long enough to take on fresh water and provisions. Unlike the other impressed men, Diego was locked below deck in a tiny storeroom where galley supplies were kept. Here, amongst the sacks of flour and barrels of olive oil, he pondered his position. He realized that he was treated differently from the others. Money had changed hands. His brothers had paid the captain to make sure he never returned. Something would happen to him, maybe even before the next port.

"Diego bided his time. The next stop was Colombo on the island that hangs like a pearl below India."

Ra pointed to the old fly-spotted map on the sitting room wall.

"Sri Lanka!" Te Arepa barked, as if it were some sort of competition with Rawinia.

"Ceylon, it was called in those days. Once again he was locked in the storeroom before the island was even sighted. He could smell the thick tropical air, even deep in the musty hold. He lay on a pile of sail cloth in the darkness, waiting, listening. Through the wooden hull he could hear the deck hands calling to the hawkers in small boats; the scraping on the deck as barrels were hauled aboard; then finally silence. Everyone had gone ashore.

"Some time later he awoke to unfamiliar noises. Something was wrong. He heard running feet. Fighting. Screams. Then voices from different parts of the ship. Foreign voices. Raiders. After a while the voices became less frantic. There were new sounds. Hammering and smashing. The voices came closer. It was only a matter of time before he met the same fate as the men left on watch.

"Soon, the raiders were on his own deck, then in the next room, and finally just outside his door. A flicker of light showed beneath it. Someone began to attack the thick wood with an axe. Stripping off his shirt, Diego rubbed olive oil on his arms and upper body. He would make himself as slippery as an eel. Perhaps he could barge past the invaders and down the narrow passageways. Surprise was his only weapon. As the door began to collapse, he reached into a flour sack and coated his face with powder.

"The door split down the middle and yellow light flooded the tiny room. The raiders were greeted by a glistening figure with a glaring white face, who rose up from a crouch, hissing and waving his arms. The men's eyes widened and they turned and ran off screaming. Diego waited, as their shouts echoed up and down the ship.

"As he reached the deck, the last of the invaders was struggling down a rope to a waiting boat. The moon was full and it was easy to see the trail of loot left behind. Nearby, two small boats were being frantically rowed to port, half a mile away. Diego walked to the railing and peered over. A heavily laden man was so startled by Diego's glowing white face that he half jumped, half fell, into the waiting boat.

"Diego looked about him. The barque, deserted now, seemed his for the taking. With a lantern he hurried through the dark passages, searching to see who remained. There were only three men still on the boat. All dead. The blood and debris made it easy to see what had happened.

"Diego was faced with two possible choices. He could swim ashore and hide out until the boat sailed on. Or he could take the ship."

Ra paused, letting the decision play in the children's heads.

"This ship was a barque, built for a crew of thirty. Ten men per watch.

"Diego did what others could never dream of doing. He took the ship.

"The first and most difficult task was to raise the anchor. Turning the bollards was usually a job for three. He found a saw in the carpenter's cabin and freed the ship from the sea floor. Once unsecured, the vessel immediately felt the tug of the outgoing tide and began to drift."

"Yea!" cheered Rawinia.

"But a drifting ship cannot be steered, so he made busy, unfurling a sail. With a single sheet he could luff and head the barque towards the open sea."

Ra sank back in his chair. "That's all for now, you two. It's late and my voice is tired."

"But you've hardly started!"

"A little more then.

"After weeks of captivity, weeks brooding on a fate that was monstrously unfair, Diego was now once more in control of his own destiny. Now, mokos, it is one thing to achieve freedom, but it is another to keep it. Chance is a fickle friend. Before long, he saw a ship on the horizon, bearing down on him. The wide ocean has pathways, and a ship with one sail will always be outrun. How could he explain himself? How could he avoid further capture, imprisonment, maybe death?

"Little more than an hour later the speedy clipper drew up next to him. This ship, the *S.S. Devon*, was bringing settlers to the new land, Aotearoa. To the captain, Diego's ship represented the bounty of the ocean. The salvage reward would be enough to fund his retirement.

"Diego's ship was grappled and boarded.

"Diego struggled to make himself understood in English. One look at the destruction wrought by the pirates and it was as if he was wearing a sign saying 'lock me up'. The captain ordered that he be taken to a small cell below deck. A skeleton crew was assigned and the two ships headed off to their distant destination.

"His situation, once bleak, was now hopeless. He was imprisoned, shackled, aboard a ship where he could not make himself understood; facing charges of piracy, and heading for the scaffold in a foreign land. In such times a man's true nature is tested. Diego had to look deep within himself to find the courage to continue. Here our ancestor Diego Santos was reborn and became one of us.

"His cell had no light, and was deep in the bowels of the ship. His needs were taken care of by the lowliest member of the crew, the cabin boy. This boy and the cook would visit him once a day to bring him food and water and to take away the bucket of excrement.

"For the first few days, the boy was terrified and the older man stood in the hallway, drawn sword in one hand and lantern in the other, while the boy rushed in to exchange the vessels from the day before. As the days went by, Diego perfected a posture that presented no threat. He smiled and greeted the pair and soon they were happy enough to be able to exchange the few words they had of each other's language.

"The boy's name was …"

"Oliver Twist!" Rawinia bleated.

"No, a different Oliver, this one."

"Carry on, Ra." Te Arepa was not one for digressions.

"This Oliver was an orphan who had earned his keep on ships since he was seven years old. Diego gradually befriended the boy, and managed to give an account of himself. This lad hungered for Diego's halting stories, and soon began to find time to steal down and talk to him through the locked door.

"Inside us all, no matter how old or young, there is a sense of justice. The unfairness of what this young Oliver heard lit a fire in him — as Diego knew it would.

"After a while the cook allowed the child to take the meals down unaccompanied and sit with Diego while he ate. This was something they both looked forward to. Each day Diego thought of some new episode, and, with Oliver's help, told a series of wonderful tales: stories of storms, of fights, of races and feats of strength or cunning, stories that made the boy wonder how anyone could be treated so cruelly, stories lightly delivered that made them both laugh out loud.

"One day Oliver brought news that made the pirate cry out something in his own language. The coastline of Aotearoa was there, on the starboard side of the ship. Landfall would be only hours away.

"Diego told the boy that from here he would be taken to a prison and from there to the gallows. The law had no time for pirates. He said, 'I have no regrets but one last wish.'

"'What's that?' Oliver asked.

"'To stand on the deck and breathe the salt air. To feel the wind in my face … if only for a minute. It is a sailor's wish.'

"And so it was that night, when all aboard were asleep, the boy stole the key. He found Diego up and pacing about in his tiny cell like a hungry leopard. The two crept through the passageways that led up to the rear decks, Oliver timorously navigating the black spaces, Diego carrying his chains so they made no sound. There was a bright full moon when they eased open the hatch. Not thirty feet away was the helmsman, his back to them. Sure enough, on the starboard side, across a few miles of white-flecked sea, was the dark outline of an unknown shore.

"Oliver looked at Diego uneasily, perhaps regretting what he had done. Diego had assured the boy that he would stay on the deck for no longer than a minute, but now they were in the open he seemed a different person from the prisoner Oliver had talked to in the cramped cell. They walked to the railing. Diego offered the boy his hand. Oliver shook it solemnly. The older man then stepped carefully over the railings, threw his head back, and yelled the word 'Libertad!' and …"

"And leapt into the wine-dark sea."

"You know this story as well as I do, Te Arepa. You should be telling it."

"No, I like to listen to it. My head fills with pictures."

"What does 'libertad' mean?" asked Rawinia.

Ra sat back silently for a while as if the effort of recollection had drained every ounce of his strength. After a while he said, "It means freedom in Spanish." There was a wistful tone to his voice. Then he sat forward. "That really is it, you two. Look at Rawinia." She had curled up in the nest of her blanket and could hardly keep her eyes open.

The following night the children arrived early, waiting for Ra to resume his story. There seemed to be an endless number of small tasks that needed his attention, and for a while the two children thought they were going to miss out. When he finally appeared he carried a small, shiny adze.

He passed it to Te Arepa who examined it carefully before handing it on to Rawinia. Neither of them had seen it before. It was black and glossy, like glass, and completely smooth but for two small grooves running up each side.

"What do you think this is?"

Te Arepa felt its weight again, heavier than he expected, and cold too, but there was something else about it, something a bit scary, something he couldn't define.

"Put it next to your lips, boy."

He did and immediately sprang back. "Ae! What's that?"

"That's the mauri[41]."

Rawinia took it in her hands to try it next to her mouth, but she could feel nothing.

"This stone has drunk men's blood. It has a history that our iwi shares with others."

"Where did it come from?"

Ra laughed. "Boy, that's a big question. If I was to tell you that story you would have no time to hear the last episode of Diego's history. So which do you want?"

"Diego!" they chorused.

Ra sank back into the old armchair, his eyes focused on some spot above their heads. They knew he was trying to remember. Trying to find the words to continue his recitation.

"This is a tale of death and birth, a tale of blood and trickery. It is the tale of our family and the tale which ties us into the history and genealogy of the greater group. You asked, boy, 'Where does this come from?'"

Ra held the adze between finger and thumb.

"Well, the easy answer is, from the head of Ngahuia's ko. It was brought into our tribe when she arrived with Tamehana."

Te Arepa was about to speak but Ra held up his hand to stop him. The stream could not be broken now.

"Tamehana was the first husband. The one who died of the strange sickness that took so many of our people. Maybe today they would say it was due to some foreign sickness, something missing from the diet, the land, or maybe we had become too isolated, and our families had intermingled and weakened. Who knows? But Ngahuia was destined to bring new life into our dying iwi, and the first thing she brought was this strange ko which had the sharpest, hardest blade we had ever known. Those grooves, boy. They were made when Diego drove the stone through the rivet that held the flanges of his leg irons together. This ko stone was hard enough to break the iron and free Diego. It was from here that his history begins to blend with our own.

"Diego was quick to learn our language and our ways. Many said that now, freed of his chains, he would be gone. That Ngahuia would wake one morning to an empty bed. But they were wrong. In us he found something that he had lost in Spain, or something perhaps that he had never really known. He found aroha, love. Not just the love between a man and a woman, but the love of the whanau and the love of the iwi. Here no one expected anything of him but he brought to us the seed of our liberation. Just as we were able to liberate him from his chains, his death sentence, he was able to finally liberate us from those northern demons who were poised to wipe us out. To take our land and our women … to obliterate our history.

"We had come this close to becoming extinct, boy." Ra's eyes gleamed as he showed the small gap between finger and thumb.

"Like the moa and the huia ... all the other manu that one never sees these days. The ones who live on only as bones or fading memories."

There was a sadness in these words that made him pause a moment before continuing.

"Within a year, Ngahuia was carrying a baby, one who was very important to you and me. It was my father. By this time, Diego had begun to draw down some of the knowledge he carried. His whakapapa went back all the way to the Carthaginians."

Once again Ra anticipated Te Arepa's question.

"They were the people from the top of Africa who challenged the ancient Romans for the control of Europe. The most famous was Hannibal."

"Hannibal with the elephants?"

"Yes, he was the one who crossed the Alps, but it was his father, Hamilcar Barca, whose history Diego carried. Some say he founded the city of Barcelona, its very name recalling his, but like all old histories no one can be sure. The thing was that the old families, the ones who felt they were the aristocrats, the high born, they took the ancient Carthaginian history as their own, and Diego's family was one of them.

"Whakapapa is full of buried treasure. Not gold and jewels or boxes under the ground, but lessons and answers to the big problems. Even problems that have never faced us before. Extraordinary problems that call for extraordinary solutions.

"This Hamilcar, before he settled in Barcelona, was the hero of his people. Like his son, he was able to save his people from obliteration because he could see further than other men. Past the limits that wall us in. He had a vision, like Te Kooti, strong enough to unite his people. It is a talent, this vision. Something that can't be taught, only recognized and fostered.

"Everyone knows the story of Hannibal and the elephants, but it was his father, Hamilcar, who set him on his way, by luring the fearsome

Roman legions into a bog where they could be slaughtered like cattle."

"Not a fair fight!" Te Arepa scowled.

"War is not fair. All through history, from the Trojan horse onwards, the really important battles have not been won by numbers or force of arms, but by intelligence, by strategy, by surprise."

Te Arepa sat back, arms tightly folded.

"Soon after Ngahuia became hapu[42] with my father, the word came that once again the Ngapuhi were on their way down from Te Rerenga o Whangarei[43], the meeting place of the whales."

"Whangarei?"

"Yes, the place that is called Whangarei today. They came in mighty waka taua[44], keeping close to the coast, decimating all who stood before them. They had given up some of their most precious land to the settlers to get muskets: fire sticks. These brought a new level of bloodshed to the land. The old grudges used to be settled by testing the other's strength: man to man, eye to eye. Now armed with these muskets, the Ngaphui saw that all of Te Ika o Maui was up for the taking.

"Now Diego quickly made his mark amongst our people. Although he knew nothing about us, about food gathering, or even this country, he had an intelligence that was different from ours. He saw things we didn't. At this stage our people all lived at the pa by Whakaruru Bay. There were other coastal pas we would move to when some rahui was laid down because kai[45] was scarce, but Whakaruru was the main one. With its sheltered harbor and fertile land it had much to offer. The Ngapuhi knew of it, and our people knew it was where they would land.

"We had a few inland pas, too. Small places mostly, just camps for hunting or maybe a refuge from coastal storms. When Diego learned

42 pregnant
43 *Meeting place of the whales,* North Island city
44 war canoes
45 food

of these, he insisted that the old people show him. He selected one up the Kahu Valley: where your eel creek comes from, Te Arepa. The Pokaiwhenua."

Ra lowered his voice. "It has another name, a darker one not used now. I will not say it. It means 'Rivers of Blood'.

"News came that the Ngapuhi had passed the tip of the East Coast. They had landed at Te Araroa, and were waiting for the weather to settle. It was only a matter of days now before they descended upon us. Our hangi pits were gaping reminders of what would happen next.

"It takes a desperate people to throw in their lot with a man who has floated ashore from a passing ship. To trust this … alien … to be their deliverer was a great risk, but our iwi had reached such a point of depletion and defeat that it seemed there was no one else.

"When the Ngapuhi made landfall, it was not at night or at a safe distance up the coast. So confident were they of their power and of our submission, that their canoes nudged the beach just below the pa while the sun was shining directly overhead. Their rangatira, Te Manukawa, stood on our sand and called out a challenge to the palisades of our pa, saying, 'Are you not men? Show yourselves!'

"Now Diego had told us that in his country there is a particular kind of bird. When some danger, a prowling cat perhaps, gets too close to her nest, she will land heavily on the ground nearby and appear to have injured herself. As the animal pounces, she flutters and flops away some little distance, not far, just far enough. Gradually she leads the predator away, until it is far from her nest. Finally, she flies back."

Te Arepa gave a "so what" expression.

"It shows the triumph of intelligence over force. This was the strategy that Diego chose.

"When Te Manukawa's men walked into the pa they found only one person: a young boy. And his name was—"

"Te Arepa!" the children chorused.

"That's right, and he was not much older than you are today, Te Arepa."

"And he saved the tribe."

"Slow down, we aren't there yet. When I say 'found him' what I mean is that they saw him squeezing between the tightly lashed manuka poles which made the rear wall. He appeared to be stuck. The men rushed towards him, hungry for the first kill, the mana of first blood."

Ra licked his lips and his eyes bulged. For a moment he was terrifying but the look disappeared so quickly that neither child was certain it had been there.

"When they were almost upon him, Te Arepa squeezed free of the poles, and limped off down the path, as though he had injured himself getting through.

"He was that fluttering bird. The one the Spanish call 'pajara'. Easy prey: but there was another reason to chase him. He was carrying something that may have explained why he was there, all alone. It was a korowai, a cloak made from the feathers of the brown kiwi and the kereru. A prize of great value.

"At this stage there was huge excitement. The Ngapuhi could smell victory. They poured over the palisade fence because none of them were small enough to fit through the gaps.

"Now Te Arepa had been chosen for the task because he was the fastest, the nimblest. He was also a fearless boy. He had to be: one slip, one tiny mistake and that would be the end of him. A fate too terrible to think about.

"At first it was easy. The ground was familiar, and apart from the korowai he had nothing to carry. Te Arepa was able to fake a few falls to encourage the warriors on, deeper and deeper into the ngahere[46].

"Soon, though, his pursuers became impatient. What they thought would be a short run, an easy capture, was beginning to torment them. They couldn't outrun the boy, so they tried to shoot him. Musket balls ripped through the leaves just above the head of the terrified Te Arepa.

"Te Arepa took off. His pursuers were now some distance from the coast and they waited for everyone to regroup. The fatter members had been left far behind in the chase. They bathed themselves in the water of the Pokaiwhenua just where it enters the tight little canyon that marks the beginning of Hikurangi[47], our maunga[48].

"Less than a hundred feet from where they sat, our people waited. They could hear their enemies' voices, smell their sweat. The Ngapuhi were angry, frustrated by the chase. When they had all caught up, and rested, almost as if they knew they were being watched, they gathered together for an earsplitting haka. The narrow gorge echoed with the sound of their voices and the thunder of their stamping feet.

"When our people heard the power of that haka, sensed the numbers and the strength of those who had come to kill them, even the bravest now feared that they were near death.

"But there was one who didn't.

"One whose face was the mask of calmness.

"One unworried by the challenges that rang out or the fate that now seemed inevitable.

"It was Diego.

"There was an enormous rock that overlooked the mouth of the valley. It was known as 'Te ngutu o kaka', the beak of the kaka, because of its shape. It was a local landmark and meeting place. Beyond this, the valley became so narrow that it was single file from there on.

"For days Diego and others had been digging away at the earth the rock sat on, until it was precariously perched. A small earth tremor, rain, a strong wind perhaps, could bring it crashing down. Diego had built up pillars to support it: flat boulders from the stream below stacked one on top of the other. It had been a slow and exhausting business. Now only these stone pillars supported the great weight, as with the ancient temples in Diego's part of the world.

"As the Ngapuhi picked their way carefully up the valley, cautious now, ready for attack, they heard a strange call ring out high above

---

47   The home mountain of the Tuhoe tribe
48   mountain

them. It was in a language the Ngapuhi, seasoned though they were with European contact, had never heard before. There must have been a moment of doubt for them. A moment when they wondered what they had stumbled into.

"The call was followed by a deep rumble of this kind that signaled an earthquake. The mighty rock where they had rested minutes before crashed into the canyon, completely blocking their retreat. It was followed by other rocks, some rolled, some hurled straight from the walls of the canyon. There was no shelter, no retreat. All they could do was rush up the valley.

"In the turmoil that followed, their discipline vanished. The fighting force that had terrorized the top half of the country became a white-eyed rabble. They must have thought Papatuanuku[49] herself had awoken and was about to swallow them up where they stood.

"But their troubles were only just beginning. Up ahead, the walls of the canyon became so steep that the only way forward was by a narrow ledge around a sheer face. As each man carefully picked his way around the rock, there was a thump or a muffled scream and he fell into the rocky stream forty or fifty feet below. Suddenly, moving forward was no longer an option either. They were trapped. Death came at them from every direction.

"One by one, the Ngapuhi were obliterated. By the end of the day, they were all dead. Those who hadn't been knocked into the river bed were killed when they tried to surrender."

Te Arepa gave his grandfather a fleeting look.

"It was not our way, but Diego demanded that not a single Ngapuhi should live to speak of it.

"It is said that the Pokaiwhenua ran blood that day all the way to the sea and it was many years before any of our people would take eels from it for fear of utu from the spirit world.

"There were two things left to achieve.

"These were the capture of the Ngapuhi's two waka taua and the defeat of those waiting at the pa.

"Not a word was spoken on the long walk back to our pa. All the elation of our victory had to be contained and all talk was in sign language. So sure were the Ngapuhi of victory that they had left only two old men and a boy to look after the canoes. When our people came over the last hill and saw their beloved bay with two huge war canoes pulled up high on the sand, they could be contained no longer. They ran screaming down the slope and overwhelmed the three Ngapuhi as they struggled to launch one of the waka."

"What happened to them?" asked Te Arepa.

"You know what happened to them."

"Killed and used for fish bait?"

Ra smiled. "Oh no. Nothing that ordinary." He slipped back into the past again.

"Their hearts were ripped out. Minutes later the smell of burning flesh and manuka smoke hung low over the beach. The rest of their battered carcasses? They would have lined the hangi that night and our bellies later on. It was a sweet victory. It was the story of Diego. It was where the strands of his whakapapa join our own, how his blood came to mingle with ours, in your bodies and in my own."

Ra sat back now for a long time, resting. The effort of telling this tale had drained him. He seemed for the moment pale and weak. Then in a little while the color returned to his cheeks, and Te Arepa asked, "What happened to the waka?"

"Diego wanted to burn them on the beach. This was the protocol of his people, but it was not our way. We took them out to the reef, just beyond the place people call Shag Point, made holes in the bottoms, and sank them. I have been told that the prow carvings of one is still there but I don't believe it. The fierce storms we get here would have smashed it to pieces long ago."

At this point Ra slowly eased himself out of his chair and moved through to the kitchen to make himself a cup of tea. Te Arepa was not to be fobbed off this easily.

"And Diego? Did anything else happen to him?" Te Arepa could not bear the thought of the story ending.

Ra laughed. "A whole life happened to him. Where do you think my uncles and aunts came from?"

"But did he do any other famous things?"

"My word, yes. He received a moko[50]. Became a famous Pakeha-Maori[51]. A land court judge. Returned to Spain too, as an old man."

"Why did he do that after everything that had happened to him? After his brothers had betrayed him and his fortune had gone?"

"That was the reason. Some small part of him had to know. Had to be sure that what he thought had happened to him was the truth. It had been the great turning point in his life and after years of land court hearings he had come to know a little about property, treachery and lies. He had to know."

"So he just sailed off and left your grandmother?"

"She had died some years earlier. He was an old man by then. But there was a restlessness in him that had never gone away. He knew the only way to get rid of it, the only way to find any peace, was to return to Barcelona and confront his brothers. This time he had no desire for their property or wealth: he wanted something else. Something hard to pin down. Justice, maybe."

"So he sailed all the way back to Spain?"

"This time he went back as a passenger on the Shaw Savill line. He had money now, and must have cut an interesting figure, with his European clothes, his brass-buckled sea boots, his moko and his beloved cigars."

"He smoked cigars?"

"Always. He claimed it was the only thing about Spain that he missed, and no one returning here from Auckland or Wellington would think of doing it without bringing him a box of cigars."

"So what happened on his trip?"

50 facial tattoo
51 European adopted into a Maori tribe

This time Ra was more matter of fact. Gone was the spell that had held them rapt.

"It was a long one. He was gone a year. Many of our people thought that we would never see him again. That he had gone home to his own country to finally rest with his ancestors. It made sense to them, for his bones to lie with their bones. That is what they would have done. But finally, Diego was not like them — or maybe because he was now one of them — he returned.

"His voyage was long and stopped at many places and he saw many things. It was these stories that I remember him for. As kids around the pa we would nag him until he told us another, and then another. We were greedy for images. Don't forget, this was the age before television. We never even had a radio. He told us about Sulawesi and Torres. About trading with the Chinese at Mallacca. About visiting the royal city of Kandi on a rickshaw. About these little plants that would wither and die before your eyes, when you touched them with your finger. He told us about his trip up the Ganges to the holy city of Benares. Of the smell of burning flesh from the cremation fires. About passing through the Suez Canal.

"Anyway, when Diego finally made it to Barcelona he found a different place. In forty years it had grown to a loud and busy city with street cars and big buildings. Little remained of what he remembered. All those years of living among our people had changed him, too. He and the city were strangers. The place he remembered now lived only in the fondness of his memory."

"Did he find his brothers? His fortune? Was it all a waste of time?"

"Nothing is ever wasted in this life, Te Arepa. Everything happens for a purpose. Part of him knew what he would find: the brothers dead, the fortune scattered to the four winds, the family in unweeded tombs. The city moves on. So it is with us all. His line had already been reaching its end at the beginning of his life. His dream of taking his place among the mighty was a boy's fantasy. For a family to survive through many centuries takes a powerful vision. An ethos. A certain ruthlessness. His brothers were ruthless, but they didn't maintain the vision that had been carried from generation to generation. Without it, the stone walls crumble and fall. The great families of Barcelona had survived by knowing this, and by eating the weaker of their number."

"It's horrible."

"It is their way. It is our way too. The Ngapuhi were after more land, more sovereignty. The coming of the Pakeha rocked the boat and the scramble for guns changed everything."

That night Te Arepa tossed and turned endlessly in his little bed as images of Diego flashed through his head. It wasn't just that he had listened to the stories, but rather that he was inhabited by them. Everything seemed to be meshing together: the rahui, the taniwha/eel, his whakapapa, and there he was, in the middle of it all.

THREE

"Haere mai[52], Te Arepa!"

It was Ra calling him from the kitchen. He stood at the bench with a letter in his hand.

"What's the story with this panui[53]?"

"Mr. McLintock called me into his office. He said he wanted me to do a test. He was going to tell you about it in the letter."

"Is that all he said?"

"He said other things, but I can't remember."

Ra looked at him, his head slightly tilted. He didn't like Te Arepa saying "I can't remember" and usually told him, "That's what stupid people say. Or people who are lazy, which counts as the same thing. Can't remember, won't remember!" But he didn't this time. He returned to the bench where he was preparing the vegetables for a boil-up. Te Arepa went back to his room where he had been reading. Rawinia came by with her deck of cards. She stared in for a while with that

---

52 come here/greeting (howdy)
53 letter

special look on her face. She wanted him to play but he was at a part in

his book where it couldn't be put down.

"When are you going to stop reading?" she asked.

"Half an hour."

She seemed satisfied and went out to the kitchen.

The following day, after Ra had taken them to school, Te Arepa saw him over by Mr. McLintock's office. He knew the letter had opened a door that couldn't be closed. All day, as he sat in the classroom, he wondered what it would mean.

That day after school, Ra was at the gate.

"I've talked to the headmaster," he began. He spoke slowly and deliberately, as though his words had been carefully rehearsed. "He says you're a smart boy. That you need to go where there are other boys like you. In the big city."

"Are we going to leave Whareiti[54]?" Te Arepa asked. That couldn't be right.

"No boy, listen. There is a scholarship exam that could get you to a famous school in Auckland. Mr. McLintock seems to think that you might have a chance. Evidently this is all because of a poem you wrote."

"'Taniwha Dream'?"

"There are others?"

"Lots."

"'Taniwha Dream' is the one he read to me."

"It's about that day at Goldsmith's Bush."

"Something about the 'tohunga clawfingers tearing the fabric of time.'"

"Yes. Then it goes, 'drenching the boy with his poisoned dream,/ blighting his life with an ancient malice,/a thorn-filled garden,/an empty chalice ...'"

"And how does it finish up?"

"The last part goes, 'Knowing now, till the end of his days/ He

---

54   name of the small village; literally, *small house*

could never alter, never erase/With angry tears, or happy lies/What's etched on the walls of paradise.'"

"Where did you get these words?"

"I got them from you, Ra." Then he added, "From the books I read. Some from the Bible. It's about that day on the river. The eel. The goat cave."

"I know that, Te Arepa. McLintock says it's good. It's more than good. He says a boy your age can't usually write poems like this. It's like the poems adults write. But then he said he saw you do it, so he knew there was no mistake."

"I wrote it."

"He says you have a gift."

"What gift?"

"The talent you have with words. You've got to use it. To do otherwise would be a crime against God. Remember the parable?"

Te Arepa nodded.

"Yours has been buried, but it's out now and we have to do something about it. It's what your mother would want."

"You've spoken to Ma?"

Ra shook his head.

Te Arepa was stung. He rarely brought up his mother now, it was too huge.

"So there's an entrance test. If you do well, then they'll offer you a place. A free place in the boarding house."

He could see that Ra had been already won over by the idea so he said nothing more. All he could think about anyway was that it would soon be Guy Fawkes and he knew for a fact that they had no fireworks.

A few weeks later he was off to Auckland with his cousin, Paikea. She drove the courier van. "From the Coast to the smoke, 3X a week" was written on the door in gold letters. No one messed with Paikea.

She had played softball when she was younger and it was as though her short wiry frame was always tensed, as though ready to catch a fastball. She would leap from the van, as tireless and springy at the end of a thirteen-hour run as she was at the beginning. Her theme was black. Black trousers, black shirt, black jacket and black boots. Her hair, which luckily was naturally black, was cut really short, like a man's. The only jewelery she wore was a big chunky watch, and a ring in her left ear. She lived with a Pakeha woman called Jinny on a little farm out of town.

It was still dark when the red van pulled up in the driveway. The gleaming wheels and blacked-out windows had made it famous the length of the Coast.

"Kia ora[55], Ra, where's this parcel?" she bellowed as soon as her feet hit the ground.

Ra said, "Kia ora, Paikea!" They kissed. "He's inside, all wrapped up and ready to go."

And so he was. Ra had told him to dress his best because they would judge him by what he was wearing as soon as they saw him. Te Arepa had polished up his black school shoes and Ra had even ironed his grey trousers and white shirt. He had borrowed a rugby club sweatshirt from his cousin Errol. Everyone respected the Whareiti Pirates Rugby Club. He liked it for the skull and crossbones emblem. Because of Diego, this had become his personal symbol.

The trip to Auckland took forever. Paikea claimed six hours twenty, but he reckoned it was much longer. They wound their way up the Coast through the darkness. As it grew lighter the towns began to get bigger. It was all new to him. At every post office Paikea leapt out, van hardly stationary, and disappeared for a few minutes, before reappearing with a bag over her shoulder. As the towns got bigger so did the bags. The van filled but the speed never varied. Paikea drove at one hundred and nine kilometres an hour. She said the cops allowed a ten percent speedo error.

Paikea was shocked to hear that he couldn't drive as if he didn't know his seven times table. Even though Ra didn't drive, and they didn't have a car, somehow she thought it was Te Arepa's duty and that he should have found a way. She was "born to drive", "lived for it", "only really came alive behind the wheel". And it was true. Behind the wheel Paikea had an intensity that he hadn't seen before. It was like her whole body became a part of the drive train. Te Arepa watched the muscles in her wrists, her restless eye, the nimble flick of her gear changes. All her movements were quick and precise. Two fingers pulled the gear stick back; the palm of her hand slapped it forward.

"Listen to the motor, boy, feel the power band flatten out and bang! Change up. As easy as that."

She taught him about picking a line for the corner. "Look ahead as far as you can around it. Pick a line that lets you through the fastest. I call it the sweet line."

She flashed him a serious look as if he had said something. "Never brake on a corner! It'll be the end of you. Brake in, power out, that's the rule."

After a while she got him to steer from the passenger seat. She rolled a smoke and gave instructions. "Go wider ... pull in ... pull in, man! That's better. You got it! Beauty!"

No one passed them for the whole trip.

They reached the outskirts of Auckland at about twelve o'clock. Te Arepa spotted its crenulated skyline as they crested the Bombay Hills.

His heart kicked when Aunty said, "There she is boy, Sin City."

About forty minutes later she dropped him at the gates of a huge school.

"Good luck, Te Arepa. I'll be back around five," she said, and then roared off down the road, leaving him bewildered and daunted beside a rugged stone wall.

The gateway was a massive arch. Along the drive there were little cardboard signs lettered with the words "Scholarship Examination" and an arrow. They led to the hall. This too was on an enormous scale.

The whole of Whareiti would be lost in this place.

At the top of the driveway there were lots of family groups, each with a boy his age amongst them. The boys were all wearing blazers, trousers and ties: he was the only one in a sweatshirt. The only one alone. The others were nearly all Asian or Indian, only a few Pakeha. He was the only Maori.

They gathered on the steps outside the hall, waiting for a word. The boys all carried pencil cases and rulers; he realized he was empty-handed. A bad start: he didn't think to bring his stuff. A tall, red-faced Pakeha man came out onto the steps. His hair was funny. It could be a wig, Te Arepa thought. The man cracked the knuckles on his long fingers then began to speak.

"Welcome to Barwell's Collegiate."

He smiled and waited as if he expected a response, then continued slowly and deliberately, as if he was talking to someone very old and deaf, or maybe someone very young.

"I am sure you are all eager to show us what you can do and, believe me, we are eager to find out. The test will take about two hours so I would ask all the parents and guardians to reassemble here at three thirty ... and we will give you back your little men."

Most people had a quiet laugh at this point. Te Arepa didn't.

The man continued like this for some time, stopping every now and then for the adults to have a chuckle. Te Arepa didn't listen to most of it; he kept looking around at the big buildings, wondering what went on there.

Then, at some cue given in the man's speech, all the boys surged up the stairs, as if there was a lolly scramble. Once through the big doors, they all stopped again. A woman at a desk was writing names on nametags and a man was ticking everyone off a list.

When Te Arepa reached the table, he had to say his name three times because the woman couldn't understand him.

"Your name isn't there," the woman said. "There's some mistake."

Te Arepa leaned over and pointed to it on the list.

The man intervened, speaking sharply. "So Santos is your name. How do you expect us to find you from your Christian name?" It was as though he had been cheeky. "See if you live up to your saintly moniker."

The hall was huge and filled with desks like a giant classroom. The walls were lined with dark panels inscribed with lists of names. The names of the fallen. The scholars. The sportsmen. The leaders. And the dates. All the way back to the 1880s. It was more like a wharenui[56] than a school hall: the meeting place for the tribe of scholars and sportsmen who lived out their times here, in the olden days. Handisides, Harris, Harris, Heremaia. Not many Maori names, he noted. Maybe his would be there, and one day, far from now, a boy like him would be reading it, thinking the same thing.

There must have been two hundred desks and chairs, each a metre from the next. He thought for a moment that someone was going to teach the whole group from the stage with a loudspeaker. The hall was filling up fast so he looked for a lucky spot to sit at. He saw the back of a brown boy near the front, so he went up and sat behind him. The boy turned briefly and smiled. He was Indian. He turned to the front again, ready to go.

After a while an old man — he looked a bit like Mr. McLintock — got up on the stage. He was wearing a black robe over a suit. Te Arepa could see the legs of his grey trousers coming out the bottom. He stood for a while in front of the microphone, looking about the hall and waiting for the huge room to settle, then he began to speak.

"Welcome, gentlemen. Welcome to Barwell's Collegiate. Look around you. This is called Memorial Hall. It commemorates our finest. The achievers, the leaders, the fallen. All like you once, little boys seated on hard chairs in this great hall. Their destinies were mere potentials, waiting to be unlocked and revealed. And that's what this place does. Has done. And will continue to do." He waited for everyone to decode his syntax.

---

56 traditional meeting house

"For now, though, it's a matter of 'Into the valley of death rode the two hundred', to re-phrase Tennyson."

He paused, as if expecting some glimmer of recognition, and then continued. "You are the few, the final few, pruned back from many more, and when you leave this hall we reduce your ranks to a humble ten. It's a harsh process. I am sure you are all worthy, boys. You have all known academic success. You all deserve to come here. But life is short and cruel and it is our responsibility to ensure that the culling is fair, if nothing else."

He paused again, giving time for this to sink in.

"This then, is your arena of choice. From this room lead many pathways. Once, long ago, I too sat here, in this room, pen in hand, anxiously waiting for a grey-haired headmaster to stop talking. Never guessing that years later I would be standing up here, doing the same." He paused again as if re-living the moment.

"Think carefully before you write. So much of what happens to you for the rest of your life could be determined by what happens between these four walls today. Give the best of yourself. Impress us. Thank you, boys."

Then he stepped back from the microphone to allow another man, younger and with glasses, to step forward and begin his lengthy instructions. After he had finished, booklets were given out and everyone seemed to ready themselves for the big test. Te Arepa was the only boy without a pen. It was too late. How could he put his hand up now? Whakama[57]! Everyone else started. The room filled with the deafening swish of the first page being turned. A hundred or so heads dropped down low over their pages. He looked around. The man who had mangled his name stared back and then walked towards him.

"What appears to be the nature of your problem?"

"No pen."

"No pen?" he repeated incredulously.

Te Arepa nodded.

The teacher looked around angrily and took one from his pocket. "Make sure you return it."

Te Arepa took the pen and read through the booklet.

Eighty tick-the-box questions and an essay. The topic: Who are you? Where do you come from? Where are you going? No other choices.

The first part of the paper was all odd man out. Which is the correct rotation? What is the next number in this sequence? Which is the correct sentence? He flew through, finishing it in twenty minutes.

Then he closed in on the essay. He liked that question. It was the perfect question for him.

On days when I feel lost or caught between two paths, there is a room I go to. It is a long narrow room and I stand on the threshold, peering into its darkening depths at the line of figures who await my call. Stretching out from the famous to the nameless, they are my army, my tipuna, and when I turn and once again face the open doorway with this legion standing behind me, I know there is no river that can't be crossed, no battle that can't be won...

By the time the next hour was up Te Arepa had written eight pages. He settled back in his chair, head drained and feeling as light as air, and then, slowly, he became aware of his surroundings again. It was like waking from a pleasant dream.

The papers were collected and he looked around for the man he had borrowed the pen from. It had seemed important that he return it. Te Arepa found him talking to a parent by the door, as the others all fed slowly out of the building.

"So, how was that, Santos?"

"A lot easier once I got the pen."

"And do you think that you are one of the chosen? One of the elite?"

Te Arepa looked at the boys, filing out. There was no answer to that question. Perhaps, because there were no other Maori present, he was a sort of elite already. He nodded and went out and sat on the steps. All around him was the excited clamor of boys telling their parents about the test. They were heroes today and could rabbit on uninterrupted to their attentive family clusters. He recognized the over-dramatization. The arms out beseechingly. The hands slapping foreheads: "If only…" He wished he had someone to perform to, someone who would let him milk the situation.

After a while everyone had gone. The big doors behind him were bolted and the man he had borrowed the pen from emerged with a box of papers.

"Are you staying the night here?" he said cheerfully. "Like it that much?"

He shook his head. "I've got to wait for my cousin to take me down the line."

"Down the line." The man repeated. "It seems that every Maori we have ever had here has come from one of two places. Down the Line or Up North."

He felt his face redden as the man strode off to his car.

It was nearly five when Paikea's van swung into the car park.

"So how was that, boy?"

"I thought it was easy."

She looked at him to see whether he was joking and then said, "You're a smart fulla; I'm sure that Ra's right about you."

After a few stops, they were back on the motorway and heading for the Coast. This time the van was full of parcels and moved sluggishly. It was even slower as Paikea detoured here and there to drop them off. Te Arepa soon found he couldn't keep his eyes open. It was very dark when they arrived.

Ra came out in his dressing gown and led him inside.

"Well boy, did you do good?"

"Hope so."

Ra smiled and nodded.

FOUR

Te Arepa was surprised to see Ra waiting at the gates of Whareiti Primary School. Rawinia was with him and they all walked home together. They made slow progress because Rawinia kept stopping to pick up lucky stones. There was tension at the corners of Ra's mouth. Something had happened. He knew that Ra would speak in his own time.

Halfway back they all stopped at the bridge, which was their custom. He sat next to Ra on the grassy bank while Rawinia fossicked about in the stream bed, washing her stones.

"You see the awa[58], boy? It's something that had to be bridged, and now we cross it every day. So we hardly think about it. Those people in the cars, I reckon they don't even know the river's there. But it was always there. When I was your age, there was a ford here and there was no way you got to school without wet feet, unless you were on a horse, maybe. And it's a pity. Dry feet might be good, but we learned something from every river crossing. The depth and temperature of the water told us what had been happening in the hills. Our journey crossed another journey. And when our feet touched that water for a moment or so ... it was a meeting, and in some tiny way, we were both affected."

A car rushed by across the bridge above their heads and they both looked up.

"People today in their cars, they miss that. It's the modern way, I know, but they miss that. What began as drops of rain on a leaf in the ngahere one day ends at the sea. So much happens to the water along the way, but the beginning and ends are always the same."

Te Arepa couldn't see where the old man was going with this, so he waited. Down near the water's edge the willow branches and reeds swirled lazily in the current. He thought about the eel. How its huge blunt head had terrified them, but had excited them too. He remembered the challenge, the greatness of the task. The glory. He thought about the goat cave. The makutu. His nightmares since that day. The feeling that he had been infected. Like his mother, with her TB. Lungs rotting away in the hospital.

"A letter came today. Barwell's has offered you a place."

Te Arepa said nothing.

"Think carefully, boy ... do you want to go?"

He had thought very little about the big college since the long journey with Paikea. It had been one of those things he had done because he had been told he should. Like going to the dentist.

"Some would say it is a great honor, a chance to make something of yourself. I am sure you have heard all the reasons for you to accept, but I want you to decide."

He looked at Ra. He could see this was what Ra had been struggling with. It had become a burden.

"If you want me to go, then I want to go."

The answer gave Ra no relief, he just chuckled and shook his head. "That's the one thing I hoped you wouldn't say. Why can't you just say 'yes' or 'no' like other boys? Then that would be the end of the matter."

Ra got slowly to his feet and they all walked on home.

That night Te Arepa was awoken by noises outside his window. He got up and peered out into the blackness. Down by the clothes-line, near the horse paddock, he could make out a figure. He tiptoed out the back door and crept up to the wash house. It was Ra. He was chanting. Chanting in the soft rain. The boy knew immediately that this was because of him. Because of his answer. He felt guilty, putting the old man through this. Even though he was sleepy, he knew he had to wait up and listen.

He went back to his room and pulled a blanket off the bed, then returned to sit on the back steps. The chanting continued as Ra worked his way through layer after layer of whakapapa.

He went all the way back to Hawaiki. Then into the dark generations beyond.

The regular beat of his voice soothed Te Arepa, and the names he had heard so often before paraded past him like a line of figures. He dozed off in the doorway and in his dream he saw them. The fierce eyes, the moko, the feathers. They gathered in a group before him, staring and shivering and swaying to the beat of the chant. There was one there, paler than the rest, who stood aloof. One with sea boots and a gold earring. His cold green eyes kept drawing Te Arepa away from the group. It was Diego Santos. The pirate. Te Arepa was mesmerized by him: his fearlessness, his arrogance. Nothing could stand against it. He had crossed from one world to another. He had faced down betrayal and risen again. He could not be denied. Te Arepa felt as if a choice had to be made. Join the warriors or go with Diego. He knew immediately what he had to do.

Ra shook him awake and they wandered into the little kitchen. The old man reached under the sink where he kept lumps of pumice floating in their bowl of methylated spirits. Plucking several out, he placed them in the grating of the coal range. Onto this a nest of dry kindling was carefully constructed. Then he lit it and waited for the water to boil. Day was breaking and the chorus of birds was building to its final raucous fury. Te Arepa watched Ra's plume of white hair as he moved about the kitchen, buttering bread and making tea.

They ate and drank silently. He could tell Ra was waiting for him to say something.

"I saw the pirate."

"Does that mean 'yes'?"

He nodded.

Ra seemed relieved. "It was hard, boy, and you didn't make it any easier for me. What did you see?"

"I saw the tipuna emerging from the darkness and assemble before me. They looked awkward and angry at being called forth. But the pirate was there. Near them but not with them. He was pleased. He grinned at me."

"Old Diego, eh? All the way from Spain. His hands soaked with blood. A price on his head. Tired of running, he chooses our whanau to plant his seed in. Our whanau to live out his days with." He paused. "And now he calls to you, boy, eh?"

"He was there. His green eyes shining like wet mussel shells. He had no fear … no doubt."

"The tipuna choose their own. We are their servants. They always walk before us."

His good clothes didn't fill the old bag Ra had packed for him, so he filled the remaining space with his journals. The Bible went in too, but this was just to please Ra, not because he planned to read it.

Three of them sat across the bench seat in Uncle Jimmy's pick-up truck: Jimmy driving, Ra by the window and Te Arepa straddling the gear stick. After a while they left the Coast and began to climb inland. Te Arepa could feel his feet heating up on the engine wall. The whine of the diff and the smell of Jimmy's cigs made him feel nauseous. They had only been travelling a few hours before the sadness began to bite at his heart. When the truck returned it wouldn't have him in it; he would be in some room, far away, in a strange city.

When they reached the outskirts of Rotorua[59] they turned off down a narrow, muddy road to where an old whare[60] stood amidst the steam. These were his father and Uncle Jimmy's people: only names to him. He knew that this would mean an hour or two but didn't mind. It would delay what lay ahead.

Uncle Jimmy's whanau came out and they all hongied[61] and then went into the kitchen for a kai. Jimmy's brother and another man were there, along with some women and a few little kids. No one his own age. Two little boys stood looking at him shyly, like he was something to be afraid of.

The adults settled in for a good talk so he slipped outside for an explore. The thick groves of manuka growing around the marae[62] concealed plumes of steam. Te Arepa squeezed through the bush towards the closest one. There was a small clearing and, in the middle, some bubbling mud. The grey crust around the edge was built up with endless, frozen high-tide marks, and covered in leaves and sticks, but in the centre it was smooth and shiny like grey paint. He stared, fascinated by the slow plop and gurgle. The eggy smell cleared his head. He remembered all the stories about Rotorua: Hatu Patu and the bird woman, Hinemoa and Tutanekai, Maui and the fire sticks. There was something about this place, something about how the earth's thin skin talked to its fiery heart.

"Te Arepa!" It was Ra, calling.

He picked his way out, taking care not to muddy his shiny black shoes. A group of them had gathered in front of the whare, around an old man who was sitting on the paepae[63]. Ra signaled him over. As

---

59   prominent North Island city, famous for geysers and mudpools
60   house
61   touched foreheads in greeting
62   the area around a meeting house
63   the area around the meeting house where people wait to speak or be introduced

he grew closer, the wall of bodies parted and he was confronted by this ancient kaumatua[64]. He was the oldest person Te Arepa had ever seen. His face was wrinkled leather, eyes pale and dribbly. The old hand clasping the tokotoko[65] reminded Te Arepa of a bird's claw, gripping a perch. It looked hard and bloodless.

They both stared at each other for a long time. The fierceness of the old man's gaze made it difficult to return but he had no choice. His head was locked solid. Then the kaumatua reached over and drew Te Arepa to him. Te Arepa shut his eyes and felt the old head hongi him, long and hard. Something was happening: it felt like someone had pulled a plug in his brain and everything was pouring out. Then the man released him and turned to Ra.

"Not much to him. Hardly fill a hangi basket."

They laughed.

"This boy …" the old man said. "This boy … will make a rain that will drench us all."

Ra seemed pleased by this comment, although the others were not so sure.

There were farewells and handshakes, but Te Arepa felt the old man's stare boring into him. He writhed before it as he struggled to remember each person's name. As he moved through the sheltering clusters of bodies, it caught him in steely flashes. He couldn't hide and it unnerved him.

At last they made the truck, and he and Jimmy waited while Ra went from person to person with a handshake or kiss and a few words for everyone. At last he joined them in the cab, and they were rattling back up the long driveway.

"Who was that old man? He was scary. His hongi … something happened …"

Ra turned. "That man is your father's grandfather. No one knows

---

64   elder
65   stick belonging to an orator

how old he is. There are many stories about him all through Tainui[66]."

"But the hongi ..."

"That was your mauri, Te Arepa. Sometimes ... how should I say this ... sometimes there are people whose mauri talks to your mauri. Spirit to spirit."

"I didn't like it," said Te Arepa.

"It's the old way. He's close to the tipuna, that old fellow. He has knowledge that few will ever have. He knows the past, so of course, he knows the future."

"Still ..." Te Arepa began.

"He is many things, this kaumatua, an ariki[67], a kaitiaki[68]." Ra continued, "That old head is a storehouse, packed with whakapapa. He is a great taonga[69], and he asked to see you."

"Because of my father?" It was difficult for Te Arepa to even mention his father, so steeped was he in shame.

Ra shook his head.

"You're part of his blood, his seed. He asks for himself."

The journey took a more somber turn. Each passing power pole seemed to be taking Te Arepa towards some inescapable destiny.

When they once again reached the Bombay Hills, his stomach was spiked by a sharp feeling of dread. The weight of what was happening sank in. There would be no going back now. The city spread before them now was huge and threatening. Filled with people he didn't know. People who didn't care about him. So different from Whareiti.

The boarding house was alive with purpose: boys carrying bedding, little family groups huddled in earnest discussion, younger brothers

---

66   central North Island tribe
67   Chief
68   guardian
69   treasure

and sisters peeping into the mouths of open bedrooms. Everyone else seemed excited: pleased to be here, sure of what they were doing. Uncle Jimmy was like Te Arepa, a bit shy in these situations, so the two of them held back and let Ra do all the talking.

Te Arepa was to stay in Marsden House, which was named after an early missionary, Ra said. His housemaster, Mr. Simmonds, showed them all to his dormitory. There were four narrow beds and a partition between each and the next cubicle. Mr. Simmonds explained that this was where the new boys were placed. As they progressed up the school, they moved to two-person dorms and finally to single rooms which were strictly "seniors only".

Te Arepa put his gear down next to a bed but was immediately told to move it to another one, as all the beds were allocated alphabetically. At this point a large, white-haired woman appeared with a note for the housemaster. He read it, grunting quietly, and then barked, "They would!" and hurried off without a further word.

The woman turned to them and smiled. "You must be Te Ireepa. I'm Mrs. Wilton, the matron for Marsden. I'm the one you come to when you need something. Why don't you just settle in here, then come down to the common room to meet all the other new boys at five o'clock."

As they left, another boy came into the little dorm. He was red-haired and crying. His stiff-jawed father trailed awkwardly behind him. It made Te Arepa feel like crying too, and he had to fight the impulse. The last thing he needed now was to cave in.

Jimmy and Ra strolled around the school with him, filling in time before the meeting. Compared to Whareiti Primary the school was huge. Three-story brick classroom blocks. Sports fields that seemed to go on forever. Cavernous gym. Out on the field there were two big boys doing kicks and catches. Te Arepa watched in awe. He had never seen a boy kick the ball so high. The other, who wore an All Blacks jersey, caught it easily and launched a rocket of his own. The ball seemed to hang in the sky forever. The three of them stood watching. There was something about these two boys: they were like lords of the school. Te Arepa was an invisible, insignificant outsider. Would he would ever get to their stage?

By the main hall where he had sat the test, there was a memorial plinth to the boys who had gone on to be killed in the two world wars. It drew Uncle Jimmy and Ra, who stood before it for a while, reading the names. There were a few Maori names here, he noticed: more than there had been inside the hall. Ra knew some of the whanau they had come from.

"You'll be at home here, Te Arepa, our blood and theirs, they run together."

A bell sounded. It was five o'clock: time to head back to the dining room for a cup of tea. Time to say goodbye to the families. Te Arepa knew that tears were never far away. Ra mustn't see them. Ra's last memory of him must not be that.

The big lunch room was thronging with small groups like his, family seeing off their boys. Most of the sons seemed to be his age: older boys evidently didn't participate in this.

After a while there was the ting-ting-ting of a teaspoon rapped against a cup. It was Mr. Simmonds, the housemaster. He spoke for a long time but didn't seem to say much. Most of it was about how lucky the boys were and what rosy futures lay ahead of them if they were willing to "put in a first rate effort". This first rate effort seemed to be a catch-cry ... he said it several times. Te Arepa looked around the room. Many of the other boys were now growing tearful. They knew what was going to happen next, and were dreading it. He tried not to look at them. It made it so much worse. He had to clench his whole body, which fought to surrender to sobs. At last Ra turned to him.

"Well, Te Arepa, they seem to be giving us the old heave-ho. I'm not going to give you any advice now. Your head must be full of it. This is the first term at your new school, the one where everyone will form an opinion about you. Make sure it's a good one ... I know it will be."

He leaned forward and quickly kissed him on the cheek. It was something he hardly ever did. Uncle Jimmy shook his hand. And then they left.

Te Arepa watched Ra's white head for as long as he could see him walking off to the car park. More than anything in the world now he wanted to run after him. To beg to be taken home. To say he had made the wrong choice. That it was too big, too hard for him. That he wasn't ready.

FIVE

For the first time he felt completely alone.

Many of the other boys went with their parents to the car park. He watched from a remove. They stood close to the departing cars, then watched them shrink into the distance. Te Arepa went to his dorm and sat on his hard, metal-sprung bed. There was a cabinet next to it. It was small but his clothes filled barely half of it. He waited for the occupants of the other beds to show their faces.

It wasn't long before two of the others turned up. One was a tall, thin boy with long brown hair he kept flicking out of his face. The red-headed boy, who had been crying, climbed onto his bed and rolled over so he faced the low wall that separated each of the sleeping areas. The other stood with his father awkwardly as if each was waiting for the other to say something.

"Well, Stephen, here we go again. You'll be okay here?"

The boy looked at Te Arepa and then into the body of the dorm.

"I'll survive."

"I'm hoping you'll do more than just survive."

"You know what I mean."

He began to unpack his clothes from his bag. Te Arepa noted that he had a number of thick novels which he shoved into his locker. His shoes were black slip-ons with stitching up the side. A bit different from his own snub-nosed earth-movers from the Warehouse. There was something careful and deliberate about all the boy's movements, not shove this, bang that, like most kids.

His father kept looking around restlessly and at last looked at his watch and said, "Oh well, Stephen, probably time I bid you a fond farewell. Study hard, endure the rest. For my part, I can guarantee we'll be here a bit longer than the other places. You should be able to put down roots. Make a few connections."

Stephen looked at him with the suggestion of a grin. "Now, when have I heard that before?"

"I'm repeating myself, am I? Senility is closing in on me. Want to come out to the car and wave me off?"

Stephen shook his head.

"Well, I guess it's goodbye then." He reached his hand forward to be shaken. Stephen touched it briefly, in a token sort of way, and then sat on the bed looking at Te Arepa. The man said "Bye, Son!" and the boy replied "Bye, Father!" without turning his head. That was it; his father walked off quickly as though he had left the car running in the driveway.

"Had to let him go," said Stephen to Te Arepa. "He was driving me mad. Whenever I go to a new school it's the same routine, the same words. It's like being stuck in the same episode of a sitcom."

Te Arepa grinned. "You've done this a few times before?"

"Oh yes. My father's in the diplomatic corps so I've been shoved into international schools as he's kersproinged his way around the world. Now he's the one stuck … in Wellington. For a few years, anyway. He didn't want me at any of the local boarding schools. It was his alma mater all the way."

"What's an alma mater?"

"His old school. Have a look at the scholarship board tomorrow:

you'll see Stackford in the dux's column. He probably hopes that this is the beginning of a family tradition. You know," he put on a deep, fruity voice, "Barwell's for my lad, be the making of him. Pass me another pink gin, will you?" He gave a bitter little laugh. "What's your name, anyway?"

"Te Arepa."

"Te Arepa, eh? Well, you're the first one of those I've met." He extended his hand to be shaken. "This place part of your family tradition?" He had an ironic tone.

"My grandfather reckons some of the dead guys are ours. I'm here on a scholarship. I don't know Auckland. I've hardly been outside the Coast."

"What coast?"

"The East Coast, man."

"Oh!"

"You sound like you've been around."

"It's over-rated. Airports and taxis. The only thing that changes is the view out the window."

Stephen got up and went over to the other boy, who was still lying on his bed with his back to them.

"Hey. What's up?"

The other boy rolled slowly over and looked up.

"Just a bit tired, eh man." His eyes were fiery red with tears.

"Okay." He paused as if weighing this up. "I'm Stephen Stackford, and this is Te Arepa ..." He turned to Te Arepa "What's your other name?"

"Santos."

"Santos? Mmm, Spanish?"

Te Arepa nodded.

"Spain's good." And then he added, "Dusty though."

"My name's ... Wade." He said it slowly, as if it was difficult to remember. "Wade Royle."

"I've always wanted to meet a member of the royal family." Stephen offered a hand to be shaken. Wade dug his arm out and shook Stephen's hand, then shook Te Arepa's.

"Where are you from, Wade?"

"Te Hoi. Or near Te Hoi, anyway."

"Where's that?"

"Over from Taupo. My family have a farm there."

He seemed to cheer up at that point, and was able to tell the other two that he was the youngest in his family, and that his three older brothers had gone through this school, but that he didn't want to; he wanted to go to the local school forty kilometres away. All his friends were there. And how he had this dog, Rex, that could jump fences, and a horse called Rags that could talk. And he used to have a pet wild pig called Pilgrim but he got eaten last Christmas. And that his mother said he didn't have to come here but his father was determined. And that this was even worse than he expected. And that he felt like dying.

"Yeah?" said Stephen, "I've been to a few of these before. In a few different countries. This one seems okay but it's too early to tell. It all depends."

"On what?" asked Te Arepa.

"On the seniors, particularly the ones in our dorm. Forget the food, forget the housemaster. That's stuff 's always the same, the real stuff happens after lights out."

"Bullying and stuff?"

"Yeah, particularly the 'and stuff ' part."

A bell rang and everyone began to move downstairs. The three of them followed down to a sort of lounge-assembly room. It was big enough to hold all sixty boys from the dorm. There were a few old couches and easy chairs around the walls and a big TV mounted on a shelf up in the corner. Stephen sat on the floor next to a group of boys his own age, and Wade was pleased to have someone to follow. Te Arepa sat on an old easy chair near them, the last one left. The housemaster appeared and began to sort through a bundle of papers. The talking began to tail off, as everyone waited for the first address.

All of a sudden, Te Arepa copped a terrific slap on the head. He ears rang as though bells had been set off inside them, then his eyes watered, and he strained to see who had done it. There was a big fat-faced boy behind him with the thickest eyebrows he had ever seen on someone so young.

"What's with that?" Te Arepa asked, voice quivering with rage.

"That's a bump, man. Get off or you'll get another."

Te Arepa slid slowly onto the floor next to Wade and Stephen, his head still buzzing from the blow. The other boys cringed, pleased it wasn't them. Eyebrows sat down on the chair as if it were a royal throne, and leaned back with his arms folded. He grinned around the room to all who had been watching.

One of the other boys on the floor leaned over to Te Arepa and whispered, "We're not allowed to sit on a chair if a senior wants one." Another added, "It's always risky. They never want one until you're on it."

"Watch him. He's trouble," said Stephen. "If he can do that in full view, then imagine what he can do after lights out."

The words lingered on in his mind: "… imagine what he can do after lights out …" Te Arepa glanced back at Eyebrows. He was sprawled out and looking around, the ugly smirk still smeared across his face.

"Quiet!" The words were bellowed by a senior sitting next to Mr. Simmonds. Everyone stopped talking immediately.

Mr. Simmonds sat back with his legs crossed and a clipboard on his knee. He wore a pinstripe suit with a yellow carnation in the button hole, like people wore at weddings. The senior who had screamed "Quiet" sat on the other side of the desk. He seemed too old to be at school. He was huge and had a little tuft of chest hair peeping out the top of his polo shirt.

When Simmonds spoke, he did so softly. The boys all had to strain to hear him, leaning forward as though they were eavesdropping on a private conversation. Two men talking. Sixty eavesdroppers.

"Thank you, Michael. How nice to see you again."

"Nice to be here, sir. May I ask, why the button hole?"

"You certainly may, Michael. I wear this button hole on the first day of term each year to demonstrate how pleased I am to be here: in the best house in the best school. I wear it to remind the boys how lucky they all are to be here at Barwell's. It's a ritual, Michael, and I for one happen to believe that rituals are important."

He turned to the boys with a slightly surprised look on his face, as if he hadn't noticed them before.

"My goodness, where did they come from, seem to have sprung up like mushrooms…"

Te Arepa looked at the other boys who all seemed to be grinning. This was some sort of game.

"Well, boys, how nice to see such a veritable garden of shiny, pink faces, all attentive, all ready to have knowledge poured into their waiting ears. I can see that this is going to be a very good year for Marsden and I trust it will be a good one for each and every one of you, too."

There was a pause and then hurried applause from all the boys filled the gap.

"Well, that was, I think, an adequate preamble, so it's time we all introduced ourselves in Marsden fashion. You've got two minutes to find out everything about the boy next to you and to give us a summary in no more than thirty seconds. I want no repetition, hesitation or street talk."

With that there was an immediate clamor as boys paired off and began to question each other all over the room. It was as though someone had switched on a radio and turned it up to full blare.

Both Te Arepa and Wade turned to Stephen, as everyone around them seemed to be paired off. There was an awkwardness about who was going to be left out. Stephen suggested that they do it circular fashion; he would introduce Te Arepa, who would introduce Wade, who would introduce Stephen. All around them, boys were interrogating each other at the top of their voices. Even Mr. Simmonds and Michael were lost in conversation. After a few moments there was another earsplitting "Quiet!" and everyone stopped mid-sentence.

"Being the eldest here — although looking at the facial hair on some of you gentlemen I am not so sure — I will start."

Looks were exchanged amongst the seniors dotted around the common room.

"I would like to introduce you to Michael Reeves, Head of House, Intermediate Athletics Champion last year, First XV member, chorister, and not forgetting Victor Ludorum in Barwell's Latin quiz last year. I am certain you are going to extend to him the same respect and obedience that you would to me. He is in all things my substitute and I am sure he will do the job famously."

Michael then stood up and detailed Mr. Simmonds's CV. It was rapid fire and included such things as the names of his children, the type of car he drove and the fact that he held the record for completing the Herald crossword, which was ninety-four seconds.

There was a polite chuckle amongst those on the floor. It was clear that anything these two said must be automatically greeted with approval and light laughter. Then the other boys began popping up all over the room, giving brief CVs of their partners. As the boys got younger, any attempt at humor or cleverness was greeted with a derisive honking: they were getting up themselves; they were way too new to be given any form of approval.

When it was Te Arepa's turn, he began, "I'd like to introduce Wade Royle who comes off a farm down the line…"

There was a loud "No!" from Mr. Simmonds.

"We avoid colloquialisms like "down the line" or "up north". They are just shorthand, lazy thinking. Again, from the beginning."

Te Arepa began again "I'd like to introduce Wade Royle, who comes from the land of Tuwharetoa[70], his moana[71] is Taupo[72], his

---

70   Tribe located near lake Taupo
71   sea
72   Large central North Island lake

awa the Waikato[73] and his maunga are Ruapehu[74], Tongariro[75], and Ngaruahoe[76]…"

"Thank you! Point made! Next!"

The whole room honked as Te Arepa slowly sank to the floor. He felt his face heat up. He put his hands over his head and tried to disappear into his shirt. Next to him Stephen flawlessly recited the details Te Arepa had given him and finished with "Sic itur ad astra."

Mr. Simmonds beamed his approval. "Ah yes, thus shall you go to the stars. Very gratifying. What can one say except, dum vita est, spes est. While there's life there's hope."

With the introductions finished, Mr. Simmonds reminded them that Marsden House was "a happy house, one big family really", and that his door was "always open". That there was a strong tradition of excellence here and he expected every boy, whatever his level of ability, to strive for personal achievement, to always be able to say "I did my best". After this it was back to the dorms for teeth cleaning and reading before the progressive "lights out".

The houses were constructed so that the juniors all slept in a big room, broken up by a head-high wall into a series of what Mr. Simmonds called "carrels" but which were referred to as "pens" by all the boys. The older boys lived in rooms upstairs called the gods. The younger boys (piglets) weren't allowed up into the gods unless they were on some errand. For a third former, being up in the gods at all meant that he was liable to be caught and beaten. Even if a junior was enlisted to do some job for a senior, there was still a strong likelihood of a thrashing unless the senior was there watching over him: "vouching" as they called it. With no one to vouch for him a junior was dead meat.

---

73 The longest river in NZ, also the people who live on its banks

74 The tallest mountain of the North Island, also the parent mountain of the Tuwharetoa tribe

75 The second mountain, of the group of three central north Island mountains

76 The third mountain, of the group of three central north Island mountains

This wasn't the case the other way round. Seniors could wander the piglet pens whenever they wanted.

There was a senior sitting on the unclaimed bed, waiting for them, when they got back to their sector. He was a big boy with glasses. He introduced himself as Adam Neeson and shook their hands, one after the other.

"Simmonds told you that all the juniors, you piglets that is, have a senior attached to them. In your case that's me. He mentioned all the things that we are meant to expect from each other: loyalty, obedience, reliability, blah blah. Some seniors are really into this, it's like their big reason for staying on. They wander around the place like squads of storm troopers. I'm not one of them. My reason for being here can be summarized in the words 'the McLay Willis Scholarship'. Everything else is just detail. I'll be giving you guys jobs, checking your pen for tidiness, and you can come to me if you need help with something. Don't overdo it; I'm pretty busy. I guess there are a few questions. Fire away."

"I got a slap in the head down there in the common room. What's that for?"

"That's a bump," Neeson said, smiling. "You were on a chair. Juniors don't sit on chairs if a senior wants one, and if there is one thing that makes a senior want a chair, it's seeing a piglet sitting on it."

"I would've got off."

"Hey, don't take it personally. There's no malice in it, it's just a custom. All the little house rules are enforced by bumps. The seniors were all bumped when they were piglets. It's just what happens, comes with the territory. I'm not into bumping, but some of those guys ..." He glanced to one side, as if checking for eavesdroppers. "You watch out. Talking in the shower line? Bump. Grinning at a senior? Bump. Shirt hanging out? Bump."

"So they can belt us whenever they like and there's nothing we can do about it?" Stephen asked.

"Oh, there's always a reason. There's like this scale of punishments here. Bumps are allowed by the house staff but sometimes there are beatings. They happen after lights out. Some kid, usually a junior, needs sorting out. He gets pulled from his bed by a couple of seniors and held while he's given a few well-aimed punches, right in the gut. This is what happens when a bump's not enough. Believe me, bumps are okay. You get used to them."

"Do you know who's going into that bed?" Wade seemed eager to change the subject.

"There's a rumor going round that the kid who was meant to be there died during the holidays, so they're trying to find a replacement. There'll be someone there in a day or two, don't you worry. If there's one thing Barwell's can't stand, it's an empty bed."

After Neeson left, the three boys climbed into their hard little beds. Te Arepa looked across at the other two. Stephen, his hands behind his head and his knees up, was staring at the ceiling. Wade lay facing the wall. The regular movements of his back and shoulders showed he was crying silently, again. Immediately Te Arepa felt the grief and loneliness closing in on him. He clenched the muscles in his stomach, determined that he would not submit to tears.

Adam Neeson was right about the empty bed.

A couple of days later, Mitch appeared.

Mitch was a sportsman. He looked it too: the muscles on his legs and arms were already well formed, like those of an older boy. He was on a scholarship, like Te Arepa, but his was a sports scholarship. After a rugby league game, his father had been approached by a scout who offered Mitch a chance at Barwell's. Providing he swapped codes. League was strictly for bogans[77].

"Hard choice?" Te Arepa asked.

Mitch shook his head. "The way I see it, the choice was coming

---

77 scruffy working class youths

here or going to the local school, carrying a blade."

"Sounds terribly West Side Story." Stephen's remark was ignored.

"Survival, man. My dad drives a tow truck. Left school at fourteen. Booted out for assault. He always says, 'Mitch ...'" Mitch pretended to be smoking and drinking while he said this. "'I was too smart to listen at school, so they sent me to Rock College. I got a diploma in car conversion, took a degree in B and E ...'"

"What's that?" asked Wade.

"Breaking and entering. 'Now I'm looking at taking a course in GBH.'"

"GBH?"

"Grievous bodily harm. That's when you leave a few marks."

"So that's why you came?" asked Te Arepa.

"Didn't have any choice. Mum shot through with one of Dad's mates. This dude doesn't really want me around, cramp his style, eh? My real dad's too busy dodging people he owes money to. He tries to be, you know, the dad-figure, but he's crap at it. So I reckon it's better here than in some dump run by CYPS[78]."

Te Arepa had no idea what "sips" was but reckoned it had to be pretty bad. He liked Mitch: he was a straight arrow. The same as Wiremu. He just told you stuff, like his dad had been to jail. Like it was no big deal. Nothing bothered him.

There was something else about Mitch. This became clear on his first day when one of the seniors decided to give him the bump in the dinner line. There was this unwritten rule that seniors could push in at the front no matter how late they came. Mitch and Te Arepa were almost at the front and getting hungry, even though the meal was only some dark, slimy stew. Graeme Hartnell aka Eyebrows, appeared beside them with his tray, waiting for them to step back and let him in. He fixed them with his bushy brows for a moment, waiting, but nothing happened.

"Hey you, I'm in here," he said to Mitch.

"I don't think so," said Mitch. "You're over there."

"Getting smart?" Hartnell aimed a half-hearted slap at the side of Mitch's head.

Mitch's arm came up instantly and bounced the slap away with his fend. The two stood there staring at each other. Suddenly the whole dining room went quiet; there was an acute radar for this sort of thing.

"Make some room, man, seniors go first," Hartnell said, a bit diffidently this time.

This was greeted by Mitch's expressionless and unblinking stare. He wasn't moving and he sure as hell wasn't intimidated. Hartnell looked around nervously as if to say the whole thing was a joke; they were mates really.

This was an unheard of back down. The consequences were unthinkable. The age-old hierarchy was being challenged. Then, to the relief of everyone except Mitch, Mr. Ansell, a young English tutor on his gap year, shepherded Hartnell into the line farther back. It was a victory of sorts, but whose exactly was hard to tell. One thing was clear: Mitch was labeled fearless.

When the older boys came through the pens throwing their weight around, he stood his ground. After a while they tended to avoid Mitch. He was an unknown quantity so the older boys treated him a bit differently. With a grudging respect.

The first few weeks flew by because they seemed to be scrambling back and forth just trying to get on top of the routines. Every minute of their day was organized to keep them busy. It started at six-thirty in the morning when they were shaken awake for their run by the duty senior. They pulled on shorts and T-shirts, then blundered out down the school drive, back through the stand of native bush, then past the chapel and on to a couple of laps of the playing fields.

Mitch and Wade would shoot off out the door, trying to be first back. Mitch bolted because he didn't like the idea of being beaten at any physical contest, and Wade because he had a farm dog's eagerness to please. Te Arepa soon discovered that Stephen, like himself, had an aversion to compulsory exercise, although in Stephen's case, it was to all other forms of exercise too.

"Enforced physical exercise, especially first thing in the morning, is for race horses or Jack Russell terriers. I am neither of those lowly beasts," he proclaimed.

Te Arepa supported him, so they would complete their laps at a quick walk.

The assistant housemaster, Mr. Faull (or Farty, as he was universally called), was a PE teacher in training. He had two goals in life. One was to show others the beauty of a life shared with Jesus, and the other was to get every boy fit. He was a good-natured, gentle man, who saw Te Arepa and Stephen as a challenge to his ministry. Sometimes he ran alongside them, barking encouragement all the way. Other times he had them out on the playing field doing stretches. The squatting exercises inevitably made him fart: hence, Farty.

"Like this boys ... down to the count of five. One ... two ... three ... four ... five (fart) and up." His facial expression stayed blank: there was no acknowledgement of the arse trumpet, as some of the boys called it. Stephen and Te Arepa found it hard not to laugh. At this point he would get grumpy and start shouting, and not long after that he'd give up in exasperation and focus on the more motivated boys.

Back at the shower block the speedsters were already lathered up and enjoying an extended spell in the hot water. It was a big booth that did six boys at a time. No privacy, no secrets here. It was strip ... wash ... dress. The rest of them would all loiter in towels, waiting for one of the tutors to arrive and clear the stalls so they could run in. They were meant to take a maximum of three minutes, with Mr. Simmonds or some substitute looking in from time to time to check that they were washing properly.

What Te Arepa found worse, though, was that there were no doors on the toilets. Everything was done in full view of everybody else.

"No chance to indulge in self-pleasure," as Mr. Simmonds put it when he explained this architectural oversight to Stephen during the first week.

The seniors, whom Mr. Simmonds called the "old hands", wandered around the bathroom, nude and hairy, chatting away as if it was the most normal thing in the world. Any attempt by a junior to cover his cock was met with scorn. "What've you got to hide?" "Do ya think that's worth hiding?" Sometimes this was emphasized with a flick of a wet towel that bit at the cold flesh and left a red mark that took ages to fade away.

Wade copped more than his share. It was as though there was an understanding that if anyone had time on their hands it was a duty to flick, punch or trip him. He made out it was a game, that he was somehow "okay" with this, but in the showers Te Arepa saw him crying, face raised to the water so that no one would notice.

From that first day, and for many days after that, they were instructed on conduct and routines. Every last detail was covered by a myriad of rules. There was an impossible number of them.

What items they were allowed on the top of their cabinets.

The order and positions of clothes inside it.

How the clothes were to be folded.

Bathing, when and how often.

The food.

Table manners.

Terms of address.

Mr. Simmonds seemed to have made the teaching of these rules his life's work. Even something that appeared to be straightforward was embedded in a complex schedule.

"Can we go to the dairy?"

"Let me see," he would say, slowing the whole thing down. "Juniors are allowed between three-thirty and four. The As to Fs are Monday; you, Santos, and the other denizens of Sector C, from L to S, will need to wait until Wednesday. If it's urgent you can trade with one of the others, but remember, you are only allowed two of these trades per term and they should be recorded in the trades book."

Another of his specialties was the organization of personal property. His own desk was an example of this. It showed three personal items, in his case photos of his two children (a pair of freckly girls) and his wife (a freckly middle-aged woman). His diary was central, opened at the correct page. To the left were the duty roster sheets. To the right the accounts. The lockable money box which contained phone cards and petty cash waited temptingly on the corner nearest the door. It was like a moral challenge, "something to test their mettle", Simmonds claimed.

Like most of the masters, he had a pet, or in this case, a clone. Peter Newell. Newell was a third former who had become obsessed with Mr. Simmonds. He believed that Mr. Simmonds was the pathway to a brilliant life and modeled himself on him in every way. This included not only keeping two pens in the chest pocket of his shirt at all times, but even imitating Simmonds' backward leaning handwriting. This last piece of imitation was particularly difficult because Simmonds was left-handed and the style came naturally. Whenever Simmonds was wandering around the boarding house doing his rounds, you could be certain that Newell was following him, waiting to do whatever needed to be done; straighten a bed, remove some extra item off a work desk.

To Te Arepa, who had never expected to enjoy them, the lessons were a revelation. At his little school back at Whareiti there seemed to be only three subjects: reading, writing and math. Now subjects multiplied and became much more difficult. The work was harder, but at least in 3B he didn't have the geniuses to deal with.

The subject he liked most was Latin; in particular, reading and translating. The Punic Wars totally consumed him. They made sense of things. It was as though he had been waiting for this all his life. Slowly translating the texts was an experience more powerful than reading; it was like being in someone's head ... seeing the world through their eyes. Caesar's eyes. He loved the Caesars. He understood them. There was a cold logic to everything they did. His favorite was Augustus. He flew high above everyone else, like an eagle. Moving troops like chessmen, outsmarting his opponents. He had held the world in the palm of his hand.

Then there were the Carthaginians. The underdogs. Hannibal, and his father Hamilcar. Defiant in the face of impossible odds. Contemptuous of their destiny. Outflanked, outnumbered, poorly armed but triumphing through bravery, audacity and imagination. Finally there was the tragedy of their eventual and inevitable defeat. It all made sense. They were the Maori.

His other subjects were like school anywhere, except that work was piled on from the first day. Mitch and Wade both struggled, so Stephen and Te Arepa usually helped them. Seniors were allowed to study upstairs in their rooms; juniors had to sit together below in shared prep areas for the compulsory quiet hours in the evening. These were supposedly supervised by an older boy or a prefect, but usually the only checks were in the form of a tutor or duty senior strolling by to see how things were going. The lazy ones didn't even do this. They just bugged the room by reversing the intercom and never came down at all. After this was free time until lights out.

The first few weeks was a period when everyone sorted each other out. People made mistakes and suffered the consequences. A junior would wander into the senior section of the dorms and return sniveling with a bleeding nose. There were the boys who were left out. They hung around trying to ingratiate themselves into the established groups, usually unsuccessfully. There had to be a reason to take them in. They had to have something to offer.

Then the enforcing began for real. They were all given nicknames. Stephen became Stephanie. Wade became Dumbo. Mitch was Tarzan and Te Arepa was called Maori. They struggled to keep their old names but it was hopeless. They all had to be re-branded, with a Barwell's name. Even the tutors used them. Te Arepa hated his. He knew survival depended on getting a new name. A name like Te Arepa was like saying "I'm Maori" every time he introduced himself. "Maori" tied him to all the things at school that were inferior or didn't work properly.

A bad kick on the sports field?

"What a Maori one!"

His old shoes?

"Maori shoes!"

Bare feet in the dining room?

"Maori shoes!"

A new name was crucial.

Even Adam Neeson (his so-called "Buddy") called him "Maori" and (when he was trying to be funny) "Chocolate Thin".

It was like he carried the mark of Cain.

Stephen seemed to be an expert on these matters. There was an early bid to call him Girl because he was a bit girly but he managed to head it off with "Steph". It was a name he'd had at other schools and it seemed a perfect fit.

So it was Steph whom Te Arepa approached, asking what he could do.

"It's difficult. You can't really control what people want to call you. All you can do is to think of a name for yourself and then work hard at getting it to stick. What does Te Arepa mean, anyhow?"

"It doesn't mean anything … it's a name. I'm named after this ancestor … the boy who saved the tribe."

"Hmmm," said Steph. "Ancestor name. Any others? What would you like to be called?"

They both thought for a while.

"What about Diego? I have this Spanish ancestor, Diego Santos."

"Not bad." Steph weighed it up for a while, then he discarded it. "No, too foreign. You'll probably end up being called wog or dago. What else?"

"Well, all the other names are Maori names, or Pakeha versions of them."

"How did this Diego come to be part of your family?"

Te Arepa laughed. He immediately thought of the full version, the "authorized version" as told by Ra. "It's a long story, believe me. Takes about a week to get through. But in the end, he was being taken back to Wellington to be tried for piracy on a ship called the *S.S. Devon*. As it rounded the East Cape, he jumped overboard and swam to shore."

"Then he became one of you?"

"He did a few other things first but that's it, more or less. My people took him in because he was such a good fighter. Not a big man, but a cunning one."

"How about Devon?"

"What about it?"

"How about Devon for a name? It's sort of halfway between Maori and wog and you've got a claim to it."

Te Arepa thought about it for a while. He liked the idea: it was a sort of happy compromise.

"Okay," he said uncertainly. "So how do I go about changing my name?"

"Just tell everyone that's what you want to be called from now on. Ignore your old name and all the other tags people try to lay on you, otherwise you'll end up being 'Nigger', like Graeme Hartnell calls you. He was the one who named Wade Royle 'Dumbo'. He hung that on him the first day."

"He's scary, that Hartnell. I don't like him too near me in the showers. There's no telling what he might do."

Steph glanced around. "True, he's bad news. He grabbed my balls in the lunch room when I was carrying a full tray of food. He made out it was a joke but I reckon he gets off on it."

"So, Devon you reckon?" said Te Arepa.

"Yeah. It suits you. Put it there, Devon." And they slapped palms.

Later, the two of them took to rebranding Wade. They changed his name to the usual for a kid with sticky-out ears: Wingnut. Mitch was fine with Tarzan, but in the end it always came back to Mitch, because Mitch seemed so right for him.

The Mitch incident: it was a bit like this.

They were all lining up for the showers. Just the juniors at this stage; the seniors were allowed an extra half an hour in bed. Hartnell was the duty senior, in charge of feeding the juniors in and out of the showers for the regulation three minutes. As each new set of six boys put down their towels and scampered into the shower with soap and flannel, Hartnell scored a well-aimed flick on their arses. If any boy was too quick for him he ordered him out of the water and made him present his arse for an extra-special flick. Steph and Devon walked into the showers, slowing for the regulation branding. It smarted but not for long. Hartnell was so busy giving Wingnut an extra-special stinger that Mitch walked right past unscathed.

"Come back out, Tarzan, I've got something for you."

Mitch either didn't hear or pretended not to, so Hartnell dragged him naked and slippery out of the shower stall. The others watched in awe as Mitch, eyes full of soap, neatly slipped out of Hartnell's headlock, hauled the senior's thigh upwards, and they both crashed onto the hard tiled floor ... with Mitch on top. There was a sickening double crack, as first Hartnell's back and then a moment later his head smacked the wet tiled floor. They both lay there, stunned for a moment. Neither boy said a word. Then Mitch clambered up, went back into the booth and carried on showering as though nothing had happened. Hartnell got up slowly off the tiles and stood quietly against the wall, his face drained of color. The others all stood around in the steamy enclosure waiting for the inevitable.

But nothing happened.

After the regulation three minutes they moved out and the next boys were gestured in without as much as a flick. Hartnell just glared at them, the back of his shirt soaked from the fall on the wet floor. Devon and the other two sneaked looks at Mitch while they stood together at the wash basins cleaning their teeth. Everyone knew Mitch had broken something that should never be broken. By dropping a senior he had shaken the foundations of every rule they slavishly obeyed.

And yet, he seemed to have got away with it.

The following day the incident was the talk of the whole school. Even the house staff talked about it. The only person who didn't talk about it was Mitch.

That afternoon was the school swimming sports. Devon, Steph and Wingnut had already been eliminated from the competition during PE periods but Mitch was a finalist in every event he entered. The glamour race for the juniors was the one hundred metres freestyle. The race came down to a competition between Mitch and another boy called Paul Swain, from Pompalier House. Paul looked like he was born to swim and he trained with a swimming club outside the school three nights a week. He had beaten Mitch in the longer distances but couldn't match his raw power over the short hauls.

Around the pool the tiered seating was swarming with boys clothed in house colors. Marsden's house color was yellow so many boys had loyally yellowed their hair with food coloring. Some of the younger teachers, especially those who were old boys, wore colored clothing, or the old striped blazers that had been part of the uniform twenty years ago.

"Regardez!"

It was Steph. He was pointing to Mr. Simmonds, all decked out in a short-sleeved, white safari suit.

"My God, he's fresh out of Africa. Fresh from sorting out the fuzzy wuzzy on the greasy Limpopo."

"Except for the shades. They're new, I think," Devon replied.

"Could be right. Let's go down and take a closer look."

They climbed down from the bleachers and wandered towards the gateway to the houses. It was clear that the swimming sports were not Simmonds's chosen duty: he lurked in the shade, just "putting in an appearance".

Steph sidled up to the housemaster. "Love the glasses, Mr. Simmonds. Dolce et Gabbana est?"

"Pro patria mori, Stackford," he replied dryly, then added, "Where are you two going, might I ask?"

"A quick comfort stop before Mitchell's big race."

"Make sure you come right back."

"You can rely on that sir, veritas lux mea."

"Hmm … in the parlance of the plebs, I would possibly say, 'Yeah, right.'"

Devon was quiet for a while, but when they were some distance away, said, "I don't know how you get away with that, Steph."

"That's the advantage of a Latin education, Devon. It's like being a Freemason. Special treatment whenever you bump into a fellow member."

The one hundred metres was the last event before the relays and it would decide the Junior Swimming Champion: Mitch or Paul. The final eight swimmers stepped up on the blocks as their names were called. They stood there, proud and twitching and shaking their arms, big in the shoulders, small from the waist down: they all had swimmers' physiques. Mitch was different, brawnier. Thicker in the waist and legs. The Marsden supporters erupted when Mitch's name was called. He gave them a wave and then swung his arms like rotor blades. On the other side of the pool, Devon could see Hartnell, all scowls and eyebrows. The gun went off and Mitch did a high, show-offy dive and then powered along the surface of the pool. He had no style — most of his body seemed to be out of the water — but he made up for it with unbelievable power.

By the end of the first lap he was two body lengths ahead. On the second lap Paul Swain began to close in on him. He glided through the water with hardly a ripple. It was just a question of whether Mitch had enough lead to hold him off. They seemed to touch the far end at the same time, but Paul was declared the winner. Mitch lunged up onto the side and ran along to pull the exhausted Paul from the water. It was clear to Devon that he had let him win: an act of breath-taking generosity.

That night, Paul Swain came and joined them in the dining room. He told them about his dream: to go to the Olympics. Mitch said it was a cool thing to wish for, and reckoned if any.one could do it, Paul could.

Later, in the dorms, the talk was still dominated by swimming. Steph told the story of Cassius, who had swum the Tiber in full flood. Mitch must have been tired, because he went to sleep almost straight away. After that it was just whispering; there was a rule about talking after lights-out. Devon heard the click of the door at the end of the passage and shushed Steph immediately. The last thing they wanted was an extra duty, the standard punishment. For a while it all went quiet and Devon wondered if he had been mistaken. He was about to give the "all-clear" when he heard muffled whispering. Something was going down.

Three figures burst into their pen with hoodies up over their heads and handkerchiefs covering their faces. It was impossible to see who they were. Two of them pulled the blankets over Mitch and held them down tight. The other one began to thrash him with a hockey stick. Hard blows, like chopping wood. Again and again. Up and down the length of Mitch's body. There was no let-up. Devon longed to do something but couldn't move. He lay immobile, frozen with fear, while his friend was being beaten not two metres away. For a while Mitch thrashed around making noises like an injured animal but couldn't even raise his arms to shield himself from the next blow. Devon lay motionless, listening to Mitch groaning and crying. Gradually all movement ceased and he seemed to go limp.

The two who were holding down his legs and arms released them. "Jesus you've killed him, you fucken idiot," one said, and then both ran off. The third figure, with the hockey stick still clenched tightly in his hand, stayed still for a moment, checking to see whether there was any movement in the other beds. Devon closed his eyes until they were just slits, terrified of giving himself away. The last assailant leaned close; Devon caught the sharp stink of his sweat. He straightened up, and Devon was certain that this was the prelude to a blow to the head, but the attacker wandered off, hockey stick resting jauntily on his shoulder. As soon as the door closed, the roommates jumped out of bed at the same moment and rushed to his limp form. Steph pulled back the covers. Mitch lay still. His eyes had rolled back in his head; the whites stood out in the murky light.

Devon was aghast; he was dead. He certainly looked dead. Steph ran off somewhere while Wingnut stood beside the bed waiting to be told what to do. Then Mitch began to whimper. The two of them carefully lifted his head and shoulders. He was surprisingly heavy. Devon squeezed in at the head of the bed, trying to support him. Steph returned with a wet towel and a basin of water. He dabbed it about on Mitch's bruised face. Devon could feel life trickling back into Mitch's body as he slowly returned to consciousness.

No one said anything: they all knew who had done this, and why.

"Let's get him into the shower." It was Steph.

He and Devon took an arm each and they half walked, half dragged him to the shower room. Devon hated himself, was ashamed of his cowardice. If only he had done something when it counted.

In the glare of the bright lights Mitch looked like he had been in a car accident. They stripped him off and put him in the shower but he was unable to support himself, so Devon went in.to the water with him. There were welts all over him; the worst were on his arms and legs. They were wide purple bars, angry around the edges. After a while Mitch leant against the wall of the shower, face against his arms, and began to take his own weight. Every now and then he spat blood on the floor.

"Who's going to get the housemaster?" Devon asked the other two. They both looked back blankly.

"We can't," said Steph. "It doesn't work that way. Mitch knows that. Housemasters are for official stuff. This isn't official."

"You're going to let these arseholes get away with it?"

Mitch turned to Devon, bleary eyed, but said nothing.

After a full thirty minutes, of rinsing, spitting, coming to more fully, Mitch hobbled back to bed. Devon listened to him sobbing now that he was back in the dark. He knew how lonely and miserable he must feel. How abandoned.

Devon couldn't sleep; he had to do something, anything to numb the guilt that raged about his body. He got up and climbed into Mitch's bed. The two of them lay in the dark, wrapped in each other's arms. It was the right thing to do, Devon thought, but at the same time, it was unbelievably wrong. After a while Mitch stopped crying and went to sleep. Devon climbed out and got back into his own bed. He saw Steph watching him in the darkness for a moment, before he dropped off into a dreamless sleep.

In the morning, Mitch looked even worse than he had done the night before. He struggled to get out of bed at alarm call. Devon told him to stay down, that he would get matron, that it was time to make a big noise about this. But Mitch wouldn't hear of it. Steph agreed.

"It will just make things worse for him, Devon."

"This sucks," Devon said, "It's just not fair …" his voice faded away.

With the support of Devon and Steph, Mitch struggled through to the showers, where a spotty sixth former called Muir was on duty.

"You guys are ten minutes after …" he yelled, but then stopped when he saw Mitch's injuries. They could tell from his face that the news didn't need spreading by them. A few minutes later, when they were getting dressed, Mr. Simmonds the housemaster appeared and took Mitch away. The bell rang, so Steph and Devon went to breakfast not knowing what was happening. Wingnut claimed that Mitch would spill the beans, tell the full story from first to last and that then everyone would see some action. Steph gave a scoffing laugh. Devon wasn't so sure either. There was a code that Mitch followed. A toughness to him.

Sure enough, at morning interval they found him sitting on the seats outside the math classroom.

"Did you tell them?"

He shook his head.

"Why not?"

They waited for details but he said nothing more.

Devon carried his friend's bag for the rest of the day because Mitch struggled. He had been offered a couple of days in the infirmary but he didn't want to get left behind. The work was hard enough anyway without missing a chunk.

SIX

The last day of term, when it arrived, was an anticlimax. Steph disappeared mid-morning on a flight to Wellington. Wingnut's dad whisked him away dead on three p.m. Soon after, Mitch was picked up by his dad in a tow truck. It was Saturday afternoon before Paikea's courier van swung into the driveway. Devon was one of the last to go.

"Bet you're pleased to see me, Te Arepa."

The shock of his name being spoken aloud surprised Devon.

"Yeah. Yeah, Pike. It's great."

But it wasn't.

"So how's it been then?"

"It was hard. So different. I've learned so much. Couldn't believe it."

She looked at him and smiled.

Paikea paused briefly where the school drive met the busy road and then powered into a small gap in the line of cars. Her driving had an ease to it; but there was something more to it than that, too, a sort of grace. There was nothing in excess. She gave every turn, every gear change, every little maneuver in traffic just the right amount of effort, and no more. She made the van seem as if it was part of her body, and she seemed to move it without conscious thought. Devon was mesmerized.

"Will you teach me?" The words came out before he knew it.

"What?"

"Teach me to drive. I'd like to drive like you. I've never seen anyone who could drive like you."

"Well ... you put it like that ... what's a girl to say?" Then she added, "Wait till we're off the motorway ... too many cops around these parts."

Devon tried to repay her with an account of some of the things that had happened at Barwell's. He found that he was changing and softening things. Things she wouldn't understand. He told her about Steph, Mitch and Wingnut. About the fights and the rules. But there was another huge part of the whole experience that he couldn't tell her about. A part that went beyond all that ... something less tangible.

"It's an old school and they have their own way of doing things. I guess it is a sort of boys' world, with its own kaupapa[79]. Some of the stuff they do is really harsh. You got to look out for yourself a lot. It pays to have a few mates, I reckon."

"Sounds like my old school."

"Where did you go?"

"Rangiatea Maori Girls' College. It's a little private school in the Manawatu[80]. I wonder if you're doing the same sorts of things that we got up to?" She looked at him with a smile and a chuckle. "I reckon you are. Yep, I see it in your eyes."

Devon waited for the interrogation but it didn't come. About an hour later she pulled the van over without warning.

"Get out then. I need your place."

He paused, wondering what she meant, and then climbed out and walked around to the driver's side, which she vacated by sliding across

---

79   the protocol for doing something of cultural significance
80   a Province in the lower North Island

the seat.

"Now look, steering is easy. Fix on a point about twenty seconds up the road and your hands will do the rest. The big thing is to get the feel of the engine and let your feet learn the clutch."

He made a few shabby attempts that had the van bunny hop and stall but then suddenly it came to him. He got it. The changes that were at first jerky maneuvers, he now negotiated easily.

"Later I'll teach you to double de-clutch — really good for trucks — but for now we'll get up to about ninety ks or so, so you can learn a bit of road craft."

At first the van seemed to be moving at a blinding pace, charging at corners and difficult to keep in line, but after a while he relaxed into it, forgot about gear changes and focused on Paikea's instructions.

"Wide in … clip the line … wide out. Don't! Never brake on the corner — you'll lose it that way. Power out man! Remember in fast. Brake. Take a line. Out fast."

By the time they had got to the curvy coastal road he was feeling confident and in charge but Paikea took the van off him again.

"That's it for now. I can see your shoulders are all hunched. You're freezing up. It's just tiredness. You've done well."

He must have looked disappointed.

"You done good, Te Arepa, eh fulla." Doing the old-world Maori accent.

Devon settled back into his seat. He was suddenly aware how tired and sore he was. He began to think about Ra for the first time in ages. It was something he had carefully avoided but now there was no escaping it. He knew that at heart he had betrayed Ra; he hadn't "kept the fire burning" (te ahi kaa), instead, he had become invisible. To pretend otherwise was a lie. He knew it would fester between them.

"Hey, Te Arepa! Wake up, man! Wake up! We're here!"

And they were: the big red tin barn on the outskirts of Whareiti loomed into view and moments later they drove up to the old house, which now looked smaller and older than it ever had before.

As soon as he saw Ra's head at the kitchen window, something exploded in his chest. He jumped from the van and tore across the lawn.

"Hey! Hey! Who's this, Paikea? I thought you were bringing Te Arepa home but you've brought this monster. You will have to take him back."

Devon's arms wrapped around his grandfather's waist and tears spurted from his eyes.

"What's this water on his face? Is it raining here? What's going on?"

Paikea walked over and hongied Ra over the top of Devon.

"Thank you, Paikea. Your mother would be proud of you."

At this remark, everyone stepped back a pace. Paikea looked near tears for a moment. Devon was aware again how quickly his grandfather got to the heart of things.

"Come in for a kai."

"Can't. Can't, Ra. I let Te Arepa drive a good chunk of the way so we're a bit behind schedule. Jinny will be waiting. He's been good company. I'll pick him up in a fortnight."

The two of them watched Paikea's van until it disappeared into the night then they went inside. Ra fixed them both some mutton sandwiches. Salty with copious tomato sauce. It was the first Maori food Te Arepa had had since he'd left for Barwell's. He looked around the little kitchen and through in.to the sitting room. A bulldog clip over the stove held a clump of yellowing bills and official letters. The fly swat lay on the bench, next to the dishes drying on a tea towel.

"Where's Rawinia?" It seemed quiet.

"I sent her off to stay with her Pakeha cousins."

"Rawinia is staying with the McGregors?"

"Ae[81]."

"In Taupo?"

"Ae. I have been too busy trying to get these local boys organized

---

81 Yes

for an iwi tourist venture. They're a hoha[82] bunch. Good kids but when they get to be teenagers ..." He paused, looking thoughtfully at Te Arepa. "When they get to be teenagers ... I don't know what gets into them. You can't get through to them."

"What's this 'iwi tourist venture' then?"

"All sorts. White-water rafting. Fishing. Guide work. Everything you can think of. Anyway I'll tell you about this stuff tomorrow. You go off to bed now. It's nearly eleven. I'm going down myself. Just been waiting for you and Paikea."

He paused thoughtfully. "So, Te Arepa. What've you learned, eh? What've you learned that you can call your own?"

Te Arepa longed to tell him everything. To let it all pour out. To be told that he had done well and that everything was all right. But he couldn't.

"I've just learned this, Ra. I carry a huge weight and it slows me down. I never knew I had it until I started at Barwell's, but now I know about it, I carry it everywhere."

"What is this weight?"

"I can't tell you."

He expected Ra to keep on, to try to get to the bottom of this, but he didn't.

"Well, no wonder you're tired. Carrying a weight around like you do would tire anyone out. But the good thing is, your bed is made up and it's waiting for you to get into it."

It was good to lie on his old bed, with its old saggy mattress and heavy blankets. For a while he listened to Ra moving around the house, fixing up things for the morning, and then he soaked in the silence of midnight in the country.

In the morning he was awakened by a smell. Methylated spirits. He reached the doorway just as Ra was beginning his morning ritual. Before long the fire was growling away in the grate and Ra had the porridge in place. He looked at Devon, reading his interest.

"A bit different from what you're used to?"

Devon nodded his head and then went back to get changed. He was still sitting at the breakfast table when Wiremu arrived. They heard the scrabble of gumboots being kicked off at the back door, and then moments later Wiremu's face appeared around the corner.

"He's been asking me for days, 'When's Te Arepa coming back from that flash school?' 'Is he all different now?' Well, Wiremu, here he is at last. Judge for yourself. Looks much the same, bit bigger maybe." Then Ra added mischievously, "Except that he carries a big weight now."

Wiremu looked to see what this weight could be and then came over and sat at the table with him.

"Youse can go. I'll clear up. Get out of here, go do boy stuff."

Ra sounded cheerful.

So they went out the door and down the road towards the shops. Wiremu wanted to know everything that had happened since he'd been away, and for a while Devon was willing to comply.

He told of the fights he had been in. The friends he had. His enemies. Stuff he had to learn. The things they learned at school. The names of things that didn't exist in Whareiti. But there were many things he didn't tell Wiremu; things he couldn't tell. Stuff he had no idea how to explain, and didn't really understand himself. When they reached Anderson's store, Devon wondered why they had walked down there. True, he had a few dollars in his pockets, but what would he want to buy in such a shop after the glittering malls and arcades of Auckland?

He found he was tiring of Wiremu, too. Tiring of trying to explain things to this guy who had never been anywhere or done anything.

They bought Cokes and sat on the slatted bench in front of the shop, watching the infrequent traffic.

"Tell me about the weight."

"What weight?"

"The one Ra told me about."

"Oh that." He thought for a while. This could be a good time to practice on Wiremu what he would eventually have to tell Ra.

"Well, for one thing, I am not called Te Arepa anymore. I'm called Devon."

"Devon? Why?"

"We all have nicknames at school. Mine's Devon."

"But you used to have a nickname here in Whareiti. Remember when you got top in the exam and everyone called you the Prof?"

"It's different, Wiremu. It's different at boarding school. Hard to explain. It's like … you have to make yourself into something otherwise you get teased."

"Everyone gets teased."

"It's different."

"It's different. It's different," Wiremu mocked him.

"Yeah, well it is."

Later that day he tried to broach the subject with Ra. It hung over him and he hoped that maybe he could clear the air.

"Ra, about the weight."

"Ah, the weight!"

"I tried to explain it to Wiremu but it was no good. Maybe I can explain it to you." He fidgeted with an old pack of cards left out on the table. "This weight I carry at school, it is nearly everything I am, you know. All the stuff you have taught me. Even my name. It all drags me down. Makes things tough for me."

"Your name drags you down?"

"Yeah. People … everyone really … pronounces it wrong, and then it's the Maori thing. It's like I got 'Maori' stamped on the front of my head."

"Well, I suppose you have … what's wrong with that?"

"Here in Whareiti, nothing, but at Barwell's … everything."

"Then you got a big job ahead of you. You got to show them you're as good as they are."

Te Arepa was about to speak, when Ra held up his hand.

"No, you've got to be better than they are. You're not the first, you know. It's just that here in Whareiti, we are the tangata whenua[83]; we set the rules. At the big school in Auckland, it's another matter. You can do it. You've got a whakapapa behind you that's the equal of anyone's. Think of your ancestor Diego. At first he had nothing for us. He was like a man from outer space. A freak. Couldn't even speak our language. But after a while his qualities shone through. Our old people recognized them. Found a use for him. And it paid off. He saved us from the plague of Ngapuhi. Be like Diego. Find a way."

For a few days Devon felt better. Even inspired. But by the time it came for him to return to school he knew he had to armor himself once again with all the tricks and evasions that made him the same as everyone else, just a little browner.

Paikea came for him on the Sunday morning before the beginning of term. Thirty kilometres up the Coast road, Paikea turned back. She had forgotten something of Jinny's that she was meant to be taking to Auckland. A few kilometres before they reached Whareiti she swung off the main road and headed in towards the hills. At the point where the farms seemed to be turning into wilderness they came to a gate and a cattle stop, then another gate and finally a cottage with a thin wisp of smoke coming out of the chimney.

"Come in, Te Arepa, meet Jinny." There was a pride in her voice.

A short, frail-looking woman appeared at the door as they climbed out of the van. She had her head tied in a bright red scarf, which made her look even paler. They kissed and Paikea took the package from her hand.

"I was so busy remembering to get Te Arepa that I forgot the main reason for going."

"I should have reminded you. We're both hopeless," said Jinny. She seemed more amused than anything. She turned to Devon and touched his arm. "So you're the scholar?"

Devon felt shy. He nodded.

"My husband went to Barwell's ..."

Paikea put her arm across her Jinny's shoulders. "This was before Paikea came along and rescued her for ... a life less ordinary."

They both giggled. Their private joke.

"Anyway, he was a top scholar at Barwell's, the poster boy for academic success."

"So he liked it?" Devon asked.

She shook her head. "He used to say that Barwell's was a religious experience. After five years in hell, the rest of his life was like living in heaven. He hated the place."

"Poor, poor pitiful me," said Paikea pretending to wipe her eyes. "It's not easy being rich and privileged."

There was a hesitation between them, as if things had been exhumed that were better left buried.

"Dr Kendall? Pacific Studies?" asked Paikea.

"Thank you, darling. I can't wait to see what holes she picks in it this time."

"We better fly. I reckon Te Arepa is dying to get back to civilization."

They moved out to the van and Jinny reached in and gave Devon's shoulder a pat before Paikea swung the van around and they headed off.

"What's happened to her hair?" asked Devon as they reached the main road.

"All came out with the cancer treatment."

"Oh."

"Remember, Te Arepa," said Paikea after they had driven a few more miles, "I hate to be the one to tell you this ... but it's hard all over." Her mouth tightened. "Now I suppose you'd be wanting to try your hand at the wheel again?"

The day after he returned Devon got a message to say that he had to go to the headmaster's study at the start of prep. He tried not to panic but it niggled away at him like a fish bone stuck in his throat; perhaps Ra had become sick, or Rawinia. He asked Steph, who was always the authority in matters like this.

"Doubt it. Simmonds wouldn't have given that sort of message to a third former to deliver. No, this will be something else. Are you in some other sort of trouble?"

Devon couldn't think of any, but by the time prep rolled around he was completely preoccupied by speculation.

The headmaster's study was approached first through the huge double doors of the foyer, then the reception office, then through the headmaster's secretary's office. Each new passage required a higher clearance. They were normally closed by four p.m. but tonight everything was lit up or wide open. He could hear the headmaster talking to a parent on the phone from the outside office so he stood at the doorway awaiting instruction.

"It may be considered normal at other schools, Mrs. Wallace, but here at Barwell's we do things differently."

The call seemed to come to an abrupt end. Devon heard the creak of a chair being pushed back and then the headmaster peered through the two sets of doors.

"Santos? Come through now."

Devon walked into the huge office and then waited near the door. The headmaster seemed to suddenly feel the need to write some notes on a sheet of paper, so for the next minute or so all that could be heard was the slight scratching of a fountain pen across school stationery.

The room was paneled and lined with shelves. The only windows were tall and thin with a lattice of diamond-shaped panes. Glass cabinets displayed silver cups, shields, pennants and some very old school caps.

The room held a couch and chairs, a coat rack with big brass hooks, and on the wall there hung a huge photograph taken on the school's centenary, with all the boys sitting on the sloping embankment. It was hard to believe that there could be so many boys at one school.

"They're gone now."

Devon jumped. The words had broken the silence without warning.

"Many are married with children. Most are leading successful lives. They are what we do. They are our purpose, our clientele, our raison d'être."

The headmaster was a small man and he spoke from the depths of a high padded chair, which made him look even smaller. The only point of animation was his large head, which transmitted an authority and menace that made Devon's face begin to twitch.

"Which brings us to you. Do you know why I have summoned you?"

Devon shook his head.

"Is that how you answer a man?"

"No."

"No sir." The headmaster's voice was so soft now that Devon had to strain to hear what he said.

"No sir," he repeated.

"It seems to me that you are languishing. Languishing in 3B. Do you agree?"

"I don't know … I don't know, sir."

"I had you placed in 3B because I wanted to see you fight your way up into 3A. To earn a place amongst the elite by dint of your own efforts. But it hasn't worked. You seem to be languishing. Resigned to it. Happy to coast along in the class without any particular effort. Is this the case?"

Devon thought for a while and then said, "I suppose I've just been getting used to Barwell's. It's a big change from what I've come from. I expect that this term I'll try to lift my grades."

The headmaster leaned over the piece of paper in front of him and wrote on it. As he wrote he muttered the words "… a term to adjust …"

"At my old school I was always top. I never had to try. Everyone knew that. Here, it's different. Much tougher."

"Oh yes. You can be sure of that. Well, let me spell out my expectations. Maybe I should have done this earlier." He leaned forward over the desk and spoke in a more personal tone. "I stuck my neck out, offering you the scholarship. I staked my professional reputation and judgment on you. Maybe even excluded other more worthy candidates. The school's board of governors sees these scholarship choices as an expression of my judgment. They keep tabs on how they are going and want regular reports. My first report to them at the end of term reads …" He picked up a piece of paper. "'… appears to be coasting. Has not really shown his capabilities …' Which is a slightly more verbose version of the old chestnut, 'Could do better … must try harder …'"

He stared at Devon as if reading him. "So let me speak plainly. You could do better. And you must try harder. This is a big school but you are not forgotten nor over-looked amongst its ranks. People are watching you. This is term two. The work term. The mid-course exams are coming. I expect you to show me your best in these exams. You owe it to your people and to the school."

He flicked open a little book, picked up the phone and then looked up at Devon, as if in surprise. "Off you go now, Santos. The next time I see you I expect to be the bearer of glad tidings." He turned slightly in his chair and squinted at the phone number he was about to call.

Devon left the office and walked out into the cool night. From the front steps he looked at the glittering harbor and its rim of lights. There was the slight rumble of cars on the motorway. He felt small, insignificant. As though he was nothing more than a piece of information in a vast computer. Something that could be deleted by a key stroke.

When he arrived back in the dorms, Steph was reading on his bed. "What was that about?"

Devon recounted everything, including the end where he was told he owed it to his people and the school.

"It's a wonder he didn't say you owe it to your race. He sure gave you a truckload of the guilts."

"Yeah. Trouble is, Steph, I don't know what I'm going to do. I'm working hard. I reckon 3B is my limit. It's great to be told that you're smarter than you are, but it's another thing to carry it through."

"You can do it."

Devon was stunned. There was absolute certainty in Steph's voice.

"Doubt it."

"Sure you can. And you will. I'll help."

"I haven't got the brain-power, man."

"It's not brain-power. It's just technique. I'll help. You'll do it. You'll see."

Mitch and Wingnut arrived, red-faced and sweaty after playing badminton in the gym.

Mitch sat down beside him.

"Hey, Devon. What's up? We heard that you'd been called to the headmaster's office."

"Jeez, everyone knows."

"No secrets at Barwell's."

"He's being groomed for academic success," Steph quipped.

"What does that mean?" asked Mitch.

"The headmaster reckons I should be in a higher class. And if I don't make a bigger effort to get there, well … well, I don't know, but it won't be good."

"And he's going to do it. And I'm going to help him," said Steph, picking up his book. Then he added with fake drama, "Failure is not an option."

They all laughed and then left it alone.

Over the next few weeks Devon did make a special effort. He

focused on his areas of strength, which were English and Latin. He and Steph had those subjects in common. They rattled through the declensions. Boned up with endless detail on aspects of the Punic Wars. Steph was always clear what he would have done if he had been "in Julius Caesar's roman sandals". Maths and science were a different matter. There were no short cuts or recreational discussion here: it was all hard graft. Devon went through endless exercises and examples for the maths until he was able to slide through layers of equations, reducing them to simpler forms, or navigate his way through formulae towards a triumphant bottom line. Science was more a matter of memorizing and applying methods. It was a slow process, and often continued well past the end of prep. Devon resented the fact that the other three left him to go off to evening rec while he ploughed away through the stubborn clay of half-understood principles. After a while it became easi.er. It was as though he had cut pathways into an impenetrable thicket and now could find his way quickly where he had once blundered about. The teachers noticed his efforts and took time to check his progress more regularly.

Even Mr. Simmonds allowed him more leeway now. His movements around Marsden House were not questioned so relentlessly. "Where are you going?" "What are you doing here?" "Why aren't you ...?" The stock questions were now aimed at other boys. People knew where Devon was going. He was off to the prep room to study. He became part of the furniture there.

The night before the mid-course exams began, Devon found himself in the happy position of not having much to do. He was able to help Mitch and Wingnut with their maths prep, and wondered why they found it so difficult. There was an anxious quiet in Marsden House as most of the boys realized that maybe they had left everything a little late.

Once they were all in bed that night, Steph stayed up reading an enormous book, while Mitch and Wingnut were asleep moments after lying down. Devon ran through the various conjugations of Latin verbs in his head: reciting them as a way of getting to sleep had become a habit.

"Devon?"

It was Steph.

"What?"

"You'll be okay."

"Think so?"

Easy for him, he thought. No Ra or headmaster breathing down his neck.

As the exams ended classes gradually reverted to normal. The boys' exam answers were given out and gone over. Devon had done well. Top in English, in Latin, well up in all the other subjects. The only boy ahead of him was an Indian boy called Rajendra. He had achieved virtually perfect scores in maths and his science subjects and shortly afterwards was promoted to 3A.

A couple of nights later Mr. Simmonds told Devon that he had "come within a hair's breadth of promotion" but they had been instructed "from above" to wait and make sure this wasn't a "flash in the pan".

"Divine intervention, eh?" Steph said, when he heard this. "Devon, wake up. It's not enough to do as well as the boys in 3A. You have to do better than them just to prove you're their equal."

"Doesn't sound fair."

Steph snorted. "As if fair's got anything to do with it."

Devon lay that night, staring at the paneled ceiling for what seemed like hours. Steph was so cynical. If you didn't have fair, then what was left? He mulled over what Ra had told him. It all boiled down to, "Be like Diego. Find a way."

SEVEN

At the end of the term, Wingnut invited Devon to go home to his farm with him during the break. Devon didn't fancy being stuck on a farm for a couple of weeks but weighed up his other options. Ra had already told him that he would be in Wellington so Devon would have to stay with Rawinia who was now semi-permanently with the McGregors. He would miss out on the chance for more driving lessons with Paikea and he wouldn't be seeing Wiremu, but in some ways he was quite pleased about that. Wiremu seemed a bit small-town for him now. He decided to accept Wingnut's offer.

After Saturday morning sport the two of them sat in the back of the white Fairmont while Wingnut's father, Graeme, drove. It was a long journey to Te Hoi, but a relief for Devon to be finally out of school. A relief not having to put on the "Te Arepa" costume that Ra expected when he went home.

They arrived in the dark and were greeted by the sounds of dogs barking.

The front veranda lit up and a woman appeared carrying a small dog. Wingnut left the car and ran to her embrace. There was much clucking and kissing. Devon stood around puffing steam in the cold air and trying not to look. He couldn't believe that they called each other "Mummy" and "little boy."

Couldn't believe the sing-song baby tones.

After this, Wingnut's mother turned her attention to Devon, putting her arm across his shoulders and talking close to his face. He was reminded how long it had been since any woman had last embraced him. The thought summoned up a panicky rush of emptiness, so intense that he struggled to answer any of her questions.

Wingnut had not told him much about the farm, just about his horse and his pig. The farmhouse was old and huge. It was two-storied with an "annex" out the back for the farm workers. Wingnut's room looked out onto the tennis court, and in the distance the snow-capped peak of Tongariro.

After unpacking, Devon was brought down to the sitting room for cocoa. The wood paneling and the high ceiling reminded him of the headmaster's study. There were stuffed pig and deer heads and near the front door a coat rack made entirely of cow horns. In the sitting room a fire glowed in the grate and the light came down from a glittering chandelier. Devon had never seen anything more magnificent.

Graeme Royle came in from the hallway. "All the way from Austria. My father bought it during the bumper war years."

"Didn't he go to the war?" Devon asked.

"No, most of the farmers around here were regarded as essential services. Remember Napoleon's 'An army marches on its stomach'? Well, he helped keep those stomachs full. No glory, no medals but someone had to do it."

Then, as if to change the subject, he added, "There are one hundred and thirty-two pieces of cut crystal. I know this because I used to clean them when I was a kid." And then, looking at Wingnut, "Hmm, a good job for you boys tomorrow."

"No way. Tomorrow me and Devon are going around the farm on

the quads."

"Devon and I," his mother Ruth chimed in. "His grammar's gone backwards."

"Maybe we should have sent him to the local school," said Graeme, and then with an accent he added, "Youse better hit the sack now, eh. It's been a long one, bros."

That night, as Devon struggled to find sleep, he was forced to revert to his strategy of rattling through his Latin verbs. Even then, Devon could hear the sound of voices, just beyond the clamor of his recitation. It was hard to know in his last waking moments whether they were inside or outside his head; he just knew he had to drown them out.

In the morning the farm was covered with a fine, glassy frost. The puddles in the driveway had iced over and the watery yellow sun had no heat in it. Ruth made them pancakes and then after they had "togged up well," Wingnut took Devon out to meet the animals. His horse, Rags, ambled over to Wingnut's whistle. He was elderly and had a big slump in his back. It made him excellent for bareback riding "because you can never slide off", Wingnut claimed.

There were two quad bikes on the farm and even though they were battered and slow they were fun to ride. For the next few hours they wound their way up steep hills where the low gearing seemed to crank them up an impossible gradient. They forded little streams and squeezed through pathways where the gorse had taken over and they had to lean out on crazy angles to avoid being scratched.

Wingnut parked his quad near a hole in the ground big enough to drop a car into. He signaled Devon over. As soon as he got clear of the bike he began to smell it: a stench that poured out of the hole like an invisible geyser.

"What is it?"

"It's a tomo."

"What's that?"

"It's a hole ... like a sort of cave-in. There are heaps of tunnels under here. Some of them go for miles."

"What's the stink though?"

"Oh that." As if he hadn't noticed it. "Dead animals get thrown in here. Lambs and calves, animals that Dad doesn't want for dog tucker. You don't want to fall in there." He made a move to shove Devon in.

Devon could see what must have been a dead cow at the bottom of the hole.

"I can hear water."

"Yep, it's a stream, comes out on the far side of the farm, about a mile in that direction."

"All the rotten stuff goes into the water?"

Wingnut sensed the criticism. "Always has, doesn't seem to have killed anyone. Anyway, enough of the stink, let's go and see what Dad and Grandpop are up to."

They traversed the ridge to the main farm road and then continued out to where the farm met the National Park. They came upon a bulldozer driven by an old man and connected to a stump by a thick chain. Graeme Royle was hacking away at the roots with a chainsaw. Both men waved when they came into view and looked pleased they had the chance to stop work.

"Look at Wade; he's a monster," the old man said. "We're going to have to clamp his head to stop him from growing."

He climbed down stiffly from the little bulldozer.

Once the old man was on his feet it was easy to see where Wingnut's father got his size from. The grandfather was massive, with a handshake that was cold and crushed Devon's little hand.

"Graeme tells me you're a Santos, from the East Coast. My mother was a Williams so we all come from the same area. Have you heard of the Williams family?"

"There are some Williamses who have a big farm not far from Whareiti."

The grandfather turned to Wingnut's father. "Y'hear how he said that, the real Maori way? We always called it 'worry iti.'"

Devon felt himself blushing.

"What's your father's name, Devon?"

"Manu Davis."

"So why are you called Santos?"

Suddenly Devon wished he had never agreed to come home with Wingnut. It was as though he was some specimen that could be pinned to a table and dissected in full public view.

"Santos is my mother's maiden name. My grandfather's name. I was given the name when I was a baby. It's my name." He felt his voice begin to rise in pitch along with his sense of outrage.

"Okay, okay," said the grandfather raising his hands and smiling. "Santos is good."

"So what are you doing now, boys?" Graeme attempted to defuse the situation.

"We're about to head back home, getting hungry."

"Go on then, we won't be far behind you."

The two men resumed their positions and attacked the stubborn totara stump again.

At dinner that night they all sat around a large table in the dining room. The grandfather — who had "separate quarters in the annex" — joined in for meals, and after dinner he brought out a tray of Maori artifacts. They were mostly adzes and patus. He explained to the boys what each would do in battle and how they would be used.

"But where do they come from?" Devon asked.

"Been in the family for years. Some were dug up when we were flattening the pa site[84] to build the barn; others came by way of deals my father or grandfather made when they first acquired the place. This greenstone one belonged to a paramount chief of Tu Wharetoa. He threw it in to sweeten the deal. He was after the muskets. The axe heads and blankets were all very well but the muskets, they gave him the upper hand."

Devon picked it up. It was heavy and cold. He could feel its mauri

---

84 pre-european Maori village

running up his arm. He knew what Ra would say.

"Are you ever going to give it back?"

The grandfather was pouring himself a whisky from the side board. "Which one?"

"This one," said Devon picking up the greenstone patu.

There was a sudden silence. Eventually it was broken by the grandfather's loud, dismissive laugh.

"To whom? It was an old deal. Those involved have all been in the ground seventy years or more. Return? No, this is where they belong, boy. They are all part of a deal, an agreement, and you don't welsh on a deal."

"Even if you're Welsh, like the Williamses were," Ruth added mischievously.

"What do you suggest?" the grandfather continued. "Give them back to the Maoris? No way!"

He was getting quite red in the face and Devon was beginning to feel better. Ruth promptly interceded and sent the boys off to watch TV in the other room.

"Man, Devon, you sure lit a fire under Grandpop. He loves those things. Always brings them out for visitors. Give them back? Never heard that before."

"I was brought up that way. We were taught that some things are given to bind you together. And the person who gets them never owns them, just looks after them. It's different, I guess, where I come from."

"Oh well, there's one good thing," Wingnut paused. "It meant we didn't get Part Two. The years of struggle. The stunted cattle, and bush sickness. The raupo cottage. Once he starts … whew!" But Devon could tell that underneath it all Wingnut was embarrassed, and there was a new awkwardness between them. He resolved to pull his horns in for the rest of the time.

On their last day Ruth took the two boys into Taupo to stock up. He had never seen so much food bought in one shop. They had a trolley each at the supermarket and they were filled to the brim. After this the boys were hungry and Ruth agreed to take them to McDonald's "for a feed of junk food". There was a large Maori family in a van in front of them at the drive-through. Endless cardboard containers were passed in through the window. You could see the excitement in the back as each kid got his package of food and cup of Coke.

Ruth shook her head sadly. "Benefit day, and this is how they spend it."

Devon had nothing much to say in the car going back. He'd thought that Ruth was different. His food was so tasteless he could hardly finish it.

The remaining hours dragged. Devon didn't feel like doing anything; he just wanted to get back to school where he could be free of the tension he had built around him.

Wingnut suggested they play chess. A large, heavy chess set was brought out: so different from the one he and Ra used to play with. Each piece in their set had the tooth marks of a hundred agonizing decisions.

Their game soon attracted the attention of the adults and so Devon, instead of beating Wingnut quickly like he always did at school, drew the game out, attempting to make a match of it. As the boys sat stooped over their game, the grandfather hovered, trying to give Wingnut hints with grunts and by clearing his throat.

After a while Devon sensed he was actually playing every.one else. The grandfather was leaning over Wingnut's shoulder staring at the board so hard that it seemed that he would burn a hole in it. Graeme Royle hovered occasionally and then retreated. Even Ruth picked up on the strain in the room.

For a while there was a fairly even exchange, as pieces were taken down either casually or as the result of a two-move strategy. Wingnut would go to move a piece; the grandfather would explosively clear his throat, and Wingnut would stop to see which piece was under threat. When this happened, he would inevitably lose his way and the grandfather would suggest coyly that "perhaps one of the men of the cloth needed a holiday", or that "a horse might like to canter towards the castle".

When they had swept most of the board and had an equal balance of major pieces, Devon queened a pawn and finished things off quickly. There was no fun in it any more. Later when he was heading up stairs, he heard the old man in the kitchen muttering to someone, "Wade could never beat that boy; he's too open ... he hasn't got the Maori cunning."

EIGHT

"So how was life in the boondocks?" Steph asked, on the first night back.

"Never again."

"That bad?"

"It would have been okay, like bearable, but he had this four-hundred-year-old grandfather who wanted to refight the Maori wars every time I showed my head."

"Well I did warn you about spending time in 'the land that time forgot.'"

"Yeah, you did, but it was either that or hang around the hostel for two weeks being an unpaid caretaker."

"You should've come to my place."

"Yeah? You should've invited me."

"I spent the whole time lying around reading. Watching my father come and go. I reckon we wouldn't have said more than a hundred words the whole time. 'I'm back.' Or 'I'm off now, Steph!' That was like a full-length conversation."

"You're exaggerating."

"Not much."

"How about meal times?"

"Meal times we both read. All you could hear was the sound of pages turning."

Mitch arrived.

"Hey, you two. Guess what I got?"

"I give up," said Devon.

"You, Steph?"

"Same."

"I got a car." The words spilled out into the room.

"Wha…"

"You guys gotta come and see it. Come this weekend."

"You can't drive, Mitch," said Steph, "I know for a fact that you're still thirteen, same as me."

"I know, I know. I just drive around the junkyard. This car's not street legal anyway. Half of it's missing, been chopped off. There's this little road through the stacks of cars in the yard. I've been spending the last few weeks teaching myself to drive on it. I'll teach you, too."

"Thanks, but no thanks, Mitch," said Steph. "I come from a long line of non-drivers. It's a family tradition."

"I can already drive," Devon said. "My cousin's been teaching me on the way home to Whareiti."

"So you don't want to come?"

"Course I'll come," said Devon.

"Next weekend then."

"You're on."

"You, Steph?"

"We'll see. I've got choir practice, I think." Which was another way of saying that he didn't fancy it.

That Friday night, when Mitch's dad, Big John, finally showed up, it was nearly dark. Mitch spotted the derrick of the tow truck weaving through the lines of parked cars.

"There he goes." There was pride in his voice.

The truck was moving much faster than the usual measured pace that cars travelled at on the school grounds and the next thing that Devon knew his hand was being wrung by a muscular blond man with a spot tattooed below each of his eyes.

"Yo, Mitch, Mitch's mate."

"It's Devon, Dad."

"Yo Devon-dad, that better? I'm John. Big Bad John."

"Not that big," said Mitch.

"I used to be bigger, shrunk in the wash."

Mitch turned to Devon. "That's why he stopped washing."

"Are we gonna stand here all weekend being wise arses? No? Let's roll then."

They climbed into the cab of the truck. It was crammed with RT gear, all set to different wavelengths. Fractured messages ripped out of these from time to time and Devon couldn't understand a word. Every now and then John would grab the hand piece and bark something out into the airwaves.

Before long they were belting along the western motorway and weaving through the zone of small wooden houses and graffitied fences. Then they got to an area of factories, and finally stopped at a high corrugated iron wall with mountains of car bodies behind it.

"Why have scrap yards got such big fences?" asked Devon. "I mean it's not like people are going to run off with a wrecked car under their arms."

"Why the big fences?" repeated John as he slid from the front seat. "That's to keep out people like me."

"And your friends," added Mitch.

There was the sound of a dog going mad.

John swung the gate wide. "Take her in, Mitch."

Mitch slid across and nosed the pick-up through the canyons of stacked cars until they got to an old house with all the lights lit up.

"This is it. No palace, but it's home." There was obvious pride in

Mitch's voice and Devon felt instantly at ease there. John was wandering over through the gap in the car stacks, with a couple of Alsatians going mad and leaping up all around him.

"Meet my two employees from Germany. This is Blitzen and this other guy is Schiesen."

Devon could tell that they were young dogs, very playful and eager to please. They all went inside and the dogs immediately threw themselves on the floor next to the heater.

John was more like an older brother than a dad. The house was decorated in a style that could have been called "morning after the party". The two couches had suffered from dog bites. There were oily engine parts lying in places you wouldn't expect. Nothing was tidied away, anywhere. Nothing seemed to matter much. This was all new to Devon, and he loved it.

"I know what you guys will be wanting. I know it because I was once a boy like youse — well, not as runty as you two — and I was always hungry. The only time I wasn't hungry was when I was asleep." He roared with laughter at his own jokes.

"Break out the beans, Mitch. You boys like a beer? Oh sorry, you're too young. I'll have to drink it for you."

Mitch went over to the fridge. He pulled out a massive tin of baked beans and poured them into a pot that he dug out of the clutter in the sink.

"Did you wash that pot first, Mitch? Number one rule of cooking. Hygiene."

"Stop pissing us about and give us a beer. I wonder why I put up with you," said Mitch, then he turned to Devon. "We only ever cook two things, beans or eggs."

Big John threw Devon a can and walked over and balanced one on Mitch's head.

"That's the great thing about having a kid with a flat head. Somewhere to park my beers. Started when he was a baby. Evolution."

"You were never there when I was a baby."

It seemed a bit sharp.

"Look, mate. Reality check. They don't let you out of rock college every time there's a nappy to be changed. Anyway, Gordon was doing a great job."

"Who's Gordon?" Devon asked.

"One of Mum's boyfriends. My sort of stepfather. Put some toast on, Devon."

Before long the three of them sat down to a big feed of beans.

"Ah! Genius. Feed the man beans. Keeps a fightin' man fuckin.'"

"Keeps a truckin' man fartin' more like it," Mitch said, looking at his father for a reaction. Big John's head was trained at a sheaf of invoices but he still managed to give his son the finger with his free hand.

Devon mulled it all over as he tucked into his beer and beans. He'd never had beer before. Ra never had it in the house. Mitch's place was filthy but he loved it. Big John didn't seem to care what other people thought and Mitch had inherited his attitude. He wished he could be just like the two of them. But he knew he never could.

"You guys have got ..." Big John paused to look at his watch. "... thirty minutes, then we're out of here. I've got two hungry mouths to feed and I can't do it by sitting on my bum in a junkyard."

True to his word, after half an hour they were cruising. Devon thought Big John was a great driver: like Paikea, but he was of the street fighter and trickster variety. It was as though every road rule had been invented solely for him to break, and his main role was to entertain the two boys. When a driver cut them off he tailgated the car until it pulled over in submission at the next set of lights, where he yelled to Devon, "Wind the window down!"

He leaned right across Mitch until his face was in front of Devon's, then bellowed "Cunt!" out the window. The businessman in the Lexus kept his hands tight on the wheel and his eyes fixed on the road ahead, until finally the lights changed and he disappeared down a side road.

Big John turned to the boys. "I'm all for improving road manners, aren't you?"

Later, when he was speeding along and talking to the two boys at the same time, they were alarmed to see a stationary bus looming up ahead.

"Dad, a bus ..." said Mitch as they were only thirty metres from ploughing into the back of it.

"Where? Where?" said John looking everywhere else except straight ahead. At the last minute he veered around it. Devon had never seen a vehicle pass so close to another without hitting it; the bull bars almost brushed the wing mirrors of slower traffic.

Later the call came in to pick up a stalled car on the motorway.

"We might get it," John said as they did a U-turn in heavy traffic. The idea was then to drive as fast as possible because all the other towies out cruising would be after the job too. As luck would have it, there were three other trucks ahead of them. John jumped out but made the boys stay in the car.

"He'll be ages," said Mitch. "That guy with the beard is a real chatterbox. Dad is bad enough but him ..."

There was another burst of crackle on the RT.

"It's Marj at HQ," Mitch said.

Devon couldn't understand a word, but Mitch flashed the lights again and again until Big John reluctantly walked over to find out what was going on.

He climbed back into the truck, just as a cop car arrived, lights flashing.

"Good time to leave," said John. "It's Carmody. He's a born-again."

As they waited for clear traffic, Devon saw the policeman climbing out of the patrol car. He gathered up his torch and his ticket book, checked his appearance in the rear view mirror, then swung out. He had the rolling walk, the swagger, everything that you would expect from someone coming over to ask for a dance.

They watched him, bemused.

"Used to be a car hoon but he crossed over to the dark side. No more tickets but he gets to hoon it for the cops, driving a police Holden instead of a Mitsi Evo. He's written a few off too. What a prat!"

The next call was to a repo on the Shore. "Some guy defaulted on his payments," Big John said. "If we can get the wheels off the ground without the alarm going off … well, that'll save a lot of aggro."

Before long they were powering over the big bridge towards Takapuna, or Pack o' tuna as John called it.

The main street was very busy with groups of drunk people surging in and out of the restaurants and bars. Kids no older than Mitch and Devon, too, were out having fun. Some drinking, some snogging their girlfriends, others just generally yahooing.

Mitch, as if he read his mind, said to Devon, "See what we're missing out on, locked up at Barwell's? We could be out there too. This is what everyone else does on the weekend while we're stuck in the dorms beating off."

Devon flashed a look at Big John; he couldn't imagine saying something like that to Ra.

What Big John said next surprised Devon; there was a change of tone, it almost held regret.

"Nah man, do the hard yards first. Otherwise you'll end up like me, in and out of the clink all your life. It's like smoking," he said, reaching for his fags and making a joke of it, "a hard habit to kick."

Mitch looked unconvinced. "What's the difference? We're all locked up till we're sixteen or so, all the time this …" he said, pointing at two young guys trading punches, "this is going on."

"No fair, no fair …" he added in a baby voice.

"Hold up!" said Big John, "Here we come …"

It was a house set well back from the road with a big old Jag and Legacy wagon parked in the car port.

They stopped out on the road while Big John assessed the situation.

"Here's how we're going to do this. I'm going to back up the driveway, hoist the wheels and we're out of here. Normally I'd knock at the door, do the informing thing, but this guy's been a bit of a trickster."

As soon as Big John put the truck into reverse a loud beeping noise started.

"It's a case of 'fuck the formalities, full steam ahead,' as Winston Churchill used to say," said Big John as he backed up the driveway.

They came to a stop behind the green Legacy. Big John plucked the hand control for the electric hoist from a box in the back and immediately the high-pitched whine signaled the unraveling cable. Mitch seemed to know the drill; he gave Devon the torch and grabbed the hook.

"Shine it in towards the back axle, man," he said, pulling the slowly unwinding hook and dropping to his knees.

The two of them went low while Mitch found the spot to anchor the cable. Big John put a spare tyre in place to protect the body work and then cranked the rear of the car clear of the driveway. As soon as it came up it swung slightly to the right and clipped one of the pillars of the carport. The response was immediate. The quiet neighborhood got a wake-up call.

Waa woo waa woo!

The car lights all flashed. There were signs of movement inside the house.

Big John turned to the boys with a goofy expression like, he'd just spilled the salt. "I hate it when that happens. Let's hit it." They were all in the tow truck within moments, powering the flashing, wah-wahing vehicle out down the street. Devon could see a couple of guys in shorts and singlets standing on the lawn, watching them recede into the distance.

"Maybe you should have told them what's up. They might think you're stealing it and set the cops onto you."

Big John was skeptical. "Yeah, Mitch, right. I knock on the door." He put on a poofy voice. "Hi Chief, I'm lifting your car. Sorry for the inconvenience. Maybe your people can talk to my people. Work things out."

They laughed.

"I guess," Mitch said.

"There is another old saying dear to the heart of every towie," said Big John. "Or it should be. 'Possession is nine tenths of the law.'"

Mitch turned to Devon. "He should know. The last thing he was inside for was possession of stolen property."

As they began to climb the slope towards the top of the harbor bridge, Devon was lost in the vision of the city at night. The tall buildings, the sky tower, and the waterfront restaurants all shimmered in the gleaming water. They were impossibly beautiful. This is what it was all for. This was the city of light that lay at the end of his schooling.

Back at the yard the doors were open and the house was all ablaze. It was as though every light in the house had been turned on.

"It's only your Uncle Frank," said John, turning to Mitch. "He threatened to drop over last night. He told me he's had a windfall."

Mitch laughed and said to Devon, "That usually means he's come across a swag of stuff and you can be sure of one thing: he hasn't paid a cent for it."

Sure enough, as they approached the house through the canyon of cars, two men appeared on the front veranda.

"Oh no, he's brought Baz along," said Big John.

"Baz McCurdy, that is. Dad calls him Blow Hard."

"Try hard," Big John muttered as they climbed out.

"What are you two bastards up to? Drinking all my beer? Come and help me turn off this friggin' Legacy. It's starting to give me a headache."

Baz got some blue packing tape and a screwdriver from inside the house and soon levered open the window and lassoed the door lock button. Devon was impressed. It must have taken less than fifteen seconds. Next he popped the bonnet and found the alarm relay. Peace descended, along with a sense of relief.

Baz turned to the two boys. "Pretty slick, huh? You can see why Subs are the most stolen car in New Zealand. So, John, how've you been, you old bastard?"

"Not bad, you old bastard."

"Keeping straight?"

"Straight as a sheila's hair clip." He wandered over to where the other man was lighting a smoke. "Hey, Frank, where's this so-called windfall?"

Frank looked coy. "That's why I've come to see youse. Share it about." He looked pleased with his comment, then turned to Mitch. "How's the boy? Playing footie?"

"No, we have to play rugby at Barwell's."

"Rugby poofs, huh? Rugby and cricket. Cucumber sandwiches in the pavilion." He turned up his nose and put on a toff accent. Mitch and Devon giggled. Baz McCurdy went inside with Big John and they closed the door behind them. Uncle Frank sunk into the old car seat on the veranda.

"And who's our friend?"

"Oh, sorry, Frank, this is Devon. He's here for the weekend. He's in my pen at school."

"Out on parole, Devon? Time off for good behavior?"

"I guess," said Devon. "My folks live down on the East Coast so I don't get out that often."

"The East Coast. What's your surname?"

"Santos."

"Any relation to the Santos in the Warriors?"

"We're all warriors down on the Coast."

Frank looked at Mitch. "Oh. He's a smarty. Watch out for that one, but make sure you sit next to him in the exams."

"I wish. I'm in 3K; he's in 3B. I'm in with the retards and the crap teachers."

"They still do that stuff do they? I thought it was year nine and year ten. That sort of thing. All mix and match."

"Not at Barwell's; it's traditional. They got this saying in the fourth form how the school goes all the way from 4A for Asian, through to 4J for genius, right down to 4Q for asking." Mitch paused to fire a spit off the veranda then added, "It's like we all got 'dumb cunt' stamped on our heads." Mitch had never said anything like this to Devon. The bitterness came as a shock.

Frank laughed. "No kidding? Well, out here in the junkyard things are a bit different. Come with me, boys, I might have something for you." They went inside where Big John and Baz were talking over cans of beer.

"... I won't fucken wear it. End of story." Big John sounded heated but it all disappeared when Mitch and Devon entered.

Uncle Frank went into a back room and dragged out a big plastic bag full of brightly colored jackets. He fussed around looking at the labels and then finally pulled out two jackets and threw one to each of the boys.

"There you go. It's always Christmas when Uncle Frank comes around. These two should fit youse. S.M. That your size?"

The jackets were Holden HDT Team jackets. Red and white, covered in badges. Devon looked at his in disbelief. A few of the older boys wore these at Barwell's: they were highly prized. Really expensive and these were the newest models.

"Well, don't just stand there gawking, put them on!" Frank had fixed himself another drink and was pretty pleased with his gifts.

"Thanks, Uncle," said Mitch. "Now if Dad can score me an HDT Holden I'll be the real deal. All the girls will want to be with me, and all the guys will want to be like me."

Devon didn't know what to say. His clothes were so "East Coast Maori" that he preferred to stay in his uniform, even during the weekends. Better that, than copping all the snarky comments. In a jacket like this he could go anywhere. Be anything.

Baz McCurdy made to leave. "You guys are lucky that Frank just happened to have fifty jackets on him." Then he said to John, "I'll take the Legacy now, since I'm going that way. Save you towing it tomorrow."

"There's no key," said John.

"I'll manage," said McCurdy, pulling a short length of wire and a screwdriver from his pocket. "I just happen to be carrying my own."

They all went outside and watched John drop the Legacy and unhitch it. McCurdy clambered in and had the car running moments later.

That night the boys slept in a room out the back that they shared with boxes of spares. Everything had the brand and year painted in white on the side. The walls were covered in porno calendars going way back and there was little to show that it was Mitch's room. It was a noisy house. Big John and Uncle Frank were up, talking and drinking for hours. Then the two dogs that slept on the veranda kept hearing things in the yard and jumped up, barking their heads off. Finally, when Devon got up some time in the middle of the night for a pee, he heard the unmistakable sound of rats gnawing in the walls. Even that didn't dampen the prospect of his new jacket, which had made his world seem alive with possibilities.

In the morning Mitch got up early. He wanted to show Devon the car his father had given him. It was cold but Devon wouldn't wear his jacket in the yard because there was too much oil. Too much opportunity to soil it.

The yard, by daylight, was large, maybe half the size of a football field. It had heaps of car corpses all around the perimeter, stacked higher than the eight-foot fence that contained them. There was a circular road that began behind the little house and wound its way through the teetering stacks. To call Mitch's vehicle a car was an exaggeration: so much of it had been cut away with a blow torch that it was not much more than an engine with wheels and a seat.

"Seems to be a bit missing, Mitch." Devon stared at the remaining two panels "Mmm. What was it? The body says eighties Laser."

"You're wrong there, bud, it's my own take on a Mazda, the Madaz Formula 1 series. Stripped back. Now, it's just nothing but go." He took his place behind the wheel. "Climb aboard. I'll put this little mutha through its paces."

The battery was a bit unwilling at first, but after a few tries it fired and then there was no stopping it. The sound of the engine roared straight from the manifold, coloring the sleepy Sunday morning. No further talk was possible. Devon held on tightly to the seat as they raced around and around the yard. Mitch drove like his father, but without the pin-point accuracy. He tended to clip things and Devon made sure he kept his arms tucked in as they flashed by the jagged, rusty stacks. As they were passing the house, a grapefruit exploded over the windshield. It had been chucked by Big John, who stood on the veranda wearing just a pair of tiny purple underpants.

"Hey, Scott Dixon! Knock it on the head! There are people sleeping in here."

They switched off and went inside.

"Real cruel on guys with hangovers. You two are on breakfast duty for that."

There was an old pan that seemed to live on the stove top. Devon noted that the contents showed bite marks: from last night's rats, he supposed; their feet and teeth had clearly scribed prints into the congealed fat. Mitch didn't say anything, just lit the gas and rummaged around in the fridge for bacon and eggs.

Uncle Frank had slipped away during the night, John told them; he had a few deliveries to make.

"You two did all right out of him. There you go, Devon, remember that: a life lesson. Success is just luck and timing. He's usually a bit of a tight bastard but you happened to be here when he was feeling flush."

After breakfast John went off somewhere and Mitch and Devon were left to tinker with the cars.

"He's been at me to take out the headlights so he can sell them on. Want to help?"

For the next few hours they were clambering over the tilting stacks with a screw driver and Twink pen, and loading headlights onto the back of Mitch's car. By the time Big John came back they had prised free about fifty sets. Next they labeled and arranged them by make and model. Big John appeared to be impressed and stood next to the box with his hands on his hips.

"Must be Devon, I can't see Mitch being that organized."

That night they went out to Onehunga to watch the Warriors play the Parramatta Eels. Devon was not really into this sort of thing, or he thought he wasn't, but sitting on the terraces, wearing his new jacket, he felt relaxed and accepted. He was content, almost. The crowd was more interesting than the game. The people in front of him, Mitch and his father, people they bumped into, were all part of something. A shared hope. That their team would win, or at least lose bravely.

As it happened, The Warriors did lose. It was their seventh consecutive loss, Big John said with a shake of his head. But no one seemed downhearted. It was as though they all knew that not today maybe, not tomorrow, but some day, the Warriors would rise again. They'd fill the hearts of their fans with wonder. Faith rewarded. And everything in the world would be okay for another week or three.

It was one of those things, Devon thought, like believing in God. They weren't spectators, these people on the stands, they were a congregation. They belonged.

At that moment, more than anything else in the world, Devon wished he could join them. Wished that he could shed his prickly, unbelieving skin and become one of the many.

They threaded their way out of the stadium. All around them were family groups, subdued but accepting, their faith unshaken, their loyalty beyond question.

By the time John dropped him and Mitch back at school, Devon felt he had been away for two weeks, not just two days.

NINE

For the final term the focus became study and Devon was determined this time to prove to the headmaster, and everybody else, just what he was capable of. He stayed in on the weekends and gave chess away because it drained too much of his energy and attention. The Latin was largely a matter of memorizing and recitation. It became a routine of his to run through sets of declensions and cases until they were so familiar he could chant them out to a rhythm like a rap. Later, he added the extra inducement of stroking himself at the same time.

When the exams finally arrived, Devon was looking forward to them. He was sick of the practice and now desired only to be tested. There were a number of personal scores he was going to settle here and, at worst, he risked not being promoted. As it happened, it wasn't the two firsts (English and Latin) that got him the promotion, it was the seventh in Maths and the recommendation for Most Improved (or as it was known by the boys, the "Try Hard" award.)

A week later Mr. Hockly, the fruity Social Studies teacher, was given a note by the messenger.

"Santos. Here, please." Then he added in a soft voice, "The headmaster wants you in his office now."

For Devon, this time there was no nervousness. He knew he had made it.

The headmaster's secretary scrutinized him closely and had him sit down. A minute or two later the door opened and Rajendra walked out. He looked very subdued.

"He wants you now," he said, and left quickly.

Inside the office the headmaster was not writing busily on a sheet of paper but sitting back and waiting for him.

"So we meet again, Santos, this time, I believe under happier circumstances."

Devon waited. It didn't seem to warrant an answer.

"Do you know why you are here?" the headmaster seemed a bit bemused.

"No sir."

"Well, do you recall our last meeting?"

"Yes sir."

"Yes sir. No sir. Don't be coy, Santos. It's not attractive. I think modesty is an over-rated virtue, and false modesty is craven, to say the least. You earned your place in the school. You've earned your appointment here in my office. And you have earned your place in 4A next year."

These were the words he had longed to hear, had worked so hard for, and now they clattered out into the headmaster's study like dropped coins. Surely they deserved a flourish of trumpets or at least a round of applause. But never mind; the glittering prize was his.

"Be advised, Santos, there are costs that go with every triumph. In order to make room for you in class, we had to remove a boy. Patel has only been in the class for half a year, hardly long enough to find his feet, but already he is going back to the B stream. Don't imagine that this couldn't happen to you. He was not the bottom but he never made enough progress to cement his place."

Devon suddenly felt a pang for Raj. He knew what the move had meant to him, how ambitious his parents were for him, and now he had to wear the humiliation of demotion.

"You are joining the best of the best. This is the stream that produces the leaders. The movers and shakers. The people you read about in the paper. I hope you are up to it. I believe you are. Please don't disappoint me."

On the last night before the end of term, as Devon and his three room-mates were getting ready for bed, Steph suggested they sneak out for a midnight ramble. It would need to be very late, when they were sure there would be no housemasters prowling about.

Next to the bathroom door was the fire escape, seemingly installed for the sole purpose of allowing boys to sneak out undetected. They headed for the chapel which stood in its own little grove of trees near the gate. Steph had his chorister's key, which allowed entry to one of the unused cloister doors.

Devon, who normally relished this sort of adventure, nevertheless felt uneasy being in the chapel in the middle of the night. Although silent and deserted, it seemed that it was full of invisible people. He could sense them pressing in on him. Even in the dark there was a soft glow from the stained glass windows, and he could see the faint outline of Jesus with finger raised above the altar. High above them, moldy old flags hung; a decaying reminder of "the sacrifices made by those who came before". Then there was the special seat where the chaplain perched, and the headmaster's seat with his hymn book placed neatly awaiting the next service. The forbidden territory around the altar was now trampled over willy-nilly by their irreverent feet. Devon's heart suddenly travelled to other spaces; to the wharenui, and the ruined hut in Goldsmith's Bush where he encountered the taniwha. To the other boys it was just a space; to Devon it was a realm, their games a transgression.

At last, Steph revealed the reason he had brought them there. He had a joint.

"Where'd you get it?" Wingnut asked in a hushed whisper.

Steph reached over and gave Wingnut's nose a little tug. He got the message and clammed up.

Steph produced a lighter and played it expertly over this end of the joint. He had a little puff and then coughed vigorously and puffed again. This time he was more successful and was able to keep the smoke down for a moment or two before it all came spluttering out. He passed the joint to Mitch who looked at it curiously and then passed it on to Wingnut. Wingnut stared at the glowing tip. The other three watched for a moment or so before Devon, impatient for his turn, snatched the joint and had a decent sort of pull. Mitch gave an "Oh what the hell" gesture and then demonstrated a major toke. This was too much for Wingnut; he grabbed the stub and inhaled powerfully before simultaneously burning his fingers and exploding into an endless coughing fit. He let out a loud "Youch!" and flicked the glowing roach several rows back into the body of the church. Steph laughed and Devon and Mitch went off to find where it had landed. Before long everyone was on their hands and knees crawling rapidly up and down the rows. Wingnut made a bleating sheep noise. Mitch came up behind him barking and bit him on the bum. Steph's laugh turned into a witchy cackle. Soon everything was funny; nothing was important.

"You guys hide and I'll find you." It was as though Steph had planned this all along. He disappeared into the sacristy and began counting loudly. The others hid in various parts of the nave. When Steph re-emerged he looked different. Bulkier and glowing. As he stepped into the diffuse moonlight by the altar it was clear why. He was wearing the chaplain's communion robes and carrying a decanter of wine in one hand and a shepherd's staff in the other.

"Come forth. Come forth, you sinners. Time to repent." He took a major slug from the decanter and proceeded down into the body of the church, hunting out his prey. One by one each of the others failed to contain his giggles and was flushed out with the crook. Devon was the last. He felt the pressure of repressed laughter welling up. Just when he was sure he had it under control it defeated him in the form of a fart: one of the trumpet-blast variety.

"I smell thee, Satan. I smell thy sulfurish breath …"

"Rank one!" said Mitch. "It's got to be straight to hell for you. Farting in church … it's one of the deadly sins. I know for a fact it really pisses God off …"

"Devon Santos!" Steph's voice attempted the godly tone. "Up with this … I will not put!"

Wingnut jumped on Devon's back. "I got him … I got him."

After this the four of them went up to the altar and lay about on the carpeted area where a few days earlier, they had kneeled to receive communion. The decanter only made one and a half rounds before it was empty.

Steph then wanted to propose a toast so they had to do this with imaginary glasses.

"To the survivors!"

"The survivors!"

Mitch held up his hand. After a moment or two, all noise died. There were torch beams flashing around the main doors.

"They're coming," Mitch said.

"Exit! Stage left."

Steph led the others out the side door just as the caretaker got the main doors open. In bright moonlight they sprinted through the copse of trees back to the silent dorm. There was a warmth to the air: the winter, which once seemed endless, had finally gone.

The last day of the school year began like any other. Being a Saturday without sporting commitments, there were those who tried to sleep in. Others were up early, organizing their things and readying themselves for an early pick-up. Mitch had already gone home because Big John collected him on Friday night; and Wingnut had everything packed and waiting in reception by seven-thirty a.m. When Devon and Steph came back from breakfast he was looking for them to say goodbye.

"My dad's here, I'd better be off. You guys have a great holiday."

Neither Steph nor Devon were looking forward to the holidays. For Steph it would mean being holed up in his father's apartment in a city where he knew nobody. A marathon of books, the internet and TV. For Devon the last few forays down to Whareiti had become increasingly difficult. In the long weekends or mid-term breaks he found it a real struggle to fit back into his old skin, and he would arrive back at school tainted by guilt and failure.

They helped Wingnut carry his bags down to the car park where his father was rearranging the back seat purchases to fit everything. There was another round of "what a great year it's been" and "how fun it's going to be, back home at last". Steph's "jolly hockey sticks" version bordered on sarcasm but the farmer didn't seem to notice. Devon found himself irritated by the farm boy's obvious desire to hurry home to "Mum and Grandpop". They watched the white Fairmont roll out the school gates and thread itself into the busy Saturday morning traffic.

As they walked back to the boarding house, two seniors emerged, laughing and pushing each other, looking back over their shoulders furtively.

"... I wouldn't even go there, man. Not that desperate."

"Coupla bush pigs ..."

In the foyer Paikea and Rawinia stood looking into the glass cases filled with trophies. Devon felt ill. He paused, not want.ing to go in. Steph looked at him, puzzled.

"You go on, Steph, I'll be up in a minute."

Steph looked at him uncomprehendingly.

"It's okay, it's not you, I just ... I just need a moment."

He slumped on a bench out of sight of the foyer. Steph stood waiting, wondering what was wrong.

"Go on. Go on. I'll be up in a minute."

Steph looked at Devon once more and then looked in at the two figures in the foyer before shrugging and moving off.

Devon felt as though his stomach had been ripped out. He could feel beads of sweat prickling at his forehead and neck. He was breathless and giddy, like when he'd been kicked in the balls during PE. Maybe it was the surprise, the fact that he'd dropped his defenses … he'd allowed himself to think the struggle was over now at Barwell's and that everything was okay.

When he finally made himself visible to the pair, it was Rawinia who spotted him first and charged forward, wrapping her arms around him. She had got bigger but she was still really just a baby. Mr. Simmonds appeared.

"I wondered where you had got to. I was about to send out a search party." He said something quietly to Paikea and sat at the duty desk where he had laid out the morning Herald.

"So big. So many boys." Rawinia was overwhelmed. There was nothing about Whareiti to prepare her for this.

"She insisted on coming up. I've been putting her off all year but this time she wouldn't wear it." Paikea came over and kissed him on the cheek and Devon flashed a self-conscious glance around the foyer.

"What? Embarrassed to kiss your cousin? Te Arepa!" Then she laughed.

Devon knew he had to leave as quickly as possible.

"You wait here, I'll get my stuff." And he ran up the stairs to their pen.

Steph was lying on the bed reading, his gear waiting beside him on the floor.

He looked at Devon, who stood for a moment indecisively, his hand resting on his old suitcase. Steph jumped up and wrapped him in a hug. He felt Steph's head resting on his shoulder. For a moment he was pulled between tearing himself away from this forbidden affection and drinking it in. It was too much, too sudden.

Steph took a step back and said, "What's this?" He reached out and carefully caught a tear from Devon's cheek on his fingertip.

Devon stood there, not knowing what to say.

Steph put it in his mouth. "Salty." Then, in a softer tone he said, "It won't be long … but I know it will be long." Then he went back to his book on the bed.

"Bye, Steph."

There was no response from the other boy and his eyes never left the page.

TEN

All the way out of Auckland, Rawinia pestered him with questions. He had no taste for it and tried to buy her off with one word answers. After a while Paikea joined in.

"What's the matter, Te Arepa?"

"I dunno, just feel a bit nothing really."

"I thought you would have been hanging out for this day, seeing your sister again, going home to Ra, Wiremu. Whareiti."

"Yeah, well I was, but now it's like I'm leaving the party. Missing out on the exciting stuff. Going back to …"

"Going back to the boring life?" She flashed him a grin.

"I didn't say that, but I guess in a way it's true."

Rawinia had been listening, waiting for her chance to re-enter the conversation. "So now, you don't want to talk about it."

She was right, too. He didn't want to talk about it. He needed to step clear now and ready himself to live in the other world. The world of Ra and Whareiti. The world where his name was Te Arepa and he had descended from a chiefly line.

True to form, once they hit the Coast road, Paikea let him drive. Once again he was able to pour himself into perfecting his gear changes, picking the line for the corners, making sure he was always in the power band. As they reached the outskirts of Whareiti, Paikea motioned him to turn off towards her cottage. Devon was surprised that there was no one there. He associated the place with Jinny, the van being Paikea's domain.

"Where's Jinny?"

"She's back in the cancer ward." It was Rawinia piping up from her mattress on the floor of the van.

Paikea took a breath and said, "They found it had spread to other parts of the body. That's the thing with breast cancer; the breast is just the start."

Devon looked at Paikea's face for any trace of emotion but there was none. A slight stress in her voice was the only telling sign. She disappeared into the house and came back with a couple of brown folders.

When they arrived home, Ra was at the door as soon as the van cleared the gateway: he must have been listening for it.

"Haere mai, Te Arepa, haere mai. The scholar returns."

To Devon he seemed older, smaller, and more Maori than he remembered.

He came forward and hongied Devon and then pushed his shoulders back.

"You've got taller ... and skinnier. And look at the hair. Don't they cut your hair at that school?"

"No Ra, that sort of thing is our call."

"On my notice board I have the letter from the headmaster. It's all about your success. Your promotion. You must have worked hard for that. The whole whanau is proud of you, boy. We need scholars. They're the new warriors."

Devon wanted to say that he had not done this for Ra or for the whanau, that he had been proving something to himself.

"Come inside, come in and have a kai. I bet you're hungry, Rawinia." Then Ra looked at Paikea, who seemed eager to get back in the van. "You too Paikea, I insist. What've you got there? Claim papers?"

"Ae. They're all you'll be getting for a while."

Ra turned to Devon. "Jinny's been working on the claim."

"A Waitangi claim? No one told me there was a claim."

"Well, you've been busy at school and I've been busy here at Whareiti and Wellington. It's a lot of work, looking at sale and purchase agreements, tracking down our old people. Paikea and Jinny have been helping. Jinny puts it all into good English, the sort of thing that a judge likes to read."

They walked into the kitchen and Devon put his bag down in his little bedroom.

"It's about the land that runs along next to the Pokaiwhenua, all the way to the hills."

On his bedroom walls were pictures of cars, and a couple of pennants. He noticed that Ra had pinned his Barwell's "offer of place" letter there too. It seemed strange to have a room all to himself again, rather than just partitions and the chatter of boys floating around over his head.

He went back to the kitchen and joined the others as they sat down at the table.

Ra continued as though Devon had been in the room all the time. "It includes your old stamping ground, the so-called Goldsmith's Bush. Remember that big tuna you and Wiremu caught there? Well, I guess there will be a few more coming out of there before long."

"Jinny says it's just the beginning; it's got a long way to go." Paikea's words changed the tone.

"I know that, Moko. When you get to my age, you take the long view. I don't expect anything to be sorted in my lifetime. This is for youse." He indicated "the young folks".

Ra had baked scones on the wood stove: cheese and date. Paikea made some tea, Rawinia fetched the big jam pot, and they all settled into a good feed.

After Paikea had gone and Rawinia had been prevailed upon to go to bed, Ra sat in the sitting room poring over the papers in the folder. Devon was restless. He had brought a bunch of books home but didn't feel like reading them. Nearly six weeks stretched out before him and he had no idea how he was going to spend the time.

"So you must be getting used to the school now, Te Arepa. Fitting into their kaupapa, eh?"

"Yeah, I guess."

"Using your own name yet?"

"No. I'm Devon there, Ra, I told you. Maori things are sneered at."

"Not by everyone."

"No. But it doesn't have to be everyone. It still puts me in the losers' camp. I'm there with the chinks, the Indians, the nerds, the fags." He wondered for a moment if Ra would know what the last two were. "It's different here in Whareiti. I can't really explain it … it's just something I have to do."

He looked at Ra. He could tell he was disappointed.

"I know it's not good. I'm proud of what I am, but I keep it to myself. Otherwise I would be defending it every day. It would be all that I am. I'm not ready for that. Remember what you told me: the fundamental principle, the bottom line, is always that the tangata whenua dictates."

Ra nodded; he seemed pleased that at least Devon had remembered this.

"Well, at Barwell's the tangata whenua are the boys in my house. They have their own kawa and kaupapa. Their own ways of doing everything. Those are the rules I have to fit into."

"And if you act too Maori you get bullied? That's what you're saying?" Ra seemed serious.

"It's not the bullying. I can handle that."

"Then what is it?"

"You become a loner. A no-mates. No one talks to you, except the teachers. No one sticks up for you. I've seen it."

Ra seemed to accept this explanation and Devon was relieved. He knew that it must seem like he was a coward to Ra, but he wasn't, he was a survivor.

"The boy who saved the tribe."

The words lay between them like a challenge.

"What?"

"You heard."

"I know what you said ... I don't know what you mean."

"Te Arepa: the boy who saved the tribe. That's what I mean. Maybe the time has come, Te Arepa. The end of a long cycle. A hundred years, a hundred and fifty."

Devon said nothing; he waited for Ra to continue.

"It's not the Ngapuhi this time. Not wakataua pulling into the bay. Now it's talks that we're not part of. Deals made behind closed doors. No blood. No death ... just slowly it all slips away, our land, our culture, our mana maori ..."

"What's this got to do ..."

Ra held up his hand to stop him. "The fact you can't use your name ... that's part of it."

He went off to bed. Devon was left to the creaking solitude of the old house.

For the next week or so he found it difficult to fill the time. There was a trip to the McGregors', who now seemed to have semi-adopted Rawinia. After a couple of weeks Wiremu reappeared; he had been staying with his grandparents in Lower Hutt. Wiremu was into rugby now; that and a cultural group that went around beating other groups in competitions. The gap between him and Devon seemed to have widened.

At Christmas everyone went to the marae. It was a relief to be amongst a bigger group again. Devon was feeling the weight of Ra's eyes and his unanswered questions, but here amongst the music and feasting he could forget about all the things he was holding at arm's length. He was introduced to people — distant relatives he had never heard of — as "the scholar". It was embarrassing at first, but then he got used to it. In a way it explained his difference.

Paikea was there with Jinny, who had lost a lot of weight and whose red head-scarf seemed to drain her face of color. They came over to see him as he sat on the long stool in the wharekai.

"Paikea tells me you're in the A class now."

He nodded, a little tired of talking about it.

"What's it like?"

"I'm not actually in there yet. One of my roommates is. I'll get to sit with him. He's super brainy."

"What's his name?"

"Steph."

"Have you made other friends?"

"Two others, I guess. It's hard to make friends there. Everyone's real tight."

"Paikea tells me you're a driver."

He nodded his head. "I love driving."

"Maybe you can be a courier one day." Jinny joked.

Paikea glanced towards Ra. "I don't think so. His grandfather has got him marked for bigger things."

Later that evening Paikea's remark came back to him again and again. He was marked for bigger things. So, it was not about him, it was about Ra. What Ra wanted. About taking over when Ra had gone. He thought about the life Ra lived. No money. This little house. Always travelling to Wellington and attending hearings. Being the one who was guardian for the whole iwi, while other people went on and lived their lives. It wasn't what he wanted. It wasn't what he was going to become.

A few weeks later, Wiremu showed up early in the morning. Devon hadn't seen him for a while. It was as if they both knew that their old relationship had gone and the new one had yet to form.

"Yo, Rep. Howsit?"

"Kay. What are you doing up so early?"

"My cousin Tania's come to stay. She's got this baby. Jeez, babies make a lot of noise. Once that kid's awake, there's no sleep for anyone."

"I remember Tania. She's got a baby? Can't have. She's only about seventeen."

"No man, sixteen. I reckon my uncle sent her here to get her out of the way. They argue all the time."

"You told me she was the wild one. Always in trouble at school."

"Yeah, she ran away a bit but she's not running now she's got a baby to carry around."

"True. I'll come over. Say hi. Let me wake up first. Since I've been on holiday I try to sleep in later and later. I can go past ten now, but my aim is twelve. That's the time to face the world."

Later that day he dropped around. The house was quiet in the morning because Devon made sure he got up after Ra had gone out for the day. He found it difficult to even look at Ra now without feeling the weight of his expectations.

When he got to Wiremu's, Tania was in the bathroom washing her hair. The baby was in the doorway in a playpen and Wiremu was crouching down playing with it, wiggling his fingers through the bars. Tania emerged just wearing a bra and camouflage trousers. Devon found it hard to keep his eyes on her face.

"So, Te Arepa. All grown up and citified too, I bet."

"Hi, Tania." He wanted to come back at her with a witty reply about how grown up she was too, but for the moment he found words difficult.

Tania walked over and leaned against the doorway. She folded her arms and looked down at Devon; there was something mocking about her confidence. Devon was sure that she would put on the T-shirt that lay ready on the back of a chair but she didn't. Her breasts were large and she seemed proud to show them off. The rest of her was so lean, almost boyish. Her hair was wet and knotted up on top of her head. There was something crazy and fearless about her.

"How long are you down for, Tania?"

"Till they get sick of me, I reckon, or sick of Eru." She leaned over and tickled the back of the baby's neck and he squirmed excitedly. "How about you?"

"For the holidays. It's weird being back, a bit like I stepped out of a party and everything's happening in another room."

"Tell me about it. I reckon I'll shoot through soon. There's been a screw-up with my DPB so I'm high and dry, but when that money comes through, you won't see us for dust."

She reached forward and grabbed Wiremu by the arm.

"Well, come on Wiremu, I promised your mother I'd do your hair today, get rid of that dandruff. Take off your shirt."

Wiremu complied, a little self-conscious at first, and then enjoying his display.

"We're all topless around here. Te Arepa, you should take your shirt off too, and I'll do you next."

For the next five minutes or so Tania worked Wiremu's head in the bathroom sink, occasionally plunging it deep into the suds.

"Trying to drown me!" he bubbled.

"Right, you're done, go and sit out on the step. Next, please."

Devon moved through and stood next to her. It was a small bathroom and her breasts brushed against his bare chest as she cleared away the suds and fallen hair, then refilled the sink.

"Ready for me to do you, Te Arepa?"

There was a flash in her eye, which startled Devon, but the next moment she was plunging his head into the warm water. She leaned over him, working the water through his hair and stroking behind his ears and up his neck. He could feel the soft bulk of her breasts pushing on his back and could smell the fresh, sharp smell of her deodorant. Neither of them said anything other than short instructions for a while.

"Up a bit."

"That's better."

"Feel nice?"

"Good smell, huh. Head up now, Te Arepa, I'm putting the shampoo on. Forward."

He found himself looking straight into her cleavage and holding her hip with one hand to steady himself as she worked the lather in. At this point he could tell for sure he was on the path to arousal. He felt panic but then gave in to it. No number of Latin declensions or thoughts of people he hated was going to stop this happening. There was no way of telling whether she had noticed. To look down would give it away. He gazed closely at the smile on Tania's lips as she kept working up the lather on his head. There was a knowingness there, a teasing, playful power she had over him. Without thinking, he rested both hands on her bare waist, then moments later pulled her in close and kissed her on the mouth. Anything to get rid of that mocking smile.

To his surprise, she kissed back. Everything went still and quiet. She pulled him up against her, their hips grinding together, then her wet hands slid low on his back. He shuddered. They stopped briefly for air and then resumed.

The next time they stopped it was clear that they were both committed. No one was smiling now; there was an urgency between them that required action.

Devon indicated with his eyes, out the door to where Wiremu sat on the back step in the sun. He felt her hand on the front of his jeans. Her mouth twisted slightly for a moment as she reviewed the options.

"Wiremu? Can you do me an enormous favor? Can you take ten dollars from my wallet on the windowsill and go down the shop? Get some conditioner?"

They paused, looking into each other's eyes, waiting for a reply. There was silence.

Wiremu appeared in the doorway.

"Ooooh kay".

Then he sidled off.

Tania had Devon's jeans off much faster than he managed to clear the hooks on her bra. The urgency now bordered on panic. Then she had his cock in her wet hand. He gasped. The next thing was he felt a fluttering convulsion and came immediately, draping the wall of the bathroom with a ribbon of sperm.

"Whoa. Wait for me, Tiger."

"I can still do it."

She started to stroke him.

"You sound pretty sure about that. Been practicing?"

He didn't answer, but took her breasts in both his hands and lifted them so he could kiss them.

"Come with me." She took him by his erect cock and led him through into the lounge where the baby was still gurgling happily in its playpen.

"We'd better be quick. Wiremu has been known to run. Should've told him to walk."

She let him go and leaned along the top of the couch so she could see up the drive towards the main road.

Devon stood there waiting for an order.

She turned back. "Come on man, we haven't got all day."

She straightened up, dropped her cargoes and knickers and leaned forward again, her wrists resting on the arms of the couch. Devon was still hard but couldn't find a way in.

"Not that way man, are you blind?"

She let him blunder around for a moment or two and then reached back and carefully guided him into place. At this point everything became simple. Details disappeared as he focused on her creamy back and round hips. Nothing more was said; both were locked in their rooms of pleasure, where for a while everything melted into insignificance. This time Devon was able to contain himself. He could feel her rib cage heave as she gasped for breath. Then she began to make noises, soft grunts at first, then little affirmations and then finally commands. Across in the baby pen, Eru began to mimic her calls. Finally she shuddered and went limp. Devon kept going but then stopped too. He knew Wiremu would be there soon and there seemed no prospect of coming for a second time.

Tania slid onto the couch and began to rub a towel vigorously between her legs.

"Mmm, yummy." Then she tossed the towel to him. "Better see if you can put that thing away somewhere; Wiremu'll be back in a moment."

He looked down at his cock, which was still standing to attention. It would not be easy getting that into his pants. They both dressed quickly and Tania went out onto the back steps for a smoke. "I sure needed that. You?"

"Same."

"Maybe I'll stay a bit longer, after all."

They chuckled.

"Yo, Wiremu. Ta. How much?"

"Eight dollars ninety-five."

"Small town rip-off. Right, let's do a round of conditioning."

From that day on, Devon's holiday seemed to engage a high.er gear. Time, which had been limping along, now began to gallop. The huge gap before school resumed again shrank into a matter of days. All his thoughts were consumed by the excitement, the anticipation of frantic liaisons. Very little was said. There were no claims of love, no moments of tenderness, just a hungry drive to do the act. Sometimes they would meet in the wasteland next to the old school. Other times it was in Devon's bed after Ra had gone to sleep. There would be a soft tap on the window and Devon would draw Tania in over the sill. For the next ten minutes they would fuck to the droning rhythm of Ra's snores through the thin wall. Other times, if a few days had passed without a chance of sex, Devon would sneak over to Wiremu's, silence Mangu, their excitable Labrador, and then clamber into the room where Tania and Eru slept. This was much more difficult because Wiremu's mother was always up late and the baby seemed to wake so easily.

Their desire made them increasingly reckless. They paid scant heed to the chance of being caught, or any other consequence. It was only a matter of time before everything would be known but they didn't care. Their huge hunger swamped everything. When Devon was inside Tania, life became stripped to complete simplicity. Their mutual need was the only goal and with each coupling they became more practiced, more daring, more successful. When they had finished they ran back to their other lives, still glowing with the warmth of their secret.

There was just a week left before Paikea was due to take Devon back to Barwell's. His only thoughts were how he could delay this; how he could keep Tania near him in Auckland. He had arranged to meet her at the children's playground, which was at the crèche next to the primary school. This was one of the few places where their presence was unlikely to raise suspicion. It was impossible not to hurry when he was walking towards one of these encounters. He hadn't seen Tania for two days; she had been visiting at her parents' house.

When he got there, the playground was deserted. There was nothing alarming about this, as she was often late, but nevertheless a feeling of dread settled over him. He lay on the seesaw and stared up into the leaves of a huge puriri tree that sheltered most of the rusting equipment in the playground. Once again he ran through the options of how to keep this thing going with Tania. He had grown up so much; had come to see things differently. In some ways he felt he knew more than his friends now, even Steph. It would be good to talk about it somewhere where there would be no repercussions.

Then he was aware of a shadow over his face. He opened his eyes. It was Wiremu. He gave a start.

"Shit, you gave me a shock. You sneaker."

"Expecting Tania?"

"Yeah, I was actually. We were going to play with Eru here. Where is she?"

"She's gone, Te Arepa."

There was a triumphant note in his voice. Something gloating.

"What do you mean, gone?"

"She's gone to her parents' place. You knew that."

"Yeah, but she's due back today. She staying on for a while?"

"She's not coming back."

Devon sat up. It was like the day he left Barwell's; he had a sick feeling. The kick-in-the-balls feeling.

"She was only going for a few days."

"No, she was leaving for good. Didn't tell you, huh?"

"No."

Wiremu wandered over and sat on the swing. "She's a wild one, Rep. You know that." Then he said with a smirk. "She doesn't have boyfriends."

"What about Eru's father?"

"Didn't she tell you? He wanted to marry her and everything. Still does, they reckon. She won't have a bar of it. She won't let anyone tell her what to do."

"Tania was cool," said Devon, as if defending her. "She was fun."

"Oh yeah, she was fun all right."

Devon sat up and stared at Wiremu.

"You thought you were the one and only, huh? Well, stud, you were way wrong on that score."

"What do you mean? You and Tania ...?"

"Oh yes."

"Since when?"

"Since the day after she came to stay with us."

"Bullshit!"

"Back at ya, Rep." He stood up and they held each other's stare for a moment before Wiremu turned and wandered off.

"Wait, Wiremu!" yelled Devon, jumping to his feet.

But Wiremu kept walking. As he passed through the gate he raised a hand and, without turning, gave him the one finger.

Devon slumped back onto the seesaw and watched Wiremu

disappear from view behind the school's thick hedge. It was hard to believe that Wiremu and Tania had been doing it but then he knew that Wiremu didn't lie. He didn't have enough imagination. For days after Tania's disappearance, Devon lay about, drained of energy or the desire to go anywhere or do anything. His life lacked any purpose, and yet when he reflected on it, he had to admit that this was inevitable. He hadn't realized that he had allowed a future to grow behind the sex. He had become attached to her. Not just her body, which he believed he owned, but to her funny little ways. Her staunch expressions. Her matter-of-fact, no-bullshit approach to everything. Now she had stepped out of his life as abruptly as she had stepped into it. His heart was hungry for more.

When Paikea picked him up, there were no words of wisdom or farewells from Ra. He had gone to Gisborne the previous day. Devon was packed and waited quietly in the front room in his uniform, studying himself in the old flaky mirror above the fireplace. He seemed the same, but somehow he was different. Older and sadder.

Jinny had gone back to the hospice; Paikea was in no mood for talking. Devon expected her to do all the driving, but she let him take the wheel when they filled up with petrol at a town near Whakatane. His driving had become much smooth.er and more confident now and the tips she gave him were few and far between. Sometimes he would change down too late and she would mumble, "It's laboring." Other times she would just motion with her hands. Devon flashed a look at her occasionally and could see the pain in her eyes. In some ways it gave him strength. "It's tough all over." Her words from that earlier time began to have a deeper meaning for him.

ELEVEN

Devon asked Paikea to drop him at the school gates.

"I'll take you to the boarding houses."

"No thanks, Pike, I'd rather walk. I want a bit of time to think about things before I join in and become a Barwell's boy again."

They pulled in off the busy road into the area immediately in front of the big gates.

"You sure?"

"Yeah, I'm sure. Thanks, Pike."

He grabbed his bag and slid stiffly out of the passenger seat of the van.

"No kiss?"

He looked around to check who else might be watching and leaned back in to kiss the proffered cheek. Paikea grinned, as though she knew the score but wouldn't go along with it.

"You have a good term, don't get swallowed up in that Pakeha stuff."

Then she disappeared down the road and he walked through the great gates towards the hall and admin area. Being Sunday night, there was no one in this part of the school. He reflected on that day when he had come up for the test. The little flags and signs guiding all the newbies. The headmaster and Mr. Simmonds. It seemed much longer than eighteen months ago: so much had happened. It was hard to imagine a year on from now.

In the distance he could hear voices, and car doors slamming in the boarding house car park. When he reached it, the area was filled with cars, and families and boys being dropped off. Most of the older boys made their own way to the boarding house, but the younger boys were accompanied by parents, little sisters, and in some cases a whole entourage of relatives, all eager to see where their charge was going to be spending his next few years. Among them was Wingnut. His father had a new car, a silver Range Rover. His mother and grandfather were with him. Devon kept back; he didn't feel up to going over the whole "How are you? What have you been doing? When are you coming to visit us again?" routine. He was done with that fake crap.

He followed them at a distance, and when they headed up to the pens he took his gear to the common room to wait it out. To his surprise it was already filling up with boys, even though the house assembly wasn't until much later. The place seemed to be teeming with boys younger than he was. Boys carrying pillows. Boys on the edge of tears. Swaggering boys trying to make a mark for themselves. He walked in and put his bag down, pushed a boy off a chair and sat down.

The boy, who was small and blond, scrambled to his feet. He seemed close to breaking down. The outrage. The unfairness.

"You can't do that. I was here first."

Devon smiled. "Yes I can, and more," he said, remembering his first thump.

"Devon!" It was Steph.

He ran forward and threw his arms around him. Devon pushed him away quickly, indicating all the little eyes around them.

Steph was unabashed "We're fourths now, Devon, we run the show. How was your break? Boring? God, mine was. Vast chunks of boredom, sandwiched between big hunks of sleep."

"Same," said Devon, struggling to hold back the Tania story. Since she'd taken off, a lot of it felt too big, too intimate, too much, to be shared with Steph.

"Wade Royle's arrived with a whole flock of his bleating family. I couldn't stand it, had to leave. Farming people become the beasts they eat. Big clumsy creatures with faraway looks in their eyes."

Devon laughed. It was so good to be back with Steph. What an antidote to Wiremu's dim-witted conversations. Soon Wingnut and Mitch appeared, then Mr. Simmonds with Hartnell, who they knew must be the next head of house. From then on there were the speeches, followed by the introductions, which were fairly abbreviated. Then came the mugs of Milo, and back to the pens.

That night, as they lay in bed, Mitch and Wade gave lengthy accounts of some of the things they had got up to. In Wade's case it was a list of agricultural jobs that he described in great detail. He would have gone on all night, but Mitch began to make loud snoring noises.

Mitch had met up with some guys who were part of a street racing set. He had spent most of the holidays in and around cars. Every incident figured smoke, loud exhausts and near misses.

"Near misses?" asked Devon drowsily.

"Near misses with other cars, with cops, with blowing the motors ..."

Mitch had gone from car fiend to full-blown petrol head.

Steph affected an immediate boredom with this, but there was a part of Devon that needed to hear more. Part of him had a hunger for the wild and the lawless; the head-clearing anarchy of speed and destruction. Something explosive enough to snap all the strings that held him back.

Being in 4A didn't seem very different at first, but it sure put

Devon under pressure. In his old class he was able to rely on his impressive general knowledge. Unlike the other boys who grew up in the city where there were always other options, Devon had spent much of his early life reading. He had been right through Ra's battered old Everyman's encyclopedia, studying the murky pictures and complex diagrams when the city boys had been playing computer games or sport, having birthday parties or trips to the mall.

But 4A was different.

Here he was amongst boys who seemed, like Steph, to have it all sussed. There was a resident group of Asian geniuses. The speed with which they did their maths was unbelievable. It was like they were years ahead and all school did was hold them back. In English and Latin this wasn't the case, but it would never balance out. Devon could tell that the prize for making it into 4A was going to be slaving away harder than he ever had, just to keep where he was. Running on the spot like Alice in Wonderland. There was something else he hadn't considered. Steph had got him in and it would be Steph who kept him there. There was a price. Steph demanded more from him: certain people were to be kept well clear of. And he insisted on other things too … like Devon joining the choir.

Steph had been in the choir since the day he arrived. Joining meant that you immediately had "suss" stamped on your brow. For some this meant you were a bona fide, card-carrying fag; for others just that you had become part of something that made you terminally uncool. Your jokes stopped being funny. You were the last to be picked for any team at PE. You were on the receiving end of the "noises". These noises were a call for general derision whenever the need arose, and it arose frequently. Particularly if you did something difficult or impressive. Unpopular boys were showered in honking laughter.

Devon didn't want to join; it would put his invisibility under pressure. But he had to do it. Without Steph's patronage he would never hold his place in 4A. He knew that, whatever else happened now, there was no going back.

Being in the choir meant frequent practices before school and once or twice a week in the evenings, depending on what events were coming up. Steph was quick to point out that the biggest incentive for being a member was having somewhere to go in the evenings other than the dorms, where you got picked on by predatory seniors.

The music department was housed in the Flagg-Lewis Suite. It had been built with the proceeds of a bequest left by a wealthy Old Boy who owned a ubiquitous courier firm. The yellow vans with the red flag motif were seen everywhere in Auckland: but this brand power had a different connotation at Barwell's. Here it carried a palpable smell of dubiousness because of its association with things cultural and hence dodgy. At Barwell's, if it wasn't a sport, preferably one that inflicted regular injury, then it was a poofy activity and drama and choir were at the "fag" end of the scale. As a result, the building was invariably referred to as The Fags and Losers Suite: shortened, in adult hearing, to the FLS.

Set apart from the other buildings, the FLS consisted of a number of small practice rooms built around an auditorium. There were different rules here. In the FLS everything was based around popularity, attractiveness and favor. Size and seniority counted for little and nothing was beyond the boy who played the system to his advantage. In this place Steph's success had been meteoric. It was easy to see why he had gravitated here. Not only was it a safe haven, but also a place where, in no time, he had established himself amongst all the power elites.

Like many boys in the FLS, Steph was a "pet" to some senior: in his case a quiet boy called Barry Briggs. Back in Marsden House, Briggs was not someone with whom Devon and Steph had any real contact, but here in the music suite it was different. FLS rules applied.

Briggs always had something secret to tell Steph. When he talked it usually involved whispering, his face close to Steph's ear. This was followed by frequent high-pitched giggles. None of that could happen in Marsden. There were little presents from Briggs too, and favors.

Steph was wearing Briggs's watch. He had one of his own but he wore Barry's. He got to use his phone too. Steph, for his part, just had to laugh at the lame jokes; smile and allow himself to be hugged.

Nothing was ever simple at Barwell's, though, and the FLS was no different. What made it tricky was the Director of Music, Mr. Willis (Willie to the boys).

Willie had arrived with a flourish halfway during their third form year. The old Director of Music, Mr. Walker (nicknamed Johnny Walker because of his whiskey breath) had left suddenly. When Willie arrived, the headmaster had introduced him as a "new broom". It was hard to know what had the biggest impact on the school: his haircut, his bright red Mini, or the revamped rock songs he introduced to morning assemblies. It was as though he had a license to do just whatever he wished.

Needless to say, in the FLS it was Willie who set the standard for everyone else. His "cool stuff " — his jokes, his clothes, musical tastes — became the boys' "cool stuff " when he was around. This was an unspoken understanding. After evening choir practice, the music was pumped up and everyone danced as though their lives depended on it. Even here, his moves were the ones that counted.

A week or two after joining the choir, Devon was on the receiving end of a story which all the other boys claimed to have heard many times.

Willie had been teaching Steph a long, complicated piece on the piano in one of the practice rooms. They sat together on the piano stool, hands rushing up and down the keyboard.

It was late, and Devon should really have returned to Marsden, but he sat and waited for Steph so they could walk back together.

When they had finished, Willie pushed Steph off the long piano stool and turned to give Devon a piercing stare. It was as though he was seeing him for the first time.

"So, Devon, what is it that makes you tick? Do you have a dream? Do you have a vision that marks you out from everybody else, or are you content to be one of the crowd?"

It was a loaded question and didn't need an answer.

"Do you know how I came to be here today? Can you imagine all the events and actions, great and small, that have led up to you and me sitting here in this practice room?"

Steph smiled and excused himself. He seemed to know what was coming next. Devon longed to follow him but was held back as if by some unwritten obligation.

Willie played a rapid little phrase on the piano, which Devon recognized as silent movie music signifying that something was about to happen. Willie was in his element. The tone of his voice softened and his face took on a more intense, focused look as he went back to the beginning.

"I wasn't born playing this thing. When I was young my parents were killed in a car crash and I was sent to live with my aunt in Rotorua. She was a spinster; do you know what a spinster is?"

Devon nodded.

"My aunt taught music for a living, from the front room of her huge lake-front villa. In many ways she was a dry woman ... had never been loved and could not give love. But she wasn't without passion, without emotion. You can't understand music without these things. It was just that all that energy had become channeled into the teaching of music. I know this because it lit a fire in me."

He stopped to let this image sink in, and then he continued.

"I don't remember when I first began to play but I am told it was about the age of four when she decided that it was time for me to learn to express myself musically."

Willie plinked away at some memory loosened by the notes.

"I do know, and this is a matter of recorded fact, that I won a piano competition in Rotorua at the age of eight, against all comers. I have been told that at the time, the judging panel simply couldn't believe that a child of eight would have the strength, or the hand span, to master the piece I played. Let alone interpret it with such maturity."

He stopped for a moment as if reflecting on his own dazzling promise. Then, while softly tinkling the keys with his left hand, he launched back into the narrative.

"From then on it was back-to-back scholarships as I was groomed for musical greatness. For some years I knew nothing but triumph. I set myself impossibly difficult challenges and met them with consummate ease. It seemed as if nothing could stop me. And then ... it happened. The incident that meant my future as a performer was effectively over."

"What happened?"

"I was bullied, Devon, bullied by a group of Maori thugs." Then, after a moment, "No offence."

"None taken, Mr. Willis. Include me out," Devon replied coldly.

"Willie, please. All my friends call me that." He paused, giving weight to the invitation, and then continued in a lively tone. "They were jealous of my talent. Jealous of my ... difference. Jealous of everything I was and they weren't."

"What did they do?" The question seemed to be expected of him.

"They used to go out of their way at school to torment me. They would steal my lunch, slap my head when I sat at my desk working, call me 'fag' and 'queer.'"

He turned to Devon. "So you see I know a bit about bullying. I know what happens at this school and I make certain that it will never happen in my domain. Devon, these boys made my life hell."

He turned around further on the piano stool and leant in close to Devon's face. Devon could smell the sharp, sour reek of his breath. He struggled not to recoil or let it show.

"One day when I was in the sixth form, my music case was stolen. It contained not only the music which I was supposedly performing at the prize-giving but also the pieces I had written myself. You must remember, I was made much of at school and this created jealousy. The sporties didn't like that."

He paused as if steeling himself to re-engage with this ancient battle.

"Anyway, I decided this was the end. It was time to fight back. Hell, I wasn't going to have my career ruined by a group of Neanderthals. I went to the principal and told him everything. This principal was a keen amateur musician himself (no real talent but he responded to flattery) and he declared war on this group."

"What did he do?"

"He suspended them."

"Did that stop it?" Devon asked, even though it seemed unlikely.

"As if ..."

"Why not?"

"Well, Devon, there are some things that can't be stifled easily. My success had, in some way, rocked their world. Shown them that they just weren't good enough, never would be. The principal may have suspended them but he never provided the protection I needed."

He paused and then added contemptuously, "So what happened? He imagined his word was law. The day before prize-giving they all came trooping back to school, from their three-day suspension. And they were after me. I fought bravely but there were too many of them." He held up his hand, showing a knobbly bone growth on the back.

"The rest is, as they say, history. They broke my hand. There was no performance at the prize giving. But that wasn't the half of it. Do you know many bones there are in the human hand?"

Devon shook his head.

"There are nineteen in the hand and fingers, another eight in the wrist. It's a complex mechanism, and they all have to work in concord. Mine refused to knit together or in any case they never articulated in a way that allowed me to fly over the keys like a concert pianist."

"But you do fly over the notes like a concert pianist." It seemed to be the easy compliment he was seeking.

"Oh thank you, Devon." Willie gave a little sigh. "There were some who said I could have been the best this country has seen. The new Michael Houston. But that dream died that day behind the school assembly hall."

"What happened to those boys?"

"Who knows? Who cares? Presumably they have gone on to dazzling careers at Paremoremo[85] and now are subjected to regular humiliating and degrading acts. One can only hope so. They were well qualified for that at least. But Devon, what value is revenge? Does it bring back the dreams and promises that nurtured you?"

Devon said nothing. For a moment he thought of the dreams and promises he was nurtured on. All they had done was make his life more difficult.

"No, it doesn't. But that was not the end of me; I wouldn't allow it. Although I was physically quite small, still am, 'Not a very impressive specimen,' the Scottish head of PE used to say, I had a heart and a dream that wouldn't die and I came back triumphantly as a composer."

"You write music too?" How easy it was to lead this guy on.

"Oh yes, Devon, screeds of it. Concertos, symphonies, chamber music, you name it."

"Rock music?"

"Of course. There are no genre restrictions in the world of music. I have written whole rock operas, easily the match of anything written by the likes of Lloyd-Webber and Rice."

"Really?"

"… Yes really. In fact, I intend staging one here, at Barwell's, this year, and Devon, I hope that there will be a part in it for you."

"A rock opera?"

"You know Cats, The Phantom of the Opera, a fully-fledged oratorio, and made for boys' voices."

"No girls?"

"Oh girls …? You want girls?" He seemed to milk the moment. "There will be girls. We are combining with Saint Leonard's Anglican Girls' School."

"SLAGS in Remuera?" asked Devon, the idea of those snooty girls coming into Barwell's was beyond his comprehension.

---

85 high security prison

"Yes, the same. I will be bringing girls into this school and it is not before time."

After this talk, it seemed that Devon was accepted. He had listened sympathetically to Willie's story, he had asked the right questions, he had demonstrated the correct level of adoration. Steph would have been proud of him.

Back at Marsden House, though, Hartnell began to assert himself. That he was made head of house over Briggs was a clear message from Mr. Simmonds. It was sports over the arts. It also meant that there was little Hartnell couldn't do. Somehow the lesson of Mitch's beating had been rewarded: Simmonds had sided with force. The house was a changed place now as a new regime established itself. Devon could feel Hartnell's eyes on him in the food queues, at dorm inspection. He knew it was just a matter of time before things deteriorated.

He grew to dread the days Hartnell was on duty. By becoming head of house something new was released in him: a hunger for persecution that now had few boundaries. Some of the younger boys, particularly, regarded him as a hero. This made him worse. There would always be something that Devon got picked up on. At first it was just low-level stuff like finding fault with the tidiness of the pen they shared and making the four of them do extra routines. That was fairly standard; even Adam Neeson had done that. It was a way of telling juniors that they had become big-heads.

Then Hartnell decided it was time to re-name them. It was a talent he had developed quite a rep for in the school and he took credit for many of the catchiest names. Mr. Robertson, the chubby physics teacher, was called Rubber Bum. Mr. Becker, the chaplain, was Pecker on account of his big nose. Wankin' for Mr. Rankin the groundsman who couldn't say his Rs.

Hartnell seemed to have accepted that Mitch, and by association the other three, couldn't be physically bullied so he was determined to do otherwise.

Mitch became Monkeyboy, Wingnut was Sheep, and Steph, Queenie. He kept his original for Devon: Nigger, or Nig if a teacher was around.

As Mr. Simmonds withdrew from the low-level running of the house, so it was Hartnell's voice that dominated the intercom. Here he had a wider audience for his announcements and it seemed that Steph and Devon were often on the receiving end.

"… and so they ask me, do we have a fag-free house here at Marsden? I say to them, not quite. Yep, that's N for Nigger, Q for Queenie …"

For a while the choir diversion worked and life became more bearable. Steph and Devon excused themselves from the house as much as they could by volunteering for every possible duty. Hartnell's ability to make their lives hell seemed to recede into the distance.

The FLS was only a few hundred metres from Marsden House but in some ways it was like a different galaxy. Under Willie's control the rule was "anything goes". The dress code, the age hierarchies, and enforced masculinity didn't apply. Illicit snacking, loafing and generally goofing off went unreprimanded. Although evening choir practice was meant to run from eight to nine-thirty in fact it ran until Willie felt like packing it in. Other times it continued even after he had left. Briggs was the FLS monitor and locked up when he felt like it.

Some weeks into the term, the spell finally broke. It was a particularly cold night, and Steph and Devon set off to evening practice. Devon was wearing the HDT jacket that Mitch's Uncle Frank had given him. As they were passing through the house foyer Hartnell's voice rang out.

"Not so fast, Nigger boy, where do you think you're going in that jacket?"

Devon froze. He had forgotten that Thursday was Hartnell's night. He hated answering to "Nigger" but there seemed to be no way around it.

Hartnell and Mr. Simmonds's understudy, Peter Newell, came out of the office. Newell stood in front of the double glass doors, arms out, blocking their exit.

"Choir practice! It's allowed," Devon said, the indignation creeping into his voice.

"Queer practice! It's allowed," Newell repeated, using a faggy lisp to draw in other boys who were going past.

"He's right, Hartnell. You can check with Mr. Willis." Steph tried to smooth things over. He was wearing an old striped blazer, but Hartnell wasn't interested in that.

"I'm not going to ring up Mr. Phallus. I reckon anything goes in the FLS." Hartnell winked at Newell, and then added to the growing crowd of juniors, "I don't want to even think what you arse-bandits get up to."

Newell and the others hung on every word, their faces red with excitement.

Then Hartnell came up so close that Devon was bathed in the stench of his sweat. "What I do know all about is what you can wear around this place."

He waited so that even the youngest and dimmest had time for the full import of the words to sink in.

"Everyone knows there is a no-mufti rule in the houses until fifth form. Last time I checked, you two were in the fourth form. You're a year early."

Then, turning to the gathering crowd, he added, "I reckon that over-rides all the stuff that you choir fags are allowed." He placed his hand over his arse.

There was a roar of approval from the gallery of onlookers.

"So let's have it."

No response.

"Come on, take it off."

And then louder and more insistent, "I said, take ... it ... off ... now. I'm confiscating it. You can get it back off Mr. Simmonds directly. See what he's got to say about it, Nignog."

"I'm not giving you my jacket. You can report me to Mr. Simmonds, but you're not getting it."

Devon tried to push Newell out of the way but it was no good; he had a firm grip on the brass handles.

"You're not going anywhere, Nigger; not till I say you can." Hartnell had this tired sing-song voice now, and shook his head in disbelief. He turned to a couple of fourth formers who were watching with great interest. "You two, give me a hand with this Maori will you? The jacket's coming off. I'm confiscating it. End of story."

The smaller of the two, Brian Nobles, seemed reluctant, but the other one, Josh Cockburn, held Devon's wrists low so that Hartnell could slide the jacket down. Then Newell was able to slap a headlock on Devon, forcing him face down onto the floor.

"Whoops … down he goes, just watch that jigaboo eat carpet."

By the time he was released, Hartnell had squeezed into the jacket and was adopting poses for the other boys. "Now, a lesson." He started talking "retarded" style.

"Nig, see jacket? Me wear because me senior. You no wear because you junior. Simple for your brain." He looked around, luxuriating in the adoration.

Something snapped. Devon sprang. He grabbed at Hartnell's face, screaming and swearing. For a moment Hartnell was caught by surprise and the two of them went down, but it wasn't long before Hartnell had Devon flat on the ground with his arms pinned up his back.

Devon's face was red and tear-stained, pressed against the carpet. He kept repeating. "You fucken, fucken cunt. I'm gonna kill you."

Hartnell looked up at the crowd that now surrounded them. "Whoooo! I'm real scared! See the headlines — 'Hartnell mugged by angry black fag.'"

Nobody was laughing now. Hartnell gradually released Devon and then stepped back, fists up and ready for another onslaught. Devon sat up stiffly, sucking on his bleeding lip.

"Want some more? Want some more? I got plenty to share."

Hartnell, part of the wrestling team, was very confident in the fight situation.

But Devon didn't advance. He stared hard at Hartnell for a moment, visualizing shit and vomit, all the ugly things … then he burst out through the double doors, unopposed. Steph, waiting silently for him, opened his mouth to say something and then shut it again. As they walked towards choir practice Steph put his arm across Devon's shoulders. They waited for a while outside the FLS for Devon to compose himself and then went in.

Devon ached from the encounter, now that the adrenaline had worn off. Scenarios of murder and maiming played in his head for the rest of the evening, right through the hymns and folk songs they were rehearsing for the mid-winter choir festival.

They finished earlier than usual that night because Willie had to go somewhere. Briggs tried to persuade Steph, and by association Devon, to stay on with him, but they had no taste for it. When they returned, Devon was surprised to see his jacket lying on the bed. He had been sure that he would be retrieving it from Mr. Simmonds, maybe not until the end of term. As soon as he picked it up he realized why. There was a big split under the right arm. Hartnell had been wearing it when he fought him and he remembered hearing a tearing noise, which he'd assumed was his uniform shirt. The hole was big enough to put a fist through. Repairable maybe, but now ruined. Defiled.

He showed Steph.

"What can you do? I knew from the first day he was going to be trouble, but he has reached that seniority now where there is not much anyone can do about it. It's how these places work. I know these things, remember. I've been to a few."

"Yeah, well, there is something we can do. We can get him kicked out."

"And how, pray tell? For bullying? I don't think so."

"No," said Devon, "not for bullying, for tearing my jacket. He can buy me a new one."

"I don't think that's going to work. You've got the jacket back. Anyway, legally I guess he was allowed to take it. Seniors can confiscate jackets; happens all the time."

"And the rip?" Devon asked.

"Well, he can claim it was already torn or that it happened in the struggle to get it off. Rough and tumble. 'Boys will be boys'. Anything, really."

Devon felt a sense of helplessness. Futility.

"Devon, it's like Rome here. He's like a patrician, or a senator, and we're just plebeians. In lots of ways these schools are modeled on the Roman Empire, they don't change, that's why they last. That's why people want to send their kids here."

Devon looked at the floor. It didn't wash. Steph couldn't explain this away or make things seem all right. It wasn't salvageable; it wasn't bearable.

"That's the finish. I don't want to stay here anymore. Place sucks. I'm out."

Steph looked worried. "Devon, we will get our own back. He will pay for this, but we will do it the smart way. He's got the other ways all covered."

"Yeah? Like how?"

Steph, for once, looked defeated. He had no answer, no reassurances to offer. Then something appeared that Devon had never seen before. Beyond the irony, there was a seriousness, a determination. Steph's eyes hardened and when he spoke it was with a low, calm voice.

"I'll find a way. Trust me on this."

Devon looked at him. "Promise?"

"Have I ever let you down?"

TWELVE

A week or so later the term finally sputtered to a halt. Devon found himself once again heading down towards the Coast road with Paikea in her courier van. Hardly a word was spoken for the first hour and Devon waited in vain for the chance to drive.

"I know what you're thinking, Devon. When's my turn? Well, not today. I need to do this myself today."

Devon had thought that she was angry with him. He was now thoroughly used to adults being angry with him: almost expected it. But she wasn't angry, he could tell. There was a weighty sadness about her that he had never seen before.

Back at Whareiti that evening Ra explained. "Paikea has had a hard time recently. Jinny's cancer has returned aggressively, and she's not expected to last much longer."

Later, he said, "I've had a letter from the school about stuff you have been getting up to but I'm not going to say anything about it now. I would like you to talk about it, when you're ready. We've got a bit of time on our hands, but don't leave it too late."

The holidays, which Devon had been dreading, took on their own slow, low-key torture. There was nothing for him at Whareiti. He had no interest in the local kids now, and hardly even left the house. The only thing which gave him any sort of relief was chess. The book of chess games he had brought back from the Barwell's library helped to sustain him during his long periods alone. Each day he would set up a new game to ponder over. He sensed his opponent in this sequence of moves. It had his personal signature at first, but then gently it built into a distinct personality.

He spoke to it. "Your move, Diego!"

One day Wiremu showed up. Devon stood staring at him for a while as though he was a complete stranger.

"Well, aren't you going to invite me in, Reps?"

"I'm not Te Arepa, I'm Devon. That stuff's long gone. Come in if you want." He was shocked at the coldness of his voice, as though it came from someone else.

"Ra tells me all you're doing is sitting at home playing chess all day and talking to yourself. What a sad one, eh?"

Devon didn't bother responding.

Wiremu blathered on about stuff he'd been up to and things he had planned for the next few weeks, while Devon stared out the window, waiting for him to finish. After a while there was the welcome sign of awkwardness creeping into his tone and Devon knew it wouldn't be long before he gave up.

"Why don't we play a game of chess?'

"You know how to play?"

"Course I know how to play."

"Okay," said Devon with a sigh. Anything to shut him up.

He set the game up and turned the board around to let Wiremu play white.

"White starts."

"I know."

A minute or two later he was surprised to see Wiremu clearing out the pawns on the king's side. He brought out the queen and Wiremu was in trouble.

"What's happened?"

"That's it. Checkmate."

"No way, I wasn't ready, it's a trick."

"It's called 'Fool's Mate', a bit hard on the ego."

Wiremu stood up. "Stupid fucken game, anyway. Should call it nerd's revenge."

He moved towards the door.

"You going?"

"What do you think?"

And he was gone.

A day or so later, Ra made reference to this incident.

"What was I meant to do? Let him win? Make him feel better?"

"That's not the point. That's not why we play games. Haven't I taught you anything?"

Devon glared at him. "Yes Ra. You've taught me plenty."

Ra opened his mouth to speak and then shut it again.

A few days later Devon noticed that Ra was putting on his old suit. It had the musty smell he remembered from when he was tiny. They exchanged looks but neither was willing to speak. The coldness that hung between them made it difficult now to even broach the mundane. Ra waited but when nothing was spoken he finally announced, "Yes Te Arepa, I'm off to a tangi, since you have to ask."

"Whose?"

"It's Jinny's. She died on Wednesday. She's up on the marae, now."

Devon nodded, said nothing, but inside he felt an aching regret. He should have contacted Paikea.

"I'm not going to ask you or tell you to go. But you do know it's on."

He went off mumbling to himself while Devon watched him walk out the gate from the kitchen window.

He turned back to his game, trying to nullify the gnawing guilt that Ra's casual news had planted in him. Having lost his queen so early in the game, his position was difficult. It was a knotty problem. Once again Diego had out-smarted him. He'd seemed to struggle when Devon had taken the black bishop and rook. Devon moved in for the kill but what seemed so easy was in fact just a ploy to ensnare his queen. He sat down and looked at the alternatives; nothing stood out. Nothing had a future beyond four moves. Devon was restless and agitated.

"So you think you've got it all sewn up, do you, Diego?"

It was impossible to sit down.

"What's the matter? Cat got your tongue?"

It was no good. If there was some way out of this mess then he certainly couldn't see it. Ra had put paid to that. He wandered out to the gate and looked up towards the marae. In the distance he could see the glint of cars parked out on the roadway.

Everyone would be there.

Everyone, except him.

He set off on a whim: there was no benefit in sitting around. When he reached the edge of the field, his eye was caught by the smoke of the hangi fire. There were a couple of older men with long poles digging out the stones. Three other people stood around watching. He was too far away to recognize them. Everyone else was hanging around the paepae as he expected. He could see Ra chatting to a couple of old kuia.

He climbed the fence and walked towards the fire. The thought of all those introductions and then explanations was more than he could take, especially from people who felt sorry for him because of his parents. As he got closer he noticed that two of the watchers were Paikea and Jim Herewini. He liked Jim because of his stories and dumb jokes. But it was odd that Paikea was out here in the men's domain. He expected her to be in the wharenui next to the casket. Since Jinny was a Pakeha this tangi was more for Paikea than anyone else.

He walked over and put his arm around Paikea's waist. It was an action that surprised him as much as it did her. She put her arm on his shoulder but said nothing.

It took a moment or so before Jim noticed him standing there.

"Hey, it's the boy." He smiled. "Kia ora, Te Arepa."

Devon leant in for a hongi and then stared at the pink embers shimmering through torrents of heat haze.

"I should be throwing Jinny in there." Paikea spoke more to herself than anything.

"What?" asked Devon, incredulous.

"Don't get me wrong. Ra wanted to show some appreciation for her work on the treaty submission. I know it's a big deal, treating her like she's one of our whanau." She paused tentatively. "But it's not what she would've wanted."

"I thought she was sold on the maoritanga[86]."

"Jinny's field was anthropology. Indigenous people's rights, not only here but worldwide. She took the bigger view. It drove the people in Wellington mad. She'd always go right back to the beginning of things. Then she would look at each change, who did what, and why. That sort of thing. She always wanted to know the big why."

Paikea's voice trailed off. Devon noticed that silent tears were running down her face.

"But her faith was different. She was a Zoroastrian. That's what we believed in."

"Zoro what?"

"It's a religion from Persia. Have you heard of the Bahais?"

Devon nodded.

"She and her husband were Bahais. They're a modern version, but it wasn't enough for her. She began to dig and didn't stop until she came to Zoroaster. Drove her husband mad."

She laughed softly.

"Then she met me."

"How was that?"

---

86 Maori cultural practice

"I was a wild one. I was burgling their flat in Grey Lynn. But that's all a hundred years ago. We found that we weren't so different. I was her warrior and she was my prophet. We had five years together."

"So you both became Zoroastrians?"

She smiled. "Something like that."

"Do you believe in reincarnation, all that Indian stuff?"

She nodded. "Everything comes back. The dead, they are all waiting for us you know, can't you feel it?"

Devon nodded. Yes, he thought, I can feel it. This is something I know.

"Better go. I've got a date with the weepin' and wailin' women. Coming?"

"No. I just wanted to see you. That's the only reason I came."

There was something about his tone. She stopped and stared at him for a moment and then leaned forward and lightly kissed him on the cheek. "You've done it then. Hei konei ra, Devon."

He watched her walk off to where a small cluster of women in black awaited her. Jim was giving instructions to the hangi cooks. It was a good time to go.

It was a week or so later that Devon woke with a start in the middle of the night. There was no noise, not even Ra's snoring. But there was something wrong — he knew it. He went to the back door and walked to the front gate. Somewhere in the eastern sky there was a flickering glow, but it was far too early to be the coming of the new day. Back in bed he was too restless to get back to sleep. Some time later, maybe an hour, he heard a siren.

That afternoon when Ra returned, he heard the full story.

The fire at Paikea's cottage. How the farmer had been burned trying to get her out. It wasn't until he had smashed the door that he discovered every exit had been locked and barricaded. The heat had been so intense that even the fruit trees had been charred in the little orchard out the back, fifty metres away. Ra had brought back a burnt peach to show him. Paikea's beloved courier van had caught fire before it could be moved; finally it exploded, flattening the back end of the cottage.

Ra said she was mad with grief.

Devon thought otherwise but kept his opinions to himself.

When it came time for Devon to return to school he had to take the slow bus trip. No more drive North with Paikea.

THIRTEEN

A week or so after Barwell's term had swung into action again, everyone was roused from their beds at six a.m. and sent to the common room in their pajamas.

At first the boys were sure it was a fire drill but these had never been held so early in the morning. And anyway, the alarms weren't ringing.

The juniors were all made to sit according to their pens, the seniors alphabetically. It was obviously serious. Mr. Simmonds looked very grumpy. He wasn't wearing a tie. He hadn't even shaved.

Mr. Faull was ready for the morning run in his track suit, trainers and whistle but now looked anxiously towards his boss. There was a rule of silence, enforced by seniors. A couple of juniors were dispatched to ensure that no one was missing.

Then the rolls were taken.

Mr. Simmonds stood up to address the boys, his voice holding a slight shiver of anger. "Something terrible has happened in Marsden House, something which has shaken my belief in you boys to its roots."

He paused characteristically to let every syllable sink in.

"Last night while most of us were sleeping there was a thief in our midst."

Another pause.

"I am inured to the occasional 'borrowing' that goes on here. I know you are not saints and that you take things that are not yours ... but this was of a different measure."

His gaze trained restlessly across the faces of the assembled boys, looking for the giveaway sign that signaled the "snake in the ranks". Then he told them what had happened.

"As you all know we operate here largely on a system of trust. That's the glue that holds any society together ... without it, there's anarchy."

There was the murmur of the younger boys wondering what anarchy was.

"Well, anarchy has descended upon us this morning and the consequences will be dire."

Further murmuring as other boys struggled with the vocabulary.

"You all know that on my desk I keep a box. That box is where money and phone cards are stored. The money belongs to a number of people: the bursar, various students who have entrusted me their term's allowances. It also holds the proceeds from phone card sales, and advance collections for house trips and charities. It is the financial epicenter of the house."

He looked directly at Mitch and then continued.

"It's a secure box, made in Germany. There's one key and I have it here," he said, holding it up. "One would feel ... that given all these measures I have put in place ... I would be seen as," he couldn't resist breaking into jargon, "exercising due diligence. But I was wrong. Some weasel ... yes, I use that term advisedly ... some weasel has stolen the box and I believe that he is one of us."

There was an outbreak of mumbling, harshly responded to by the seniors' glares and a few well-aimed slaps that soon restored the silence.

"At this very moment trusted members of other houses are poring over every locker, bed, nook and cranny in Marsden and you will not return to your pens until the money has been recovered. I'm not talking about a small sum. I'm talking about more than a thousand dollars. And yes, the police have been informed. The machinery for punishment is now in place and the result will not be less than expulsion but will more likely amount to a criminal prosecution."

With that he left the room. There was an immediate stunned silence followed by rapid swelling of mumbled questions, theories and accusations. This time the seniors did little to suppress the noise — they were too busy delving into this fascinating speculation themselves. The cash box had long been cited as the ultimate prize for any thief, but had normally been referred to in jest because of its believed invulnerability. Now that this bastion had fallen anything was possible.

For two days after this, whispering and suspicion ensued, with many boys being called to Mr. Simmonds's office for interrogation. It was not long before Devon and Mitch were summoned to explain the origin of their Holden jackets. There was little doubt where this suspicion had come from. Mitch explained how his uncle had gifted them the jackets, but Simmonds was far from convinced. He rang Mitch's father, Big John, with the two boys standing in front of his desk. After a minute or so of cagey explanation, there was the outraged sound of Big John's voice exploding from the phone. Mr. Simmonds held the receiver at a distance from his ear for a while and then, unable to break into the tirade, thanked him and hung up mid-expletive.

"It seems your father, Mitchell, is quite adamant the jackets were purchased and given legitimately. Please explain to your father, when he's in a calmer frame of mind, that what we're doing is quite routine and not aimed at you in particular."

"I'll try, sir, but once he gets an idea in his head, it's hard to shift."

Mr. Simmonds looked a little worried as he escorted them back into the common room of Marsden House and called in a couple more boys.

Towards the end of the week things slowed down and it seemed that whoever had stolen the money box had pulled off the perfect crime. Everyone was watched closely to see if there were any giveaway changes in spending patterns or behavior and it was clear that the whole house was going to be in a state of permanent suspicion. Privileges were suspended and the TV room was off-limits after the six p.m. news was finished. The weekend loomed and all leave was going to be out of the question. Theories ranged wildly.

Mr. Faull announced to the boys in the common room that Sunday night that he believed he knew what lay behind the robbery. It was the work of boys in a rival house who wanted to break the Marsden House spirit. Ever since they had moved into first place in the house competition "certain factions" had been quietly doing everything they could to drag Marsden House down. "But we are not about to let that happen, are we boys?"

"That's so Mr. Faull," said Steph at the breakfast table the next day. "Good old Farty, he believes that the house system really matters. He's a true believer."

Just when the following weekend also seemed doomed, Peter Newell came running into the prep room all excited, blurting out the news. There was a break-through in the case. Graeme Hartnell had been called to the housemaster's office. He'd been there for more than an hour and then taken to the headmaster's office. There was a police car in the driveway.

This seemed too amazing to be true. Everyone knew that Hartnell's family was as rich as stink; he flaunted it at every opportunity. Why would he steal the box? What proof could they have? It was impossible.

However later that evening, his parents arrived and took him away.

"He has been suspended and is 'helping the school with their inquiries,'" said Adam Neeson, who for once had been drawn away from his studies. He was interested in how the incident was handled from a legal stance and this was a great chance for him to casually toss around the jargon.

He was emphatic about it. "You juniors simply must not jump to conclusions when something is still clearly subjudice. The presumption of innocence is a basic tenet of the British legal system. The evidential process must be followed scrupulously or what chance is there of a fair trial?"

Mitch was smirking at Devon; there was something almost God-like about the justice of this.

At breakfast the following day, the word was out that there had been an anonymous tip-off, pushed under Mr. Simmonds's door, which had alerted him to the traceability of the phone cards. Telecom were contacted and that was all it took. Hartnell had loaded his phone with the cards the same night the box had been stolen. Although the evidence was "circumstantial" as far as Neeson was concerned, it seemed watertight to everyone else. Later, when some twenty dollar notes were found between the pages of a maths book in his locker, the matter moved to "beyond reasonable doubt".

By the middle of the following week it was all common knowledge. Hartnell had transferred to another private school near Hamilton. He refused to admit any guilt whatsoever but could not account for the loaded credit on his phone. His gear was packed and waiting in the duty room to be picked up.

When Hartnell's mother arrived, Mr. Simmonds called for someone to carry his things to the car park. Hartnell's mother was impressed by the boy: by his willingness to help and by the sincerity with which he relayed to her what a loss Graeme would be, both to the school and to him personally. He asked her to pass on his best wishes to Graeme, and the hope that things worked out better this time.

"Well, thank you. Who shall I say helped me?"

"Tell him it was Nig."

"Nig?"

"Yes Nig, short for Nigger. We all have nicknames here."

She looked at him doubtfully for a moment and then said "Thank you, Nig, I'll be sure to pass that on."

With Hartnell out of the way, peace reigned in Marsden House. No one was exactly sure what had happened to him, but the principle of "what goes around comes around" seemed the most likely explanation.

The weekends were still a problem. Mitch, without warning, failed to return one Sunday night. When Devon finally reached him on the phone, all he would say was that Barwell's was getting in the way of his education. So now Saturday and Sunday were like a vast uncrossable plain at the end of each week. The tedium was numbed by hanging out in the Flagg-Lewis Suite with Steph, listening to music and, increasingly, smoking weed.

Steph had a steady supply and was always inventing a reason for them both to sneak outside to the little copse of trees next to the chapel, and light up. They would lie down in the manuka and flax wilderness garden not forty metres from the main driveway to the school.

"So where does this come from?"

"Ah, there's a riddle ..."

"I know ... Briggs."

The thought of Briggs being his dealer set Steph off on a wild coughing fit.

"Get real, Devon. Look, no offence but you are a real country boy about some things. I can see why you get on so well with Wade Royle and his woolly clan."

"I don't."

"Never mind." He sniffed, rolled onto his back and said, "Let me tell you something, Mr. Devon Santos. Something which I'm surprised you don't know about. We ... that is, you, me, all of us fellow boarders, are stuck here, imprisoned week after week while fifty metres in that direction," he pointed towards Newmarket, "the world and his brother rattles by. It's no coincidence that this school's been sited close to Mount Eden prison, because we're prisoners too. We just don't need the bars." He pointed at his forehead. "The bars are all here. Or should I say there," he said, pointing at Devon's forehead. "The reason I smoke this, the reason I am able to get weed, is because I have found a way to slip past those bars. I have the tools and the weapons to do it."

Devon, the dope beginning to slow things down, was having

trouble keeping up with this.

"We have two things going for us, Devon, but most of us are too scared or too stupid to realize."

"What two things?"

"We have our youth. Our pretty faces and our young bodies." He flashed a model pose at Devon. "We are full of future possibilities. All of them — the adults, the teachers, everyone really — they're all stuck in the world. Bogged down by ..." He paused and attended to removing the tiny leaves from a manuka twig, "Their responsibilities."

He turned to Devon again. "Don't you realize that we aren't? We can do what we like. We have what they want ... we can give them some of it ... and then take what we want." He held up the joint as if to illustrate the point.

Devon mused on this, wondering what Steph would say next. But he said nothing.

Then as if he had finally exhausted the subject, Steph sat up and said, "Come on. Let's go to the music suite. I feel like I can handle a good blast of early Sonic Youth."

They carefully wriggled out of the bushes and made their way past the big hall. Steph talked loud and fast, waving his arms about and every now and then jumping up and doing a little spin ... the trademark Steph-is-stoned move. Other than this he seemed to be able to function normally in a half-stoned state; in fact, he said, it made everything easier.

It was not the same for Devon. There was a point where the dope seemed to open a curtain and expose a dark place: somewhere unpredictable and scary. First, came the creeping unease, then the feeling of being watched. It followed him everywhere, and everything he saw seemed to confirm it.

Just when they needed it, the FLS was locked up, but the sound of a piano rang out through the louvres in the skylight. Devon and Steph banged away at the door but it was hopeless: the insulation in the practice rooms was too good.

"Give me a leg up, man."

Steph knitted his fingers and boosted Devon up onto the low entrance roof. He looked around; they had been warned about climbing on the roof many times, but there was no one near. Heaving himself onto the flat roof he moved towards where the relentless piano exercises came from.

"Oi, Briggs! It's me and Steph. Let us in."

It was only a guess but a fairly safe one: Briggs was legendary for the amount of time he put into his practice sessions.

"Who is it? Devon?"

"Yo!"

"Go to the door then."

Devon and Steph were allowed in, the door locked behind them.

Steph reached up and put his arm around Briggs's neck. "Thanks, Barry, you're a mate."

It was an odd move, Devon thought. They went off to the control room and Briggs returned to bashing away on the piano.

Steph was still trying to find the tracks he wanted on the computer when the piano stopped and Briggs appeared in front of the big window separating the control room from the recording studio.

"You guys want coffee?"

Steph made a kiss sign at him and he disappeared.

Later, when they had almost forgotten why he'd left, he appeared at the door with three mugs in his hands.

Devon opened up. "Oh legend!" He made to take his and Steph's mugs but Briggs made a point of handing Steph's to him personally.

"Thank you, Barry, you are a … special person. Isn't he a special person, Devon?"

Devon nodded.

"We only came over because I knew you'd be here. He's got an amazing keyboard technique, Devon." Steph turned to Briggs. "What did Willie say about it?"

Briggs wouldn't be drawn so Steph tried a new tack. "Let's go to the practice room and you can do us something soulful."

He ran on ahead, calling back to them as they walked along the corridor. "I know ... that piece by Erik Satie, da da da da da dum."

"This?" Briggs stroked out the poignant, silky notes.

Steph clasped his shoulders and breathed huskily in his ear, "God, that's so sexy. You could get someone to do anything with that music." He caught Devon's eyes in an ironic flash.

"What was it that Willie said? Go on ... tell us. Pleasey please ..."

Briggs blushed but then said, "Oh something like, 'it's the sort of technique that can't be taught.'"

"It's true, Devon, feel his hands. Go on, feel them."

Briggs seemed reluctant to offer them and Devon felt a bit awkward, too.

Steph grabbed both their hands and put them together. Then for a moment or two the three of them were yoked together in Steph's grip.

"There. Not so hard, huh?"

Devon looked at Briggs's face. It was inflamed and bumpy with acne, but being in the proximity of Steph made him redder than ever.

Steph toyed with Briggs, treading the fine line between teasing and tormenting.

"Barry, what do you look for in a girl?"

"Do you look for the same thing in a boy?"

"Ever had a girlfriend?"

"Ever done it?"

Briggs tried to answer honestly and candidly but was being set ever more testing questions.

"Who do you think of when you're playing with yourself?"

"Ever been down on someone?"

Devon could see the relief on Briggs's face when Steph finally excused himself to go to the toilet. It was short-lived: the moment he returned, Steph was at it again from a new tack.

"God, it's weird. That music, so soft but so powerful too, sort of licks away at you." He stuck his face only inches from Briggs's. "Know what I mean?"

Briggs nodded and began to play again.

Steph leaned over his back and said, "God, that makes me so horny, why do you play it? You know the effect it has on me."

He straightened up and when Briggs and Devon looked at him it was obvious he had an enormous erection. He looked down at his bulging trousers, and then threw back his arms as if surprised, "My God, what is happening to me? Barry what have you done to me?"

Devon twigged to it a moment before Briggs lunged out from the piano stool to touch it.

Steph jumped back with a laugh and pulled down the front of his trousers to reveal the cardboard tube he had secreted whilst in the toilet. Everyone laughed but Devon and Steph laughed a lot longer than Briggs.

"I guess you guys better be going."

Steph was tucking in his pants again. "Yes, Barry, you're right, I think we'd better."

He had a fake shocked expression, as if he'd been violated, and as he walked out, he reached around to cover his arse.

They ran clear of the building, laughing and squawking, and didn't stop until they were back on their beds in the dorm.

"Steph, what was all that about?"

"I wanted to show you something. Something I learned. Something you need to know."

"I need to know that? I don't think so."

"Yes you do. In lots of ways you're still just a naïve little Maori boy from the Coast."

"Don't you call me that."

"Well, you are. And you know it. Look, Devon …" Steph stood up to see if there was anyone lurking in the other pens. "I told you that I had a boring holiday. That all I did was read and sleep, but I was lying."

"So what did you do? Go to all the gay bars of Wellington?"

"Gay? Straight? That's such shit, Devon."

"Oh yeah?"

"Course it is. During the holidays I found a friend. A secret friend."

"I don't know that I want to hear this story."

"My friend ..."

"The word is 'he', I reckon ..."

"Okay, he then, was secret not because he was a he, but because he was much older than me, one of my father's colleagues."

Devon didn't say anything.

"There were a lot of things that could have gone wrong, but they didn't. I reckon I learnt more in those ten days than I did all of last year."

Devon put his fingers in his ears. "I don't want to hear this, Steph..."

Steph came over and sat on the edge of the bed. "You know how we had that argument with Mr. Carell, the one about Achilles and Patrolocus? The great fag debate?"

"So you decided to put it to the test?"

"No, it's just that I wanted to make my *a priori* knowledge a bit more *a posteriori*."

"Yeah. So you put your posterior on the line?"

"Forget the sex stuff. That's just packaging. It opened a door and I peered through. The stuff I saw ... well, it changed the way I look at things. I stopped being scared. Nothing scares me now."

"Briggs sure doesn't."

"He's nothing. Just something to practice on."

"So you spent your holidays doing stuff for your father's friends?"

"Just one friend. He's got a boy my age."

Devon was appalled. "Poor kid, that's all I can say. Jesus, he's someone's dad. Steph, how sick is that?"

Steph continued unabashed. "The thing is, Devon, we're in charge now. I told you it's us."

"Until another cunt like Hartnell comes along. He will. Briggs might turn into one."

"Ha! He's my pet. I'll show you. You want a hamburger? Something at the shops?"

"Maybe …"

"Wait here." Steph hurried off. He was back in about five minutes.

"So where's the burger?"

"You wait."

Devon was beginning to feel a bit queasy. Steph had gone too far. About ten minutes later, Briggs came hurrying in with takeaway packs from McDonald's.

Later Devon said, "That's sick, Steph. In some ways that's even sicker than the games you were playing in the green room."

Steph looked up from the *Vogue* he was reading, "Don't look a gift-Briggs in the mouth."

As Devon suspected, the path that Steph had shown him the previous weekend had only just begun. The following Saturday morning, while the others were off doing sport, Steph proposed that they should go and call on Willie in his flat.

"I don't think so. Just because you're his little pet in the music suite doesn't mean that he'll want you turning up on his doorstep first thing on Saturday morning."

"You're wrong, Devon. That's exactly what it means. I know for a fact that he always sleeps in on Saturday mornings, so he will be thrilled to see us."

"Well, he may be pleased to see you, but I doubt he's going to be pleased to see me."

"Oh it's 'the more the merrier' with him, you wait and see."

They got Newmarket leave, as it was called, and went towards Mount Eden where Willie's flat was located. It was a big house and he rented the back half of it.

His red Mini was parked in the driveway.

Steph pointed to it. "You'd like this, I'm guessing. I'll get him to give us a ride in it later."

It took a number of knocks before Willie came to the door.

It opened a crack first on the end of a chain. Devon glimpsed a disheveled Willie lurking in the gloom.

"So it's you."

"T'is I, Willie, are you going to let us in?"

"Who's with you?"

"My trusty side-kick, Devon Santos, of course. You didn't expect me to come alone?"

The door closed and they heard the chain being unhooked. Inside the flat was the sort of chaos that Devon relished. Such a contrast from the severe order of Marsden House. Everything lay everywhere. The hall floor was strewn with dirty clothes and underwear. This led directly into the sitting room where, amongst everything else, there was a piano, an immense TV, and stereo speakers. Scattered around were mixing boards, CDs, a laptop, some bongo drums, a couple of acoustic guitars.

There was only one couch and it looked as if Willie had spent the night there. Takeaway boxes lay on the floor and the huge screen flashed endlessly as though Willie had fallen asleep in front of it. He flopped onto the piano stool.

"Take a pew," he said, indicating the couch. Willie surveyed the mess, as if noticing it for the first time. "Yeah, I was up late last night, ripping through DVDs of 'nineties musicals, looking for stuff to steal. I must've finally keeled over about three a.m."

He paused as if losing track. "The next thing I hear is you two banging at the door." He yawned and scratched his balls absently. "You could've been anyone."

"Well you were wrong. It was someone. Us."

"I feel like my head's been sat on by an elephant. My IQ must be in the single digits."

He stood up and peered through the curtains.

"What do you say we go for a swim? I need something to cut through the static."

"Yeah, why not? It's winter. The beach is logical," said Steph.

"We haven't got any togs," said Devon, more thinking out loud than actually saying anything.

"Togs? What are they? Don't need togs man, we can go to Ladies' Bay, swim in the nick." Willie searched around and came back with a couple of stained old towels.

"Here … these okay?"

So they were off. Devon squeezed into the back seat and Willie, warming to the task, fired up the sounds.

"Industrial techno …" he said, as if answering a question. "Great for straightening out battered brains. Reprogramming."

They wound their way around the waterfront. The Saturday morning traffic was frenetic with families all going places. Willie fancied himself as a zippy driver but was thwarted at every turn. At the end of the winding esplanade they climbed up to a cliff-top look out. There were a few seats and an arrow showing a path to the beach. After they had parked, Willie led the way as they threaded their way down the cliff. Steph seemed familiar with the place and Devon wondered if he and Willie had been here before.

The beach, predictably, was deserted. It was an overcast day in winter, bordering on bleak. Devon and Steph sat on the pebbly foreshore, determined that this was as far as they were going. Willie made a big point of being energetic and, looking neither right nor left, dropped his trousers, then slid off his underpants. He stood there in front of them as if it was the most normal thing in the world. His cock was large and he flapped it around as he wrestled out of his upper garments. Devon tried to look somewhere else but it was pointless. This display seemed to have been engineered for Steph's benefit.

Willie, now completely naked, was eager to get the others to follow suit. "Come on you two, let's have them off. Don't be pussy."

Devon looked at Steph. He was sure that this sort of "Yo ho! Last one in's a rotten egg" sort of thing was so un-Steph. However, a moment later, he stood up and began to slide out of his clothes. Willie stood by with undisguised interest then ran out into the grey water.

Devon waited for a moment to see whether Steph was indeed going to go through with it and then took his clothes off too. For a moment they both stood on the edge of the sea looking at each other's cocks.

"Yeah, I reckon it's the thought of the cold water," Steph said, as though answering an observation made by Devon.

"Didn't seem to have that effect on Willie."

"Willie's willie," said Steph and they both sniggered and then began to edge their way into the freezing water.

Willie turned to them as the seawater rose to the level of his balls. "Come on then, no girly noises." Then he dove forward and swam strongly away from the shore.

Devon turned to Steph — he was sure he would bale at this point — but he lunged awkwardly into the water, so Devon followed suit. It was unbelievably cold. Devon could feel his heart beat madly against his rib cage.

After four or five strokes, Steph turned to him. "I reckon we've done enough. He wants to kill himself, let him."

They both turned and powered back to shore. An elderly couple appeared as they reached their clothes. They had walked around the corner from the next beach. The boys huddled in the security of their towels, hoping they would walk quickly by.

It was not to be. The woman seemed determined to speak to them.

"It looks cold, boys."

Devon grinned. "It is cold."

"Your father doesn't seem to mind." She indicated Willie's bobbing head one hundred and fifty metres from shore.

"No brain, no pain," said Steph and the couple laughed and moved off.

Once they were a decent distance away, Devon and Steph struggled back into their sticky clothes, still half wet. What had been a very quick operation when they first arrived became tricky as their clothes bunched and caught on their wet bodies.

As the couple cleared the next cliff and disappeared into the next bay, Willie re-appeared a little sheepishly. His attempts to be nonchalant seemed forced and slightly desperate. Devon noticed the cold water had shrunk his cock considerably, but it recovered once again as he stood in front of the two of them and dried it vigorously.

"Okay, Willie, check. Got the message." Steph seemed unimpressed.

Willie slipped on his underpants, sat next to the boys and lit up. Steph put his hand out absently and Willie passed the joint to him. It was obviously a ritual of theirs. Steph took a quick hit and passed it to Devon. He had a puff and passed it back.

Willie looked on approvingly.

"You do that well, Devon. Been smoking long?"

"Ever since I was about ten."

"Hmm. Hard core," said Willie.

Steph looked away as if hiding a smile.

When they got back to the flat, Willie suggested they have a shower to warm up. Devon didn't like the idea but Steph went in like it was no big deal.

Willie dug around until he found a DVD of the movie *Platoon*. "You might like this."

For the next few minutes Devon did everything he could think of to block out the thought of what was happening in the next room.

When Steph finally re-appeared he seemed a bit distracted.

"He'll be in there for a while, a good chance to score."

Steph went and pulled a cigar box out of one of the big bookshelves at the end of the room. Inside were bunches of tinnies with rubber bands around them. He helped himself to a few and threw one to Devon.

"He never knows. I've been helping myself for months."

He then took a furtive look back into the bathroom where Willie was taking a never-ending shower.

"Willie, can I have some money?"

"I gave you twenty dollars."

"I know, but that's way gone."

There was a pause. The shower went off. Willie emerged and

fossicked for his wallet in the back pocket of his jeans.

"Here's twenty. Make it last."

"Twenty dollars each."

"What? You'll bleed me dry, you little blood sucker."

"That's the idea. Forty dollars. Twenty each."

"Well, I've got an idea."

"What's that?" There was a knowing air to Steph's response, Devon thought.

"I think since we have Devon here we should do a few more photos. I'm looking to expand my portfolio." He fumbled about in the shelves by his piano.

Steph looked at Devon. "Are you up for it?" And then, in a softer voice, "Willie wants his quid pro quo."

"To take photos of us?"

"Oh yeah, but in poses. And in the nick of course."

Devon was diffident.

"Come on, Devon. Be a sport." Willie changed his tone theatrically. "No animals will be harmed in the making of these pictures."

He held out a folder filled with black and white photos. On the top was a photo of Steph sitting on a chair somewhere. He had no clothes on, one leg tucked up, and he was staring wistfully into the distance.

"That was taken at the Urquharts' lodge on Waiheke, remember that afternoon, Steph?"

"I remember sitting on that chair for an hour while you took about six hundred photos of me."

"It's not easy to take a good photo. Any monkey can point and click."

Devon flicked quickly through the thick wedge of photos. He glanced at Steph.

"Yes, I know," said Steph, as if answering a question. "Most of them are of boys and most of them have no clothes on."

FOURTEEN

When school finished on Tuesday afternoon, Devon waited outside the FLS as arranged. Where was Steph? He never expected such a big crowd waiting to go in. Not only were there girls from Saint Leonard's Anglican Girls' School, the closest girls' school, but there was also a good number of the older "sports hero" guys who thought any association with the FLS was much the same as wandering around with an "I'm a fag" sign pinned to their brawny backs. But here they were; even Lance Hendricks, the grizzled hooker from the first fifteen. He was Samoan and looked to be about thirty years old. He sprawled on the benches near the main entry with several of his mates, eyeing the girls and laughing loudly. There were also other seniors who had famous reputations as thugs, geeks or nerds.

Devon waited nervously to one side, trying to keep an eye out for Steph but also to stay well clear of this intimidating mob. A few younger guys arrived but turned away when they saw the assembled crowd milling noisily by the glass doors. After a few minutes without sighting Steph, Devon knew it was impossible: he felt too exposed and vulnerable. Then there was a cheer; someone showed up to unlock the door. The crowd surged in.

Now that their backs were turned, Devon was able to follow them into the auditorium without drawing attention. He found a spot to sit in the darker area of the tiered seating. Still no sign of Steph. Centre stage, Willie sat at the piano, talking to a middle-aged woman clothed entirely in black except for a pair of shiny red shoes.

About this time, Steph and Briggs appeared from the wings carrying a long table. They disappeared momentarily to return with two chairs. There was something of the comedy duo about them which provoked a derisive cheer from the rugby contingent. Briggs immediately scuttled off into the wings. Steph froze mid-stride and then turned to face his tormentors. There was a moment of deliberate pause before he performed a slow and deep bow, then straightened up, gave his trademark stoned spin and skipped off the stage. There was spirited applause starting from the girls, and then reluctantly followed by the boys.

The woman walked to the front of the stage and stood staring into the audience with her hands on her hips. The whiteness of her face was dramatized by arched eyebrows, thick mascara and crimson lipstick. With her lush, glossy hair secured by a number of black combs, she reminded Devon of something Japanese he had seen in a magazine. Although she was not part of the school, there was something challenging about her: something "in charge" that gradually subdued the rabble to silence.

"You will never see a better example of impromptu theatre than that," she said, indicating the point where Steph had exited. "When I arrived here ten minutes ago, and I saw the assembled 'talent' waiting outside, my heart sank. I read your attitudes, your faces, the way you were standing and sitting. Without exception they all said the same thing: 'I want to be looked at, I want to be adored and applauded.'"

A few students squirmed, recognizing themselves in that description.

"I knew then that this was going to be a long haul. But when I saw that boy carry out the table and salute your taunts, I knew there was at least one person here who knows what it is to be an actor."

Devon felt pride for Steph.

Someone snorted loudly up behind him.

"Some of you know me. We did *Pirates* with a few of you at Saint Leonard's two years ago. My name is Dianna Davis, but here," she indicated the area around her, "you can call me DD." There was the subdued mutter of "DD" around the auditorium as the boys tried it out.

"Mr. Willis and I intend trying something a little different this year. He has written a libretto to which I am going to fit character and movement. It's called *Original Sin*. He can tell you about it."

Devon felt his ear being tugged. It was Steph, who had run around and come in the back way.

"She's been praising you. You should've heard her. 'The only real actor here ...'"

"I don't need her to tell me that," he said with a fake flick of his hair. "I have been acting since birth. My first costume was a knitted cap and a pair of Huggies."

Willie moved forward and stood beside DD, downstage.

"Thank you, DD. I know why so many of you have turned up for this. It's no surprise. *Pirates* was the talking point of the year. Sports events come and go but something happens when we perform. It goes deeper."

There was a ripple of comment at the "goes deeper". The capacity for fag puns was a touchstone for rugby heads. There was an ongoing competition to see who could get in the fastest or crudest rejoinder. Willie, however, continued unabashed.

"*Original Sin* is a musical in the rock genre. Its look is gothic. The theme is identity ... and that's explored in many different ways. We aren't looking for talent as such; we're looking for commitment. It's surprising how talent emerges from hard work. Once you miss a couple of rehearsals, as far as I'm concerned ... you're gone. Today we'll get you to read, to sing and to move. Next week we'll cast and from then on it's sweating it out ... week after week until the performances at the end of term three." He looked to DD. "Anything else?"

She put her hand on her hip and lowered her voice an octave. "This is a standard speech, a bit like a disclaimer, but I am obliged to give it. We're bringing two single sex schools together. We're not too old to know what that means." She glanced at Willie. "If I come across any impromptu or off-stage dramas being enacted, well, what can I say, there will be consequences, and a bucket of cold water will not be one of them. We have a job to do, so we challenge you to show us what you're capable of."

They were mixed together in groups and taken to various locations where they were given about a minute each to "show their goods" as DD put it. Steph was in the same group as Devon so he was able to provide the sort of clues Devon needed.

When practicing for a speaking part they were given a piece of poetry to read. It seemed easy but tripped most people up. It began with the lines, "I caught this morning, morning's minion, kingdom of daylight's dauphin, dapple-dawn-drawn falcon, in his riding ..."

When Steph's turn came, he was able to make its stop-start cadences sound like normal speech. Devon tried to emulate him but it was like walking to the end of a greasy pole: he got nearly to the end when he crashed into undignified gibberish.

The singing was easier: the choir had taught him something, and his improvisation ("going to the dentist"), was given noisy acclaim.

A week later the real auditions were held. Both Devon and Steph were given roles as clones. These were the rejected prototypes which Dr Funkenstein made before perfecting his all-dancing, all-singing monster. They were not eligible for leading roles on account of their being too small. The leads were given out to Lance Hendricks and his friend Frank Little, both in the first XV. They were big and looked their parts in lab coat and suit.

Because Devon and Steph had minor roles, they were not going to be needed for a few weeks while the hard work went into knocking the leads into shape. When they were finally called, they found themselves paired up with their equivalent girl clones: Sina and Vanessa. Sina was the sort of Samoan girl destined to be head prefect. The daughter of an Anglican minister, she wore a blazer emblazoned with her accomplishments.

"My God!" said Steph, "You must have stolen these or bought them on Trade Me. Speech, netball, choir, orchestra."

"All she needs now is drama, and she'll have a complete set," said Vanessa. Her own blazer was conspicuously bare.

"You know me," said Sina. "I'm just your typical FOB over-achiever."

"Where are yours, Vanessa?" Devon asked, disingenuously.

"I've only got one, but I didn't earn it at school." She plucked a small silver marijuana leaf on a chain from her pocket. They all exchanged smirks. It was going to be a good team.

It was soon clear who was in control. DD strode around driving the brief auditions, while Willie seemed content to sit in the background and play small pieces for them to perform to. When he tired of this, Briggs took over. Even in these short interludes it was easy to see that Briggs had something to prove.

DD quickly blocked out their stage moves, taking her cue from notes she had scribbled in a wire-spined notebook. They were repeatedly told "time is of the essence, you will only be shown once", and that detail and polish were their personal responsibility. "Whether you shine or fade comes from here and here," said DD, indicating her head and her heart.

At Saint Leonard's, the girls hurried Devon and Steph away to find a rehearsal space by the flagpole, well away from the distractions of the auditorium. There they chalked out their movements on the tarseal. Their roles as clones required them to all play the same person but with subtle ways of distinguishing one from the other. Sina attempted to inject some sa sa[87] moves into her persona while Vanessa seemed to specialize in Goth posturing. Before long they had a small audience of third form girls who were waiting to be picked up by their parents.

Steph was good at mimicking the girls' moves and suggested that they do the "boy" versions. Steph found the gloomy poses easy to incorporate in his act, but Devon struggled with the Samoan dance moves. Sina came around behind him and wiggled his hips while he shoo shooed with splayed fingers. He felt awkward in the face of her fluidity.

"Come on, Devon, get in touch with your inner brown." Sina seemed to think it was all very funny, and, as if to rub it in, Steph sashayed around in front of them, easily achieving the frenetic hip movement.

"He's a natch … Devon, you had better go with the Goth."

Devon was relieved to be upstaged here and soon they both had something worth performing. The gaggle of admirers had grown to about a dozen and they were egging them on.

Back at the auditorium doors, DD was watching with her hands on her hips. Devon could tell she thought they seemed to be onto something.

When they returned to the darkness of the auditorium all the other groups of clones were watching in the stalls as DD tried to steer the two Barwell's leads around the stage. Every action had to be spelled out by her, and her mounting exasperation was obvious. The two footballers' incompetence, combined with their embarrassment, meant they were getting worse, not better. Finally DD let out a scream and ordered them off the stage.

"Steph! You and your friend come down here and show these two how to meet in the street. Something obviously foreign to their experience."

Devon and Steph, both confident now, bounded onto the stage. They had a brief discussion and then approached from opposite sides.

With the lumbering walk of eighty-kilogram rugby players, they went into their ritual of exaggerated recognition, the shoulder-pushing and hand-slapping that they saw performed every day in the corridors of Barwell's. It worked brilliantly on the first take.

DD, who was seated at a table, jumped to her feet. She paused to hitch up her skirt and adjust the glossy black feather boa that floated behind her as she pounced around the stage. Hendricks and Little seemed to shrink into their seats as she strode over.

"See that! See that! Every step and move has a meaning. Their bodies and faces canted towards the audience for easy reading. Every aspect of the male ritual observed. Now you do it."

The two props didn't know where to look as she leaned over them. They knew they were being called to account, and that failure at this point amounted to major disgrace. They slunk up on to the stage to give it one last shot. Following Steph and Devon's demonstration exactly, they approached from opposite sides, grinning and shambling. What followed was hopelessly clumsy. The audience were exchanging the embarrassed expressions that amounted to a collective thumbs down.

"Thank you. Thank you. That's it for today, boys. I will contact you at Barwell's through Mr. Willis. Bye now."

Then she turned to the waiting clones.

"Okay, clones. Into the wings and then come out in the order I picked you."

She left the stage and sat in the stalls waiting.

Each group of clones took the stage and performed their piece. As each group performed, they tried to outdo the previous one by over-acting. Devon noticed that there was a SLAGS style about them which rendered them all much the same. By contrast, Steph and Devon's Samoan/Goth interpretation immediately assumed star quality.

Willie materialized from the back of the theatre and joined DD in the stalls. After everyone had performed their pieces, DD called over Devon and Steph and indicated that they should sit and wait two rows away. Her mouth had a pinched look as though she were trying to suppress what it was about to say.

"I'm sorry, Willie, but I'm simply not going to invest any more of my time, let alone squander my reputation, by putting on a show with those two bozos as the male leads. Sorry, but that's it."

Willie, looking as though he'd foreseen this, said nothing.

"I used to be of the opinion that one could teach anyone the rudiments of acting … it certainly has been true so far, but these two … the only thing one can do is bury them deep in the chorus and hope they become invisible."

Still silence on Willie's part.

"Well?"

He seemed awkward, as if backed into a corner. "DD, you'll get no argument from me. These productions have always been a venue for the jocks to perform for their admiring mates. It's a boys' school tradition; they have this expectation of roles."

"Boys' school tosh!"

"Oh, I know that but …"

"I wouldn't put up with it at Saint Leonard's," she said. And then added coldly, "I think too much of myself to get pushed around like that."

"These are the best of the seniors, DD, you should have seen my preliminary list. It's the reality of school musicals at Barwell's; it can't be helped, I'm afraid."

"It can be helped." She indicated Steph and Devon with a haughty swish of her hand. "These are the two leads I choose to work with and if this steps on the toes of the Barwell's elite then that's the price we'll have to pay."

"I may get a mass walk-out."

"Then we'll fill their parts with girls."

"The script calls for adults."

"Rewrite the script man, it's not Shakespeare."

That seemed to be the end of it. Against Willie's wishes, Devon and Steph had secured the roles of Dr. Funkenstein and his monster.

FIFTEEN

The immediate impact of this decision was, as Willie had predicted, a mass walk-out by the senior boys, leaving no boy in the cast older than fifteen. New aspirants were found. Girls were drafted in. The script was changed. Everything seemed to be building around the new leads.

For Devon and Steph, the next few weeks' school work — in fact all aspects of school life — seemed to shrink to insignificance, as their energy was soaked up by the production. Almost immediately they discovered that they had inherited a sort of star status, but this was mostly amongst the SLAGS girls. Their pre-eminence allowed them to exploit the house rules. There were so many special exemptions for rehearsals and other matters that in the end Mr. Simmonds gave them carte blanche and they were able to come and go as they pleased. Most evenings now were spent at the rehearsals even though their own actual rehearsal time was relatively brief. When they weren't needed they would play cards in the green room, waiting for DD's little bell to ring to summon the next group up on stage.

Steph was in demand from all quarters. Willie would take him to one side at every opportunity to work through his solos. Briggs would insist on Steph helping him with his rehearsals. DD used him to demonstrate moves for the more clueless in the cast. It seemed to be the world he was born for. At the end of the evening there was a small core of cast and crew who would repair to the green room for coffee and progress updates. Even at these, Steph's opinion was sought and in many ways he was treated as an equal by the adults.

It was about this time that Devon noticed Briggs begin to change. His willingness and generosity seemed to come at a price. That price was exclusive rights to Steph's attention. When Willie called on Steph, Briggs watched them closely, no matter what else he was doing. Later there were petulant recriminations.

"What did he want this time?" Or perhaps, "Why did you let him put his hand on your shoulder?"

"Did I?"

"Yes, you did."

But usually it was the plea for equal sharing.

"You promised you'd spend time with me this afternoon."

"I planned to but it didn't work out …"

"I've heard that before …"

What used to be a situation that Steph manipulated for his amusement now became one-sided pestering. Steph tried to placate Briggs with excuses like, "It was part of my schedule," or throwaway comments like, "Pressures of stardom, Briggs." Then it heated up to, "You were watching us? My God, what's happened to you? You're obsessed."

When this had no effect, Steph began to actively dislike him.

"Jesus, Devon, here comes Zitface, how am I going to get rid of him?"

Two weeks out from the opening night, a drama camp was organized at the school's lodge on Motutapu Island in the Hauraki Gulf. This was normally used by the PE department for leadership training but it had a large common room which they would use for rehearsals.

On Friday morning a specially chartered ferry waited for them at the city wharf. Willie went and sat up in the bow of the boat taking the opportunity to smoke incessantly and otherwise abandon the normal "duties of office".

Everyone was wearing mufti and Devon was amazed at how the girls had transformed themselves. Vanessa and Sina waved them over. They wore the standard low-cut jeans and tight tops, but added to this was the jewelery and make-up. With the new look came a heightened gregariousness. They teased Devon about his battered HDT jacket. Boguns were open season for theatrical types. Steph's striped blazer was more enigmatic.

"It's the blazer of Dorian Gray. I am actually one hundred and thirty-seven years old."

A fresh breeze sprung up once they cleared the harbor and the stocky little craft began to dip and pitch in the chop of open water. Vanessa squealed and snuggled in next to Devon. He slipped his arm along the back of the seat, careful not to touch her exposed skin. As the city grew smaller, his thoughts went back to Tania. The rules of engagement were so different here. Back in Wiremu's bathroom a decision had been made and what followed was as irreversible as plunging off a rock into a deep pool. What was happening here was not unlike the opening moves of a chess game. Pawn to knight four. Your move.

It wasn't long before Briggs appeared and heaved himself onto an adjacent bench. As the other four chatted away he tried to join in but his comments were lame and poorly judged. There was something forced about him, a change in his demeanor that made him seem almost fierce now. After a while he gave up speaking and followed their remarks with a fixed, humorless grin.

By the time they cleared the rugged perimeter of Rangitoto, the quiet bay on Motutapu came into view.

It looked vaguely familiar because of camp photos which were always part of the school magazine. There was a large central block which housed the kitchen and games room and two radiating wings which became the girls' and the boys' wings. Behind it were tall macrocarpa trees and the ropes and ladders of the confidence course. The little bay was such a tranquil contrast with their bumpy passage that everyone stood up and moved to the front as the ferry glided into the wharf.

No one was allowed into the dorm area until everything had been carried up from the ferry to the cook house. Here it was sorted into food, musical/dramatic materials, and personal belongings. Everyone sat around the long tables waiting for Willie and DD to give some instruction. When they re-entered, after a lengthy debrief on the deck, it was obvious who was in charge.

"Now that we've arrived, without incident," DD began, "it's time to spell out a few local rules …"

Willie sat with the boys, grinning while DD, rising to the new role of Camp Commandant, gave a lengthy oration about her expectations for the weekend.

"She's channeling Demi Moore from *G.I. Jane*," Steph muttered to Devon after one particularly stagey turn of phrase.

In essence the message was: no sex, no drugs, work hard, no bitchin', no swimming without supervision, everyone pitches in, no sex, no practical jokes, no drugs, no telling tales out of school, no nocturnal highjinks and of course no sex.

For the first time it dawned on Devon that sex was a real possibility this weekend.

There were six rooms in each wing, each containing four bunk beds. Willie chose the one nearest to the common room; Devon and Steph took the one at the far end looking out to sea. They had no sooner dumped their stuff on the beds than Briggs appeared in the doorway.

"So that's where you're going. I'll take this one."

"I thought you would go in with Matt Rogers or Willie maybe." Steph's tone seemed imploring.

"Yeah? No way. I see enough of Matt at school and Willie ... I wouldn't share a bus with him."

Steph looked at Devon and rolled his eyes. There was nothing to be done now but endure it.

Before long a bugle sounded and everyone headed back to the big room. Willie was holding a battered old trumpet he seemed to have brought specifically for camp. DD had a plan for the day that accounted for most of their time until ten-thirty that night. They were put into teams for most activities and Devon was pleased to note that Briggs was not in any of their groups, other than in a supervisory role in the kitchen.

After this, Willie assembled his keyboard and was soon absorbed, rehearsing the musical numbers. DD took the remainder of the students outside to the climbing frames where she had blocked out the shape of a stage for the rehearsal of set pieces. Devon, who was without Steph for most of the day's activities, found himself pairing off with Vanessa. After the first hour their awkwardness had gone and he felt easy in her company. He had not realized how demanding Steph had become. Vanessa was altogether lighter, less complicated company. By the afternoon she was leaning on him, grabbing his arm as they went off to do things, and messing up his hair when he became vague or dreamy. She hadn't arrived in his life like an express train, the way Tania had. This was altogether more gentle. He was gradually warming to her, like sun emerging from a cloud.

Vanessa was from Northland. Her parents had sent her to SLAGS because they were worried about the effect the local girls' school would have on her.

"It's all sex, drugs and hairdos ... broken up with fights."

She wanted to know more about Devon.

"Don't you miss your grandfather?"

"What's your sister into?"

"When are you going back home next?"

The questions tugged at him. He wasn't ready for this. They stirred up feelings that he kept buried and he was unwilling to tell her any more than vague details. His family was a book that he did not want to open so he had invented a simple gloss that satisfied the inquiries of most people.

They had an hour or so before the evening activities and games began. Willie dropped by to see if anyone wanted to go for a swim. As soon as Briggs dismissed the idea as ridiculous, Steph agreed. The two of them made off before Briggs had a chance to change his mind. Devon lay on his bunk, aware of Briggs's tormented presence below him. He tried to ignore it but it was impossible, so he swung down and left the little room without a word.

Outside there was nobody to be seen. He could hear the buzz, and occasional squawk, of the others emanating from the bunk rooms. He climbed up onto the headland to see where Willie and Steph might be swimming but there was no sign of them. He knew what that meant and was glad he hadn't gone with them. The next bay had been fenced off and an attempt made to replant the native forest. The tallest trees were just above head height and had already attracted the attention of a couple of noisy tuis. Out beyond the bay the sea was a sheet of beaten tin and tall grey clouds billowed above it in the darkening sky.

The hand lightly touching his shoulder produced an involuntary yelp. It was Vanessa.

"I saw you heading over the hill and thought I better follow you. Remember what DD said. 'We must always have a buddy.'" She crouched beside him with a possibly ironic grin on her face.

"Hi, buddy," he said, and leaned over, kissing her fleetingly on the mouth.

It was sudden and unexpected. They both pulled away briefly and then came together again. This time the kiss was long, hard and deliberate. She leaned across in front of him, placing one hand on his cheek and the other on his shoulder. He could smell her hair as it tickled his face and slowly lay back, drawing her onto him. They continued to kiss as he slipped his hand inside her blouse, feeling the smooth skin, the delicate undulations of her ribs, her bra straps, and then, because he encountered no resistance, the lacy bulk of her breasts.

Their mouths parted again, and still gasping, they stared into each other's eyes. Nothing was said; there was nothing to say. When they kissed again, this time slowly, more carefully, he was able to fumble free the buttons of her blouse and she lifted herself clear to help his urgent caress. His cock, which had hardened at the first kiss, now felt her hand tighten around it. What had strained awkwardly in the folds of his jeans now straightened to her touch. His mouth found her nipple as he felt her hand slip inside his zip. There were a few moments of exquisite pleasure before he came with a shuddering gasp inside his underpants. The ecstatic release immediately mutated into disappointment. The moment, the opportunity, had come and gone so quickly.

"I've come …"

"I know," she replied. "Is that good?"

"Mmm, but I wanted … I wanted to do it."

She looked almost sorry for him. "Boys must have fun, but girls must be careful." Then she laughed.

"We'd better head back. Don't want to be noticed." She leaned over and kissed him on the tip of the nose and then stood up, refastening her blouse.

He lay there a moment, aware only of the soggy mess inside his pants, wondering if it showed through.

"Come on, Devon. I'll go back first. You follow in a few minutes."

By the time he cleared the hill she was already back in the bunk rooms. He stood on the ridge amongst the whispering trees and looked down at the camp which was melting in the gloom. Everything looked different now. He knew it was different. He could smell the sharp salty air wafting up from the rocks exposed by the low tide. Above him a slew of white stars showed through a break in the clouds. He had the feeling that the universe had paused momentarily in the midst of huge change and he was able to view it in detail, like the photograph of a breaking wave revealing the impossible geometry of every viscous curve.

Around the point at the end of the bay he saw two figures picked out against the dull silver of the sea. They were holding hands but stopped as they clambered over the last of the rocks. One of them laughed. It was Willie.

Devon stumbled down the hill. He felt his breath returning and gathered speed as he ran down across the confidence course. Willie had gone on up to the big room where DD was organizing the dinner team and Devon was able to startle Steph by grabbing him as he reached for the door.

"Jesus! Devon, you nearly gave me a heart attack sneaking around here like that."

"I've been out looking for you."

Steph turned. "Why? You knew where I was going. And what's it got to do …" And then, sensing Devon's disappointment, he touched his face and added, "Just payin' ma dues," his voice little more than a whisper.

"Oh, whatever," Devon said. "I don't care what you do, Steph, I just … I just couldn't stand being in that little room with Briggs by myself."

When they re-entered the bunk room, Briggs lay on the bed, eyes closed and iPod blasting in his ears.

Steph turned to Devon. "He's a worry." Then he smiled and added, "Might have to kill him soon."

It was one of those throwaway comments Steph specialized in. A bit scary.

Briggs pulled an earphone from one ear. "What was that?"

"I was just saying you looked so relaxed."

Soon the little bell that signaled dinner sounded. Steph gave Briggs a hard jolt on the side of the head and he sat up angrily, pulling the earplugs out.

"Sorry, Briggsy. I told you three times. Dinner. Dinner. Dinner."

Steph had an innocent look but Devon knew he was being malicious. While Briggs was getting organized, Steph made a "come this way" gesture with his eyes and Devon followed him quickly outside into the darkness. He could feel his arm being tugged in the opposite direction, down towards the water's edge. In the shadow of two large rocks, Steph produced a joint and lit up.

"Come on, Devon, it softens everything."

Devon made do with a single toke; it popped and spluttered as the seeds caught. There was an instant roaring in his ears. Later, as they headed up to the cook house, Devon had to steady himself by holding a fistful of Steph's jacket.

Devon found himself sandwiched between Sina and Vanessa. For a while all the rivalries and worries of school seemed pleasantly distanced as he mellowed out and voices mutated into noise. He began to focus on simple things. Just being there, buried in the group, his thin-skinned individuality sublimated in the noisy throng.

After dinner, a game of charades was organized and this time Devon found himself in a team consisting mostly of girls. The only one he knew was Sina. The teams took turns choosing a delegate from another team to act out a song or book title for the others. DD was the timer and Willie was supposed to ensure that no cheating took place.

After a few rounds everyone had a basic grasp of mimed vocabulary and so the challenges got more difficult. The material was extended to TV shows, sayings, and even random sentences. Sina was able to achieve 'Sex in the City' in less than fifteen seconds. Devon was pleased that the others in his group were far keener than he was to accept the acting challenge; the grass he'd smoked had made him a bit self-conscious and paranoid. This was not the case with Steph. It was as though games like this had been devised with him in mind.

After a while the players in the other teams sensed that Devon wasn't involving himself. A challenge with his name was scribbled out: 'My Humps' by the Black Eyed Peas. He was still wondering how to play this title when DD announced that she was retiring for the night, and perhaps charades had run its course.

Willie decided to take over. He dragged his electronic piano into the center of the seating area and tried to run through a few of the songs from the show. No one was interested; they wanted karaoke. Steph came over and joined Devon again, his face now flushed by his exertions. Devon said he wanted to go to bed but Steph wouldn't hear of it.

"Take this," he said, proffering a little orange pill.

"What is it? Where did this come from?"

"It's E, from Willie's little box of tricks."

"Did he give you this?" asked Devon, incredulous.

"Not exactly," said Steph with a cackle. "But he knows I've got them. That's why our team won every charade. Our performance was drug-assisted. Go on, take one."

Just as Devon swallowed the Ecstasy, Briggs's head appeared through the gap. "What's that?"

"E. Want some?" said Steph, without hesitation.

"I … I don't think so …"

"You're so boring, Briggs, you wonder why I never want to be with you … there's your answer."

Devon watched Briggs, fascinated as his resistance melted and he obediently dropped the orange pill.

"Happy now, Steph?"

"Oh, I'm always happy, Briggs. I find everything sooo hilarious."

Steph jumped up and went over to where Vanessa sat. After some consultation, the two of them approached Willie to see if he could play their request. Devon recognized it from a DVD that Steph owned. It was *Diamonds Are a Girl's Best Friend*, sung in the manner of Marilyn Monroe. The singing seemed just a pretext to work the room as the two of them systematically slithered their way through the audience, finishing up on each side of Devon, roughing his hair and blowing in his ear. Across the room, Devon could see Sina, glaring at him. He wondered what had been said, what was going on between the two girls.

After this, Willie belted out a series of loud and fast rock and roll pieces which had everyone on their feet and dancing. Everyone except

Briggs, that is, who sulked in a corner, his face turning progressively redder as the pill worked its magic.

"Come on Briggs, dance it off," called Devon, but it was no good: he seemed determined to stay sullenly slumped where he was.

Someone fed some house music through the amp and the next thing they knew Willie was in amongst them trying to out-dance everyone on the floor. Devon took his sweat-drenched shirt off and was dueling it out with Sina who seemed determined to keep Vanessa at bay: shouldering her out when she danced near. Willie was dancing with Steph and Snowy Gibson, the youngest boy on the island. The music pumped into the night, while the dancers were corralled into a tight, manic throng.

When the numbers thinned to the hard core of the E-fuelled, Willie suggested that everyone cool off in the sea. The idea of night swimming was so far beyond the acceptable that it hadn't even been raised as a possibility. This meant that it also hadn't been specifically forbidden, so after brief discussion, they all followed him down to shore.

They snuck down through the camp towards the foreshore, their rarefied excitement making it an ordeal of suppressed giggles and shhhhhes as they passed the bunk rooms filled with sleeping students. Finally they were greeted by the dark curve of the bay and stood on the cold sand looking out at the lines of phosphorescence marking each small breaker. Willie, as if sensing that they were waiting for a signal, peeled off what remained of his clothes and charged in ahead. The others followed, but not with the same reckless abandonment. Their white underwear gleamed in the moonlight.

After the initial gasps and squeals, three or four swimmers, having proved their courage, raced back to the bunk rooms, Vanessa among them. The five or six pupils remaining were content to bob about in the dark, soothing water. Sina swam over to where Devon waited and climbed onto his back. She seemed determined to claim him in the on again/off again competition that had started when she tried to keep

Vanessa out of the dance circle. She wrapped her legs around his waist and gripped his shoulders tightly. Devon was surprised at how light she was in the water and wrestled her around until they were facing each other. She hung her head over Devon's shoulder and for a moment they were comfortable, enjoying each other's warmth. Devon could hear Steph and Willie somewhere off to the side, invisible against the dark mass of the headland. On the pier a solitary outline signaled Briggs's presence. He must have gone down to see what he was missing out on.

Devon turned and began to nibble at Sina's neck and earlobe. He could feel himself growing hard again, which surprised him because the water was so cold. Sina pulled away for a moment and then came in to kiss him on the mouth. He wondered what had been said between the two girls. He moved into shallower water until Sina slid lower on his body. In the shallows the steady rise and fall of the water made them rub rhythmically together. Devon sensed her recognition as his cock slid up between their tightly clasped bodies. Even though he had come only hours earlier he knew he could not delay this much longer. He pulled her pants to one side and fumbled for her vagina. He expected resistance but there was none. In a moment he was inside her. She felt hot compared to the water in the bay. He was able to raise and lower her easily in the bobbing water and she gasped in his ear as he drove deeper. This time his overwhelming feeling was one of accomplishment. He wanted to stay there forever; the two of them locked, joined and somehow completed. A moment later he sensed her eagerness to struggle free so he grasped her hips and covered her mouth with his. Her wriggling, his thrusts, her fingernails on his shoulders, his beating heart, all quickly climaxed in an exquisite shuddering burst. "God!" she said and struggled free.

There was a look of panic on Sina's face as she turned towards the shore. He floated dumbly in the shallows, watching her gather her clothes from the shoreline and disappear over the bank. He knew then that he had been wrong. Sina wasn't Tania. Nor was she Vanessa. His rush to "accomplish something" had somehow spoiled the fun he was having. The jump from kid games to adult activity had taken that away. Suddenly he felt regret. It had gone too far, too soon. Something had been broken.

As he hunted for his jeans among the garments scattered along the shoreline, he could hear arguing in the distance. It was Briggs, his voice unnaturally high, almost squeaky. Devon took off his underpants and pulled up his jeans over his wet legs. He could tell there was some sort of show-down brewing.

"You got something against people enjoying themselves ..." Willie was smoking, and looking out to sea.

"... meant to be in charge ..." Briggs was loving the moral high ground. "... I'm going to take this up back at school..."

Then he heard Steph's more measured, calm voice as they came into view. "You're such a jealous, wet-blanket Briggs ... anyway, you took E along with the rest of us. Devon will bear witness to that."

"Yep," said Devon. "But all it did was make his face go red."

"Redder," added Steph. "Just like a ... just like a bumpy old strawberry." He let out a cackle as he enjoyed his image.

"Fuck you, Steph!" Briggs stormed up over the bank.

"Someone should go after him I suppose," said Willie without much enthusiasm.

"Let him go," said Steph, "It's what he always does. That's why he's such a loner ..."

Something inside Devon winced. It was true, but the term "loner" was the ultimate insult at boarding school.

"I thought he was your pal these days, Steph." Willie seemed momentarily interested in boy politics.

"You're right, Willie, he is my pal. Do you know what pal stands for?"

Willie shook his head.

"Personal Arse Licker."

They all laughed. It was the first time Devon had heard that one.

They ambled out to the end of the pier where Willie produced a joint. He lit up, took a deep drag and passed it to Steph. "To tell you the truth," he said, looking out to sea, "I'm a bit sick of this. Sick of the whole school thing." Steph passed the joint to Devon and they both waited for him to continue.

"Don't get me wrong, this week has been fun, but the rest of it … too many rules, too much pretending required. It's just not me. Respectable, responsible, reliable …" He seemed to have run out of 'r' words.

"Call me irresponsible …" said Steph who always seemed to know the lyrics of a song to fill in gaps like these.

"Yes, I'm unreliable …" they both sang along, "but it's, undeniably true …"

"I think I'll quit at the end of the year, flap my wings and fly away."

"What will happen to me?"

Devon was surprised to hear Steph say this. He doubted his sincerity.

Willie looked at him with a grin. "You'll be all right, Steph. You're the ultimate survivor. I am not so sure about young Devon here."

Steph threw his skinny arm over Devon's shoulder. "He'll be all right. He'll have me to look after him." Devon laughed, but he knew all too well that it was true.

When they got back to their bunk room they found that Briggs had moved out. There was a note on Steph's bed.

He read it out.

"Dear Steph,

I used to believe we were friends, that we cared about each other. I know I did. Now I don't understand you. Since you have been with Willie you have turned into a cunt. There's no other word for it. Although it's difficult I am going to have nothing to do with you from now on.

Your (ex) friend,

Barry Briggs."

Steph looked up, with a twinkle in his eye. "I'm a cunt, Devon.

There's no other word for it."

"Well, I like cunts Steph, I have to tell you."

Steph put his hand on his chin, in a mock-reflective pose. "Hmm, I'm going to have to get to the bottom of what that means."

He struck the pose of a comic-strip superhero about to depart on a mission. "But first, I have work to do …." He sprang out the door and disappeared down the hall.

Devon, by this stage, was so exhausted that he didn't even have time to speculate over where Steph was going before he dropped into a deep sleep.

When he woke in the morning, his hair was stiff with salt water. He could hear Steph snuffling in the bunk below. He squashed a mosquito on the wall next to his face. It left a circle of dark blood. The events of the previous evening had the chaotic intensity of a dream. Too much to make sense of. A year's worth, in just a few hours. He thought of Sina and Vanessa. His sexual encounters. He wondered whether this had been something they planned before they came out (girls were such schemers). Maybe it was a competition between them. And what had Steph been doing with, or to, Willie? Or Briggs for that matter?

He peered over the edge of the bunk. Asleep, Steph looked much younger than fourteen. In full cry, he had the wit and confidence of someone seventeen or more, and by comparison Briggs seemed like a gormless younger brother. Sometimes even Willie seemed younger than Steph. A bit naïve. Steph seemed to be the one in control.

Devon was suddenly reminded of DD's G.I. Jane speech. That had certainly been swept away. How much of what had happened was going to resurface back at school?

It was all too much. He rolled over and went back to sleep.

Some time later, Briggs burst into their room and gave the bunk a boisterous shake. Devon woke with a start, frightened he was going to fall out.

"Oh, Barry!" he heard from below. (It was Steph's "Great Aunt Agatha" voice) "How delightful to see you in a more cheerful frame of mind."

"They called breakfast some time ago. You'd better head up or you'll miss out."

"Thanks, mate. 'Preciate it." His tone had switched to "truck driver" instantly. Steph had retained his ability to think on his feet, even lying in bed after a big drug-fuelled night. Briggs waited for action in the small room, all the time smiling foolishly, as if he was doing his level best to appear cheerful.

"Well, go on up, man. Hold the fort. Tell the troops we'll be on deck presently."

At this Briggs seemed appeased, and disappeared. Devon swung down into the vacant space.

"God, Steph, he's sure changed his tune. I was certain he'd be radioing the police this morning."

"He's a happy camper really; you just have to know where his buttons are."

When they reached the kitchen area everyone seemed to be sniggering and exchanging guilty looks. Everyone that is, except for DD, who was eating her breakfast by herself in the corner. She seemed to be acting out a role. Beyond the "aloof " and the "disapproving" there was also the "hurt and disappointed".

One of the girls told Devon that DD had already made a speech about certain "unscripted activities" that had happened after she had gone to bed last night, and how she had been let down badly by everyone.

"I guess that includes Willie?" Devon asked.

"You bet," she said. "He's crazy. Completely mad."

Devon laughed. "He's a 'no limits' sort of dude all right."

Because the ferry was expected at midday, their main aim for the morning was to return the camp to its pristine condition. Devon was assigned kitchen cleanup and Steph was in charge of mucking out the toilets. Sina was in Devon's group but she seemed unwilling to even look at him, let alone talk to him. Devon polished the stainless steel surfaces and Sina attempted to mop the floor around him. He sensed the growing tension between them. As they were finishing off, when he was leaning right over to get a difficult spot on the bench, she jabbed him up the arse with a mop handle.

"Yeow!" he yelped, turning, "What was that for?"

"For being a wanker." Her voice was cold.

"Sina ..."

She frowned and said nothing, then dropped the mop and flounced off. He wanted to go after her ... talk it through, but he knew it was no good. He had done something last night that wasn't going to be mended with a "chat". He thought of chess again. There were rules to this game all right, and he had violated them.

Once the camp was clean and tidy and all their gear had been stacked on the pier ready for pick-up, they were all called to assemble in the main area. There was to be a meeting.

Something to sum up the camp. They were all given pieces of paper and told to write on these the best and worst things that had happened on the weekend.

For twenty minutes or so there was almost perfect silence as everyone tried to find the language to describe their chosen incidents.

The only ones not writing were DD and Willie.

DD prowled back and forth restlessly in front of the window that looked out onto the bay. Willie ran his fingers silently over the keys of his electronic keyboard which sat unplugged on a table near the door. Devon watched him closely, realizing that Willie could hear all the sounds in his head, and felt envious of his self-sufficiency. The only sounds he could hear were voices telling him he had fucked up. For a moment, even amongst this crowd in the room, he felt completely alone.

"Stop now. The boat is coming!"

They all looked up and sure enough the cabin of the ferry came into view, a kilometre or so beyond the point. DD plucked the lid off a galvanized rubbish tin and wandered around the writers, collecting their papers like votive offer.ings. She placed the lid on the floor in the center of them all and they watched intently, wondering what was going to happen next.

"These are your collected thoughts, recollections, experiences. You have shaped these and committed them to paper. When we do this, we externalize experience, we strive to create a record, a permanent reminder of something fleeting. But these are personal things. They have no business outside yourself, outside your circle of friends nor, most particularly, away from the island. They are marks on the sand and need to be washed away by the incoming tide."

She produced a box of matches from her bag, and with due ceremony set fire to the nest of jottings. There were a few gasps and strangled cries as though something loved was being destroyed. Looks were exchanged. There were calls to mutiny. Quickly the flames grew and a few fragile ashes rose towards the ceiling. Behind the pyre, DD stood guarding, witch-like and waiting for the conflagration to complete itself. Soon all that was left were a few embers, as light and nebulous as the clouds out the window populating the blue expanse over the sea.

A hooter sounded as the ferry slowed for its approach to the pier. Everyone waited for DD's last words.

"If there is one thing I care about above all else, it is the power of drama. Staging a piece like *Original Sin* carries with it a series of responsibilities which far outweigh the hunger for acclaim by individual egos."

She glanced around the room, trying to envelop everyone in her accusation. Devon noted that Willie kept his head low as he played the silent keys of his piano.

"We have two weeks now until first night. We have made enormous progress since that first scruffy audition at Barwell's a month ago, but we still have a long way to go. What is required now is discipline and dedication ... in equal measure. No one is so important that they cannot be replaced, even at this late stage. I will allow no one to jeopardize the success of this show: unlike you people, I have a reputation to maintain."

Her mouth pursed as if she was daring anyone to challenge the statement. "I'm going to make no further reference to what happened last night and I expect you all to follow suit. Now let's go to the boat."

They were a very different crowd on the trip back to the city wharves. Most of the girls sat together in the main cabin, braiding each other's hair, or with head buried in a book, or just gazing blank-eyed across the choppy seas to the rising skyline. Devon thought Steph looked washed out and exhausted. His eyes were red-rimmed, and his face was drained of colour. Willie sat up in the bow with a guitar he had borrowed from one of the girls. He was strumming it Spanish style and the flourishes caught on the wind and bathed them like clouds of spray. Was it the music, or the seemingly unswimmable distance to land, or just his sense of isolation? He couldn't be sure, but something cast Devon's mind back to Diego. He sensed a change coming.

SIXTEEN

The following week there were murmurings "that something happened" at the camp. Devon expected another inquisition like the one resulting from the theft of the money box, but strangely, the events of the island disappeared into their own wake, and everyone did as DD suggested and put all their energies into pulling the show together. The rehearsal schedule was stepped up, meaning that there was something on every night after school. Willie would call for them after dinner and take them across to SLAGS for the scenes they were working on. After that he would return to Barwell's, where he rehearsed the band and the orchestra.

By Wednesday it was clear that there was something wrong with Steph. He was flat and listless on the first two days and soon growing sicker by the hour. On Thursday night he lost his voice and was kept back in the dorms. On Friday the school doctor recommended a couple of days in the Ascot Clinic for tests.

It was odd for Devon, being at school without Steph. He had taken over every corner of his life so completely that there had been no room for his other friends: Mitch hadn't come back to school after the last holidays and he hardly spoke to Wade Royle these days.

He returned gloomily to his pen at the end of school on Friday afternoon, staring into the vacuum of a four-day midterm break. Devon had been given clearance to visit Steph at the clinic but he had no taste for it. He'd had enough of drama, in all its forms, for the time being. Marsden House was almost deserted; the last of the boarders were down in the showers sprucing up before their escape. He was able to wander around its various forbidden zones without any challenge from a territorial senior. It was like being in a dead zone. Even the duty room was deserted. He stood for a moment processing the softly distant sounds, then, on an impulse, he picked up the phone and dialed.

"So what've ya got in mind?" Devon asked Mitch, as Big John edged out into the traffic.

"I plan on groovin' to the chug of four hundred and twenty-seven inches of De-troit muscle." He had this fake tough stress to his voice. Did it quite well too.

"Yeah?"

"Yeah! Mate of mine. You don't know him: Billy Revell. He's shoe-horned this massive mill into an F100."

"That a fact?"

"Yep, got a Hurst shifter and four on the floor, mags up front, chromes down rear. Grunty mother of a beast …"

"Okay, okay, Mitch, don't turn poet on me, I get the picture."

When they reached the Stock Cars they were waved straight through into the pits. Everyone knew Big John. Nearly all the cars were battered and sprayed canary yellow or fire engine red. Some had cartoon characters stenciled on the door: Pistol Pete. Beagle Boyz. Mighty Mouse. It was the only way of telling them apart.

Mitch spotted someone and they headed over to where three guys were all sticking out of different openings of an old Ford Popular.

"Rebel!" Mitch called to a jeans-clad bum hanging out of the engine bay.

"Who dat?"

"It's Mitch, man. I thought you had eyes in your bum."

The guy emerged slowly and the other two also disentangled themselves.

Rebel was a few years older than Mitch and Devon, and he looked like he'd been in a few fights. He had a scar taking off from his top lip that gave him an ironic sneer. What looked like a mole turned out to be a borstal spot, tattooed just below his left eye. The other two looked like dirty photocopies of each other. They were twins.

There was a round of intros where Devon got to shake grease-stained hands. Gaz and Snake. Snake because some punch had turned one tooth into just a sharp fang-like sliver in the front of his mouth. Now he was into snakes; snake rings and bracelet, snakes tattooed around his biceps.

Rebel turned to Gaz. "Look at him, I reckon he's on steroids."

It was true, Devon noted: Mitch was unnaturally muscular for someone his age, but then he always had been. Mitch put his fists up and closed in on Rebel with a few perfectly judged jabs. For a moment they looked like they might exchange real blows, then Rebel backed off.

"Okay, okay, I'm throwing in the towel."

Rebel whipped a dirty rag off the engine block and threw it at Mitch's face.

It was plucked out of the air and immediately flicked on, straight into the unguarded face of Snake.

"So what's up?"

"Throttle linkage snapped on the first lap and we can't fix it so we're stuffed."

"Where's Ray?"

"He's a bit pissed off with me so he's gone off to the beer tent to join the other losers. Might just go cruisin." Then Rebel added, "You guys wanna come?"

"We just got here bro, hardly even seen a race," said Mitch, who turned to Devon.

"What about you, Devon?"

"I'm a starter."

"Youse?" he asked the Taylors.

"We better stay. He's paid us."

"Your call," said Rebel. "Let's go."

Devon wasn't ready for the violence of Rebel's driving. The truck roared and lurched and swung like a bull released from a rodeo pen. It was as though he wanted to kill someone; charging at other cars innocently waiting at the lights only to screech to a halt, inches from their rear bumper. He would pass where there was no room or need to pass, and then cut in sharply. His whole demeanor changed. He was sucking his lips, swinging on the wheel and ramming the gear lever up and down as each red light tormented him into a reluctant halt. The further they went, the more wired he became. Mitch, as if sensing the call, pulled a joint out of his top pocket and lit up. It was a shock to Devon, Mitch carrying weed, a sort of sin against his athleticism. Mitch took two or three quick pulls just to get it going then he passed it on to Rebel. By Devon's turn, all that was left was a tiny, lip-burning roach. Devon, a bit rattled, took it without hesitation. It was one of those times where he'd take anything.

"Where are we going?" Devon whispered to Mitch.

"Thunder Road, I reckon."

This was something that all the boys back at school talked about. The after-hours street racing scene that constantly moved as the police shut it down. A few of the older boys claimed to have been there.

"Yeah, Thunder Road," Rebel said quietly, almost to himself. "Hey, Mitch, pass us that bottle, huh."

Mitch fished the bourbon out of the glove box and Rebel had a drawn-out chug. Then another. Then he threw the bottle out the window. It smashed against the door of a parked car on the far side of the street.

"Yee ha!" he yelled then looked back at Devon and Mitch.

"Direct hit. Skills."

They headed out to the 'burbs where flimsy houses gave way to chain link fences, huge metal sheds, and streets with no cars. Then they came to a section of new roads and half-built factories. There were cars all over the road and groups of guys parked in clusters, waiting for something to happen. Rebel slowed right to a crawl, looking for someone he knew. Near the intersection there was a maroon Holden Maloo with three people in the tray. It had a chrome roll bar above the cab with six square spotlights mounted on it. When they saw Rebel's F100 approaching, someone yelled and a moment later Devon was dazzled by a soup of white light.

"Fuck!" said Mitch. "Blind us, why don't cha."

As they slid in to the curb, Rebel mumbled, "Two cheers for Baldy Brown."

They all piled out and it was some time before Devon's eyes recovered sufficiently from the lights to be able to see who was in and around the ute.

Mitch and Devon stood off a bit while Rebel went in to connect with the others. There was a huge guy wearing a Holden T-shirt and a leather hat. He clambered off the tray and locked Rebel in the bro handshake. Rebel had a boxer physique — big chest and arms — but still the other guy was several sizes bigger. While their hands were locked together there was a short sharp assessment of each other, as if they could break and start swinging at that point. Rebel, though smaller, seemed fiercer, more fired up.

After a moment he turned to them and said, "This is Breaker, Breaker Brown." And then to Breaker he said, "Mitch and Devon. My little buddies. My apprentices."

Breaker, for his part, flicked them a bored nod and then turned away, hanging over the tray of the ute and staring into the distance. The other two declined to climb down.

Rebel continued. "These two, Martin and Gail, give us the grunt and the glitter." He pointed to the scrolled paintwork on the front. "See this: 'Mother truckers'. That's Gail's work. She's doin' a Midnight Autos one for me, eh Gail?"

Gail looked at him for a while. "Maybe." And then she said, "When you come through with some stuff."

"Ah yeah. You know I'm working on it."

Gail looked at Devon. "That's what he always says."

"This is Martin. He's a poet, and he sings a bit." Mitch grinned. "Specially after he's been tokin'. Hard part is to get him to stop singin' but what he's really good at, like he's da bomb around these parts, is makin' a motor sing."

Martin was a bit more gallant and shook both the boys' hands.

"You boys at school?" It was Gail.

"Was," said Mitch, proudly. "He's trying to escape." Then he turned to Breaker. "What's happenin' on the strip? Looks dead to it."

"You're right with that one. We was hoping to do some business but so far it's just DCs and chinks."

"Business … shee-it!" Rebel spat out the words. "I wanted to race someone. You're the only ute here, Breaker, and I know I can whip your arse. No sweat."

At last Breaker turned and looked back at the group. "Like, sure thing Rebel. My arse would be the only thing you'd be seein'."

Just then an old Falcon rounded the corner and all their heads turned simultaneously.

"Here's the man!" It was Gail, her voice taking on a sparky energy that had been absent earlier. The four older people sauntered across the road to where the car had pulled up, leaving Mitch and Devon by the two utes.

"What's that all about?" asked Devon.

"What do you think? Santa's arrived," said Mitch, and then added, "It's their friggin' dealer, man. That's what they're into. Well, the other three anyway. I reckon Rebel's still your true car man."

Devon and Mitch stood aside, watching the others doing the "try before you buy" tokes. It was impossible to see who was in the car,

other than the fact that there were two of them. At one stage Gail broke
into a sustained coughing fit but this didn't stop her; it seemed to make
her determined to score as much smoke as she could.

When it was over they staggered back to their car, clearly wasted.
Rebel was wobbly, and sort of excited, but the other three were all in
their own little spaces.

"Let's get out of here," said Rebel to Mitch. "We'll head back to
Martin's." It was clear he was fired up and wanted to go somewhere —
anywhere.

He turned and yelled, "Hey, Baldy!"

"Fuck you, Rebel."

"Sorry, I meant Breaker. It's just the dope talkin'. You okay behind
the wheel?"

"I can't see the wheel."

"Same. That's some wicked weed. These two are still straight as.
They can steer us back to Parnell."

"You're on." No more than a mutter. Breaker was out of it.

Rebel tossed his keys to Devon, and Mitch climbed into the Maloo.
Devon had only driven on the empty Coast highway, not here in the
city full of cops and lanes and rules. He wanted to wriggle out of it,
make some excuse. But he knew he couldn't. It was never an option.
Rebel just assumed he could drive. Rebel rated him. It was a chance to
prove himself. Show that he was man enough.

Devon slid in behind the wheel. The seat was lower than he was
used to. Pike's van made you sit up high and kind of lean forward. He
fired up the motor which released a throaty roar that made the others'
heads turn.

"Taste it! Taste my bum chuckle, Breaker?" Rebel yelled out the
window, taunting. "It's the Ford song."

In the Maloo, Mitch did the same, and for a minute or so they
exchanged engine roars.

"Cut it, Devon," said Rebel, and then added, "Revving's just a wank
when you do it too much."

Devon eased the T-bar into drive with a slight jerking clunk, and then the beast crept forward. The power made him sit up and take notice. He could feel every cell in his body coming alive. Becoming attuned to the task at hand. Then he knew this was what he had been waiting for.

Mitch nosed in front with the devil horn salute and Devon was content to follow along behind. They hadn't gone a hundred metres when Mitch planted the accelerator and the Maloo began to shrink in the distance.

"What are you doing, Devon?"

"Huh?"

"You gonna let him do that to ya?"

"No fucking way, man," he said, and floored the gas pedal.

Before long they were bumper to bumper again.

"Take him man. It's just Baldy Brown's heap."

Rebel wound up AC/DC on the system. Devon felt the bass drivers punching out *Highway to Hell* in the small of his back.

There was a long straight ahead where the roads went across open country to the next link to the motorway. Devon pulled out and drew level. For a moment they stuck there, mirror to mirror, no more than a foot apart. Devon glanced across to see Mitch low in the seat, eyes glued to the road ahead.

A car loomed up in front, heading towards them. Devon knew he had to hold his ground and prayed that Mitch would back off. But there was no sign of that happening. The other car began flashing its lights, but a moment later took off into the long grass on the side of the road, horn blaring.

By this stage Devon had passed the one hundred and sixty k mark and he could feel the power in the motor begin to flatten out. There was not much left to pass with. Up ahead, a big sign signaled an intersection. He flicked a glance at Rebel. Slumped in his seat, feet up on the dash, his eyes were tight shut as he grooved on the music. The decision was all Devon's. Ahead was certain humiliation. A back down.

He was the "boy". Worse than that. "Chicken".

His hands clenched and he pushed down with his foot as hard as he could. Up ahead car lights swished across the intersection. He was committed: nothing could stop him now. Out the passenger window, Devon sensed more than saw Mitch brake hard — then rapidly fall behind in the rearview mirror. He was backing off while he still could. Off to the right, Devon could see an eighteen-wheel tanker coming to meet him. Every sinew in his body was taut as a guitar string. All he could see was the safety of the far side, the empty road leading away, filling his vision like something viewed through a glass tunnel. His hands tightened still more, his eyes screwed up to slits as he hunched, ready for the massive impact.

There was the huge blare of the truck's hooter and Rebel opened his eyes. At the same moment they flashed through the intersection, just clearing the front of the braking Kenworth truck, and then shot through to the glorious empty road beyond.

For a moment it happened: a lightness, like he was floating, like he was a million miles away, watching himself in a movie. Every thought, every little worry, the countless strings that held him down were snipped and nothing mattered. It was all a game.

"Sheee-it! That was close." It was Rebel.

Devon felt himself settling gently back into his old skin again.

"I had it covered." He could smell the salty tang of his own sweat.

"Still ..."

"You told me to take him. I took him."

"Yeah," Rebel said with a sigh. "Yeah, you did."

And that was it.

They slowed down to the crawl that was ninety ks. They were nearly at the motorway by the time Mitch closed in behind them. He flashed the rack of spots on the roll bar. It was like being on the stage ... being called for a bow.

When they arrived at Parnell, Rebel directed him to a little street where the houses and apartments gave way to office buildings.

"There it is."

On one side there was a big apartment building, on the other, a construction site. The house had been left, waiting for the right offer to come along so they could tear it down and throw up a high rise. The yard was wall-to-wall cars, some fully intact, others partly dismembered, some stacked, some on their sides: there must have been twenty or more. Nearly all of them were Subarus.

"Shit, what a lot of cars!"

Lights flashed at the corner and Rebel glanced back. "Here comes Baldy Brown."

He threw his arm across Devon's shoulders and marched him along to where the others were still clambering out of the cab.

"Did you see my boy here? So who's got balls, huh? Who's got them?"

Mitch came dancing up to him.

"What were you doing, man? Were you mad? That tanker ... far out. Talk about close."

They all wandered down to the door of the little house. Martin fumbled for the keys, then threw the door open with a flourish.

"Mi casa es su casa."

"Back at ya, Martin." Rebel turned to the others as they went in. "He thinks if he says it in wog we'll all be impressed."

"It's all wog to you, Rebel." Gail had had enough of him.

"Spicks and sprouts, wogs and frogs, they're all slimy cunts ... make crap cars. Cars for poofs."

Gail just shook her head and ignored him.

Somewhere in the house Martin kicked the sound system into action. There was a table in the kitchen but otherwise just one chair and a broken stool, and mattresses on the floor in the lounge. Dirty plates and glasses filled the sink, and takeaway containers spewed out from a black garbage sack in the kitchen. Breaker passed Devon a joint and from then on everything took on a different perspective, like he was trapped in somebody else's dream and he felt slightly panicky. He followed Mitch into the lounge.

There was a coffee table and a big TV, and the walls were covered in drawings. Dragons and motor bikes, skulls and angels, flames and blood. The music became impossibly strong and rich and the dope made the images seem to pulse and slither around on the wall.

"Who did that?"

"Gail. She's an artist.

"They're cool," he gasped.

"Hey, Gail," Mitch sang out, "Devon likes your art."

Devon felt immediately exposed. Wished he'd never asked. Gail wandered in from the other room and looked at Devon as if for the first time.

"So you like art, Devon?"

"Well, I like yours, I guess."

"You'd be easy. You've got a classical face. Straight off a Greek vase, you are. Mitch, he's more of the common kiwi."

"Oh. Thanks."

She got a piece of charred wood from the fireplace and began to draw. It took a moment to realize what she was doing: the scale of the face was as big as the lid of a rubbish bin. She paced backwards and forwards, creating the outline, carefully positioning the nose, mouth and eyes.

"This is what cave people did. They would go out hunting …" She stopped for a while as she started to work the hair in around the scalp, "Then they'd come back … to their cave … and try to picture what they'd seen."

She was rapidly detailing the nose and eyes. Devon was astonished to see his resemblance emerging in her deft strokes.

"How can you do that?"

She pulled another stick from the fire and using her fingers toned in the peaks and hollows of his face, blurring out the lines and revealing Devon with startling intensity.

"I can do that …" working in a shadow under the chin "… with you keeping still."

"Come on you two, I got a donk to load up for Big John." It was Rebel.

Gail closed in on the detail she was smudging with her thumb around the corner of the mouth, and said quietly, as if to herself, "Poor Rebel, so easily threatened. You can go now Devon, go join the boys."

Devon slunk off with a rueful grin on his face.

Out the back, Martin had a motor dangling from a tripod; off to one side was the Legacy wagon it had come from. They lowered the motor onto a trolley and pushed it out to Rebel's F100. Even with the four of them it was surprisingly heavy. Level with Rebel's ute, they positioned themselves on all sides of the motor to lift it on. There was a piece of carpet in the back and some ropes to tie it down. Devon and Rebel were on one side, Mitch and Martin on the other. Devon watched the flex and bulge of the musculature in Rebel's arms. There was a scary power there, the sort that fighters had.

"Scratch the paint work," said Rebel, as they strained to clear the high sides, "and you're dead."

"Where's Baldy? The one time you need him, he's not here," said Martin as they wandered back to clean the grease off their hands.

"This calls for a brew. Come with me, you two."

"Drink up. I had better be getting you back. Big John will be spinning out."

By the time they got back to the wrecker's yard it was nearly three in the morning. Big John came down to the gate to greet them in his dressing gown. He had the dogs on leads and they were leaping all over the place. He struggled to contain them.

"Jeez, that took a long time. You been pulling it out all night?"

"We got side-tracked." Mitch sounded pretty pleased with himself. "Ended up on Thunder Road."

Big John didn't look pleased.

"Figures." He pulled the gates wide to let the F100 in.

Rebel did a three point turn up near the house so that he could back in to the big tin shed. Big John tied up the dogs and came and stood next to them.

The shed was full of engines and parts with the name and year scrawled on them in white paint. It seemed to Devon much easier this time when the four of them hefted the boxer motor onto a bench.

"I wanted the turbo two point five: What this?"

"It's the new non-turbo version. Almost as powerful. Only ten ks on the clock."

There was a shiny patch on the block which Rebel pointed out. "All ready for you to put your own number onto, then everything's legit."

"Big deal. Whatever happened to getting what you paid for?"

"Midnight Autos is not the Warehouse, man. We got a supply chain made up of broken arses from every lock-up in the country. Most of them can hardly read."

"You're speaking to one."

"No offence, BJ."

"Yeah right!"

Devon saw the uneasiness between them. It seemed that none of Big John's deals were working out. Either that or it was Rebel's cocky manner that gave no quarter to Big John's brusqueness. They all stood around staring at the engine for a while wondering where to go from here. It was like there was unfinished business between Big John and Rebel which wasn't to be discussed while the two younger guys were there.

"Better be off," said Rebel, climbing into the cab of the F100. "Good to see ya," he said to Big John who seemed uninterested.

"Wouldn't wanna be ya," chirped Mitch.

Rebel gave his wolf-grin and gunned the ute down the narrow driveway and out the gate. The sound of its revving motor hung in the still night air long after he had disappeared.

"You can stop clapping now, he's gone." Big John sneered, "He might seem like the goods to you two but I've seen off dozens like him. They pull a few stunts and they think they're King Shit until they drop their guard and someone takes them out." Big John spat in the direction of the departed ute. "His day will come."

SEVENTEEN

School resumed on Wednesday but Devon returned a day early. His pen was empty, and Steph was still holed up in hospital. He wandered over to the FLS. It was wide open and he could hear the sound of a piano coming from one of the practice rooms. There was something familiar about the piece. A sort of angry grace. It was, of course, Briggs. Devon stood staring at the back of his head through the glass panel in the door. After a moment, Briggs stopped suddenly, his fingers resting on the keys and then he turned.

"What are you doing, Devon? Come in."

"Hi, Briggsy. I just got back and I was cruising about, seeing who was here."

"Oh. You mean that you were cruising about looking for Steph?"

"Maybe."

"Well, he's not back from the Ascot yet. He's due tonight some time."

"I never thought he'd be in that long."

Briggs shot him a patronizing stare. "You're so naïve. You and

Steph, both. You think you've got it all sussed but you haven't. Look at him now. A complete mess. Not so cocky.

Everyone says it was stress. I know it was drugs." Then he added, "Something I bet you know all about too."

Devon didn't say anything. He'd tapped into a dammed-up pool of anger and jealousy.

Briggs paused thoughtfully then turned back to Devon. "I remember the day Steph arrived. And you," he added, almost as an after-thought. "There was something innocent about you. Laughter in your eyes, eh. Anyone could see that. Then Willis comes along and spoils it. Spoils everything. You couldn't see it; you were dazzled."

He resumed playing. "You were too young, all excited by Willie's attention. I saw through it because he'd ..." He stopped for a moment or two, composing himself and then tried again, "Because he ..." He dried up. There was something unsayable.

"I don't blame Steph. Not really," said Briggs, "He's only young ..."

He began to tinkle the keys at the same time. "I blame Willis. He's an evil prick and I'm going to take him down."

Devon tried to think of something to say that seemed sympathetic. "Oh well, I guess I'll get over it. You seem okay."

Briggs fixed him with a cold stare and said nothing.

Later that evening Devon was lying in the common room with a few other staybacks when Steph walked in. He was paler and skinnier than before, if that was possible. His eyes seemed to have sunk deep into their dark sockets. Everyone stared at him.

"What's the matter? You all look as though you've seen a ghost."

There was no reply to that. Devon got up and they walked out into the grounds together.

"What happened in hospital?" he asked, feeling a little coy about the past few days.

"You might well ask." It was Steph's great aunt voice. Then he broke back to normal. "It was soo boring. But I did get to talk to a shrink."

"A shrink? Why? You some sort of nutter?"

"Of course I am. Always have been. I didn't need a shrink to tell me that. I was bent since day one." Then he smiled and added, "So are you, Devon. That's why we're mates."

Devon shook his head.

"That's the reason," Steph insisted. "What else have we got in common?"

There was a nastiness coming out in Steph that had usually been directed at other people. It was startling.

"I'm not bent."

"You're not? Oh my God, I must have mistaken you for someone else. What was his name now? Te Arepa! That's right, Te Arepa, from the little town of Whareiti."

"What's got into you, Steph?" Hearing his name spoken by Steph like that, after all this time, was like having icy water thrown in his face. "What are you trying to prove?"

"Where were you?" Steph's voice rose a little. "What happened to you, Devon? I was sick in hospital. I had no one."

"I was at Mitch's place. He invited me and I went. End of story. Get over it." Devon knew he sounded angry and defensive but he didn't care.

"Great!" Steph spat the word. "It's good to know where I stand. When things go wrong for me I don't see you for dust."

"I went out west on an impulse, okay? I didn't know it would stretch out into days. What's wrong with that?"

They stopped on the steps leading up to the headmaster's office.

"What's wrong with that? Let me see," Steph continued, his voice, an angry whisper. "I stuck my neck out for you, Devon. When Hartnell was making your life hell I got rid of him. You couldn't do anything. And Mitch was terrified of him." Then he added, "Wouldn't have had the brain power, anyway."

"You got rid of Hartnell?" Devon's voice was loaded with outrage.

"That's a new one. Hartnell was kicked out for stealing. Couldn't happen to a nicer guy. I didn't see you lift a finger."

There was a tense silence, then Steph spoke slowly and carefully. "Hartnell never stole anything." His tone stopped Devon in his tracks.

"What?"

"I stole that box from Simmonds's office. It was the only way. I can tell you that I had help … and it cost me. Big time."

"How could you do that, and keep it a secret? Someone always talks in this place. It isn't possible."

"Stealing the box wasn't that hard. Maybe getting the key to Simmonds's office too; that cost me a few favors. Loading all the cards onto Hartnell's phone, that was the tricky part."

"What sort of favors?"

"You don't want to know." Steph leaned into his face, "You'd just think I was a bigger sicko than you do now."

There was no answer to that so Devon stayed silent. After a while Steph seemed to perk up and continued.

"But getting to Hartnell's phone up in the seniors' rooms, without being seen. That takes serious Steph skills. Secret agent stuff."

Devon was relieved to see him returning to type, bathing in his own cleverness.

"You remember the night I made Milo for all the seniors? It took hours."

"Yeah, what a suck-up. Not even the third formers would do that unless they were seriously beaten-up on."

"The first person I gave it to was Hartnell. I made it real sweet, to cover up the taste."

"The taste of what?"

"The taste of the five Donormyl pills I'd crushed up."

"What do they do?"

"Well, one makes you sleepy, two and you aren't meant to drive a car. I knew that three would knock out an ox, so I gave him five."

"Shit! You might have killed him!"

"That was always a chance," said Steph, adopting an air of cool detachment. "Anyway, he was out cold on the bed before I had even finished the rounds. Uniform still on. Lights on. Snoring like a pig. I was able to grab his phone and load it up with all the phone cards. Hundreds of bucks worth of talk time."

"What happened to the money?"

"I kept it, except for a couple of twenties I planted in one of his maths books. Still got some of it. I don't do these things for free you know. I'm not the Caped Crusader."

Devon glanced back over his shoulder as if to make sure no one was listening from the top of the steps. It seemed impossible, and yet Steph never told lies. Well, not to him anyway.

"You remember the day he tore your famous HDT jacket? You ended up on the floor with his hands around your throat."

"Yeah. I remember that you didn't do much."

"Do I look like a fighting man to you?" It was a rhetorical question. "I did quite a bit actually, but you didn't see any of it. I made a resolution."

"What was that?"

"I resolved that I would get rid of him, and I accomplished it inside my deadline. I would've loved to have gloated at the time, or at least shared the pleasure, but as you pointed out, this isn't a school where a secret can survive."

"How about these people who helped you? How come they didn't say anything? I can't imagine some senior sticking up for you."

"Briggs was one, and there were others, but none of them knew what I was doing. I had to smokescreen them with other motives. It was complicated, but it came off."

"Jesus, Steph, you did this for me?"

"Hartnell was never my problem. He was yours mostly."

"Was Briggs part of this?"

Steph nodded. "That's why the fallout's coming now. He thinks I owe him, for the rest of my life probably."

Devon was dumbstruck. He had thought that what happened to Hartnell had been pure karma. But now it seemed that it wasn't so, it was a case of Steph intervention. It was hard to credit, looking at him.

So pale, his skin had a transparency like watery milk. You could see the blue veins in his thin neck. Then there was his gentle, girlie manner. Not really the avenging angel. Devon had underestimated him. Sold him short. He felt cheap.

"So what have you been up to at Hoon Central?" asked Steph brightly, as though they had never had their previous talk.

"Nothing much. It was just a chance to get out of here."

This was not the time for bragging detail.

Steph seemed appeased.

"Let's go to Willie's place. Check out the final rehearsal schedules. See what he's been up to."

They headed back across the main football field to the road that led to Willie's flat.

"Do you know how many visitors I had?"

"Nah."

"Just two. Matron and Briggs."

"Big fun, huh? Who was the most boring?"

"There was nothing boring about Briggs." His tone changed. "Have you talked to him recently?"

"Yeah, I was down at the practice rooms this afternoon," Devon said, suddenly visualizing Briggs's tormented face.

"What did he say?"

"Oh, not much. 'Willie's an arsehole. He ruins all the boys, 'specially you, maybe me, and I guess him too.'"

"Yeah? He said much the same to me. But with me he was full of these revenge fantasies. Tying poor Willie up. Driving things up his arse. Yup, he's turning into a fucked-up sicko, first class. But Briggs is not boring." Then Steph added, almost as an afterthought, "I'm scared of him, actually."

"It's just talk," said Devon. But it wasn't like Steph to say he was scared. "He'll get over it. You know what this school is like; the longer the term goes on the worse everyone gets, and by the end everyone is nearly killing each other. Over nothing much, usually. Stir-crazy stuff."

They had to bang loudly on Willie's door because he had the stereo up so loud. The door swung open. Willie seemed relieved to see them.

"Jeez, what a racket. I thought I was being busted by the cops."

He gestured them in and threw himself onto the couch.

"So you're out, Steph? Like Lazarus, risen from the dead." Then he added, as an after-thought, "I would've visited but I'm paranoid about hospitals."

"So it's okay to abandon me? Great. Thanks Willie, I'll remember that when you need some support. It's nice to know who your friends are, in your hour of need. In my case, I guess it's Matron and Briggs."

"Keep away from that one," said Willie. "He's a complete head case. He's progressed from just being a sad youf ... locked in a snot ... to someone who's threatening me with hell and damnation every time he opens his mouth."

"Why's that?" asked Devon. "What have you done?"

Willie and Steph exchanged glances but said nothing.

"That bad, huh? Yeah, he's baying for your blood. I'm just glad he's not after me."

"Thanks, Devon, for those re-assuring words."

Willie fumbled about for his smokes. "I guess that has, in part, led me to my next career move."

"What's that?" Steph seemed genuinely interested.

"I have decided to leave. I'm out of here, I'm gone."

Willie, sensing the boys' unease, broke into song, in an attempt to lighten things up. "I'm goin' where the sun shines brightly, I'm goin' where the skies are blue, I've seen it in the movies ..."

"What? You're just going to walk out on us?" Steph spat the words out..

Willie was unabashed. "Steph, if there's one thing that I have no doubt about it's this: that no matter what happens, you will survive. You'll survive at Barwell's. You'd survive a nuclear holocaust. I reckon you were a hundred years old at birth and you are slowly growing younger."

Steph turned to Devon. "Another one. What did I do to deserve this? Whatever happened to loyalty?"

Devon looked away, wishing he had stayed in the dorms and not got involved in this. He was well out of his depth.

"So what's happening with *Original Sin*, and the choir and all that stuff?"

"That stuff? It seems that *Original Sin* was where it all began to unravel. There's been a shit-storm from what happened on the island. I think that Dianna was a bit naïve in thinking that it would all float away from a pyre on a rubbish tin lid. Still, as Edith Piaf used to sing, 'Non, je ne regrette rien.'"

"What's that in English, Willie? I don't like the rain?"

"Devon!" said Steph, with fake outrage. "Pah-lease."

"Anyway, like I was saying, I reckon by the end of the year, I'm gonesville. Till then I'll just hang in there and try to revert to my low-key, inoffensive self."

"And then where?"

"A friend of mine's got this bar at Noosa Heads. He's been at me to come across since … forever, so … I think it could be a good time for a re-incarnation, this time as the piano man in Queensland."

Steph clammed up, obviously angry.

Willie sprang to his feet. "Well, I'm off to Newmarket to score a Thai takeaway. You two coming?"

Devon looked at his watch and realized that dinner would be finishing in twenty minutes.

"Steph, we should be going. If we miss dinner, then roll call too, there is going to be all sorts of shit happening. I don't think it's a good time to be sticking our heads up at the moment."

But Steph was already somewhere else.

"You go, I've still got stuff to work out here."

It was asking for trouble but this was no time to argue the point. Devon left directly and jogged all the way back to school, arriving minutes before the kitchen closed and he missed the check-off. It was spaghetti and meatballs, standard back-to-school fare. Wade Royle was queuing for seconds.

"Hey Devon! Come and sit with me."

Devon could see Briggs circling and so he decided to stick with Wingnut.

Devon was on the receiving end of an endless description of a rugby match when Briggs came and sat next to him. Devon pretended to be fascinated by every detail but eventually Briggs butted in.

"Where is he?"

"What?"

"You know what I'm talking about. Where's Steph, Devon? Someone saw you two heading off together."

"He's gone to the shops I think. I'm not his secretary."

"Bullshit!" Briggs's face was bright red, which made his acne even more lurid.

"Steady, Briggs" said Devon, shielding his eyes. "They're going to blow." It was the standard anti-Briggs jibe about his acne.

"Fuck you, Devon, y'black cunt," he screamed, then stormed off.

"My God!" said Wade. "What was that all about? He looked as though he was going to kill you. What have you been up to? And where is Steph, anyway?"

"Yeah, well Wade, I've only been back in this place a couple of hours and I'm sick of it already."

When Steph did arrive, he got Willie to sign him in at the duty room, went to the prep room looking for Devon.

"I've got a cunning plan. Do you want to hear it?"

Devon was trying to do a week's prep in an hour.

"Fire away but I'll keep working."

"I'll help you with that but I can't talk here ..." Steph made a movement with his eyes to where one of the uni student tutors, supposedly supervising, was playing with a PSP.

They wandered down to the pen but it was no good there because Wingnut was holding court to some of the other country boys about farm stuff.

"We'll take the laundry bags over." This was a duty for third formers but it had been neglected during the break and sat in huge sacks in the corridor.

They both struggled with the big sack down through the duty room where they met with Mr. Simmonds.

"What's this? Attempting to lay up a few brownie points?"

"You know me, Mr. Simmonds. Always eager to please."

The irony on both sides was not something Devon felt like participating in.

Simmonds held the door open for them and they struggled out into the quad. It was dark, quiet and deserted so they sat on one of the benches outside the laundry.

"It's Briggs," said Steph. "It seems he's gone completely bonkers."

"Tell me about it. I had a row with him in the dining room. Over you, by the way."

"How so?"

"He demanded to know where you were. I was talking to Wingnut. I wasn't going to tell him anything. I made the volcano joke and he went berserk."

"Yeah? Well, it seems that he's launched a jihad and Willie's on the receiving end. Willie's actually scared." As Steph was, clearly. "That's why Willie's packing it in. That's what's behind the Australia thing. I'm going to have to do something about Briggs."

"Like what? Kill him?"

"Maybe. But I'll try money first. You know he's really poor?"

"I think everyone in the school knows that. It's a running joke."

"Well, I have a slush fund that I've never got round to spending. I'm going to see if I can put it to good use."

"You are going to buy his silence?"

"Something like that. Let's get back. I don't want Simmonds on my case."

For the next few days things seemed normal, or as normal as could be expected. Steph made sure that Devon's homework was of a high, but believably high, standard. Devon wanted nothing else but to get lost in the safety of school work for a while. Briggs kept away from the pair of them.

Then it was the final dress rehearsal for *Original Sin*.

For a while everything seemed calmer and less pressured than it had been before the midterm break. Dianna resumed control, and this time over the whole production, with Willie acting as music director only.

The first inkling of suspicion Devon had that something weird was happening was when he noticed that Briggs had taken to wearing Armani aftershave. Most of the guys at Barwell's wore Lynx or one of the cheaper brands with movie star names, but Briggs had a fancy spray bottle which he carried in his pocket. At first there was a wave of envy, because it was well known that expensive aftershaves were babe magnets, but then there were the questions.

Where had it come from? He was famously poor and he sure as hell didn't have any secret admirers. And then there was the way he wore it. He was so strongly scented you could track his progress all over the boarding house. The other boys in the dorm made a point of dropping dead in their tracks whenever he passed. They would lie on their backs and wave their legs in the air like dying flies. Briggs became uncontrollably angry when his exclusive scent was treated like fly spray. The angrier he became, the more determined the others became. A code word was invented and if anyone yelled the word "flies" every.one within earshot would drop to the ground and wave their legs in the air.

All the boys from Marsden House were invited along as audience for the final rehearsal. It was the first time that the wider school would see what they had been working on. By the time Wednesday rolled around there was a festive air. The excitement was heightened by the thought of being in close proximity to the girls. The cast were allowed an early tea so they could go down to the auditorium to have their makeup applied. Willie, who had been a bit subdued, seemed to have found his old exuberance. He wore some sort of antique dinner jacket for the occasion. Dianna was wearing her characteristic black outfit with vivid red shoes.

The entire cast was assembled in the stalls for a pep talk. DD was joined by the headmaster and Mr. Simmonds. The heavy brigade. They gave their brief version of the "you are Barwell's ambassadors" speech, then disappeared. Devon wondered what was up: Marsden House was hardly a public audience.

It wasn't until the performance was about to begin that someone noticed that Briggs was missing. There was an immediate inquisition. He had certainly been seen earlier in the evening but for the last hour or so he had disappeared. Steph put up his hand and said he would go and find him but Willie vetoed the idea.

"No. No one's bigger than the show."

He glanced at Dianna. "We'll start without him. I'll play his part and conduct from the piano stool." He was in no mood to be argued with.

Backstage, Devon saw that Steph was looking anxious and asked if he knew what was going on.

"Oh yes, Briggs has gone mad. I saw it coming but everything that's happened in the past few days has made it worse."

"The Armani …"

"Yeah, that was me. Seemed a good idea at the time but he's become so weird and unpredictable. He's probably fixing bombs to the building as we speak."

The idea had too much credence to be funny.

From in the wings they could hear the overture strike up. The piano piece, in Willie's hands, became more flamboyant than it ever was when Briggs played it, and those waiting to go on slipped into the focused state that distinguishes a performer from someone who is merely "on stage".

By half time there was a heady mist of triumph hanging over everyone. Sure, there had been a few slip-ups and missed cues, but for the first time there was a clear understanding of the power of theatre, and the intense feeling of being part of something spectacular ... of being admired and adored.

The green room was packed to overflowing at half time when Dianna came down to praise them for doing so well and to exhort them to lift their performance even higher in the second half. Devon was sitting with Vanessa and Sina. The awkwardness of their island adventures melted away as they relaxed into the concept of being players in a bigger drama.

As they assembled in the wings for the second half, they became aware that something was happening at front of house. The words weren't clear but the tone carried past the thick curtains. There was an argument going on. Devon peeped out and saw Briggs trying to push Willie off the piano stool.

"This is my part. You're not taking this from me."

"Briggs, you've missed the start and you're holding up the show. Go now. Don't make things worse for yourself."

Voices from the audience of juniors were beginning to yell things out.

"Sit down, Briggs!"

"Don't be a knob!"

"Loser! Loser! Loser!"

Briggs's voice rose to a yell. "You'd like that wouldn't you? You'd like me out of the way so you can do your dirty stuff with whoever you want."

At this point someone in the audience yelled, "Flies!"

Instantly there were boys falling all over the theatre, lining the aisles with their waving, twitching legs and death rattles.

For a while Briggs ignored everything going on around him.

"So you can stick your filthy hands ..."

But gradually it seemed to sink in. He paused mid-sentence and then climbed out of the orchestra pit and, after picking his way through writhing bodies, ran up the endless steps to the exit.

At the doorway he turned for a final high-pitched shriek.

"Fuck you! Fuck you all!" Then he disappeared.

A stunned silence descended over the auditorium. The boys in the audience realized they had gone too far. What they thought was merely ragging had driven Briggs to a state where something terrible might happen. Something for which they might have to accept responsibility. The tormentors looked around nervously, hoping that some adult would wrench back order to the proceedings.

Willie stood up in the pit and announced, "I'm sure he feels much better for having that off his chest, but we have work to do."

He seemed totally unrattled by what had gone on. "Ladies and gentlemen of the orchestra, it's time for a reprise of the overture. On two. One … two …"

Music flooded the auditorium and the second half of the production swung into operation.

Soon after this, Mr. Simmonds and the headmaster reappeared and sat near the back, watching the rest of the show. The second half rolled through flawlessly. The orchestra sounded like something more than they were, the players precise in their every gesture and movement.

At the end of the show the headmaster hurried off, but Mr. Simmonds made a lengthy speech of congratulations, referring to his own formative theatrical experiences when he was merely a "callow youth".

Although the dress rehearsal finished just after ten p.m., it was nearly one a.m. by the time the last of the excited thespians was cleared from the theatre. Steph stayed to the very end, soaking up the adulation and feeding off the waves of excitement generated by his part in this momentous performance.

It was not until they got back to the dorms that they learned about the dramas that had taken place outside the theatre: Briggs's angry histrionics, his fight with one of the other seniors, a fight in which, predictably, he had come off worse. Then there was the bottle of vodka that he had drunk immediately afterwards and finally the arrival of an ambulance which had taken him off to the emergency ward. Everyone was buzzing with excitement.

In Briggs's absence, Neeson was appointed Head of House and fed them regular bulletins about his recovery.

"Briggs has had his stomach pumped."

"Briggs is in the psych ward … with all the loonies."

"Simmonds claims that Briggs is the first genuine suicide attempt on his watch. Man, is he pissed."

"Briggs is being released tomorrow, but he's being kept away from everyone else while they keep him under observation."

It was true. When Briggs returned, he was confined to his room for a number of days. His only visitors were his mother, who came briefly on the first day, staff members, and a man Neeson claimed was an 'Education Department shrink'. It wasn't clear what the fall-out from all this was going to be, but for the days that he was away, a happiness descended over Devon and Steph that was as near to perfection as either of them had ever known.

All the cast were accorded high status, in Steph's case almost hero status. This was unprecedented for an activity that normally carried little kudos at this sports-mad school. It was if single-handedly they had brought about a change in the whole ethos of the school and for a few days the arts were triumphant. Even Mr. Simmonds, who normally adopted a haughty aloofness, was eager to discuss some of the niceties of what he referred to as "the dramaturgy on display".

As the nights progressed, theatrical hugs became the currency backstage, and no one received more of these, from both boys and girls, than Steph. Devon, the lesser player, nevertheless enjoyed the reflected stardom of being in his glittering wake. With each night Steph managed to add more privileges to his star experience. He enlisted a tame third former to act as his personal batman. When he arrived for make-up he was trailed by "my boy Jeremy" who seemed to enjoy the role, carrying a personal effects bag and dressing in similar clothes. Steph had a hauteur which admittedly had always been there but now was exaggerated and came with his carefully crafted "sayings of Steph", plus a full range of personal tics. Devon was given a new nickname, "Helloo Crunty Paws!"; Steph's approval of others was invariably accompanied by "Good idea! I was just about to think of that myself "; and Jeremy was introduced with "You have met my P.S.P.?" "What?" "My pint-sized pal?" All of this was made infinitely more enjoyable thanks to the removal of Briggs from their midst.

On the night of the final performance everyone in the cast only had one thing on their minds. The "After Party". Rumors of the wild abandon at these events made all the other boys desperate to be included. The chance of finally achieving that elusive goal of every Barwell's boy, doing the deed with a SLAGS girl, seemed to be a definite possibility. The girls, it was said, were in such a state that they would give themselves to anyone.

"Anyone?"

"Sure?"

"Me?"

"Why not?"

"A one-legged leper?"

"In with a chance."

"Briggs?"

"Don't even go there."

The momentum gathered by each successive performance meant that the last night was packed out. Many of the boys who had been to the show several times already were now standing up in front of their seats, singing along with the choruses. By the time the last big song came, everyone was on their feet and it had to be performed a number of times as an encore because no one seemed ready to leave the auditorium.

After the show everyone hurried off to the classroom where the post-show feast had been laid out. A number of teachers had been drafted in to act as security and exclude those not in the show. One of these was Mr. Faull, who seemed so excited he failed to note that Steph had smuggled Jeremy in with him.

Once inside, everyone stood around the long tables not hungry or not daring to begin this last part of the theatrical ritual. Vanessa had managed to hook up with Devon while Sina, keeping tight with a different group of girls, just flashed him the occasional evil glare.

"It's holidays soon. My family have a little place at Opoutere. You must come over and stay."

"You reckon?" Devon had no illusions that this was anything more than a drama fling.

"Oh yes, I've told my family about you and they are dying to meet you. Where will you be?"

"I haven't thought about that yet." Then he added, "My family have a little place on the East Coast too."

Suddenly his arm was wrenched out of Vanessa's grip. It was Steph. He hauled him over to a small space away from everyone else.

"Have you seen Willie?" His urgency startled Devon. "Someone said that he went off with the headmaster and another man as soon as the show finished."

Devon looked around. It was true, there was no sign of him. "I'll ask Mr. Faull."

He found Farty standing just inside the door, blocking any further people from coming or going. There was something cold and authoritarian about him now. Not his usual breezy Christian self.

"You don't need to concern yourself with that," he announced, and then noting Devon's disappointment at this brush-off, he leaned over, almost whispering in Devon's ear, "Go off and enjoy the party, Devon. Leave that stuff to the adults."

"What stuff? Is there something happening?"

Mr. Faull looked as though he had already said too much. He glanced around furtively, nodded, and said, "Off you go. Make the most of it."

Devon had the ominous sense that even now, when they were supposedly enjoying the fruits of their success, it was already over.

Across the other side of the room, Steph was forcing chocolate éclairs into Jeremy's mouth, mashing the cream and chocolate all over his face at the same time. Devon longed to rush over, exploding with this new scrap of information, ready to foment a drama after the drama … but he didn't. Something held him back.

Mr. Simmonds appeared at the door and he and Mr. Faull went off together. Devon slipped out behind them, shadowing them as they made their way to the front of the school. In the driveway was a car with its door open and in its lit doorway a man in a suit crouched, muttering into a two-way radio.

Mr. Simmonds and Mr. Faull chatted to the man briefly, then the housemaster walked quickly up the front steps. Devon scampered back as Mr. Faull returned to the party.

Back in the safety of the throng, Devon had to lean against the wall to catch his breath. Through the frenzied mass of feasting cast members, he glimpsed Steph appearing and disappearing. Steph was in his element. This was something he had worked towards, something he was born for. He was gesturing extravagantly, making killer comments, receiving congratulations and tormenting his diminutive understudy. He was a star and all those around him seemed to be glittering and glowing with the light of adulation. Devon looked back at the door as if to run and never stop, but that option no longer existed. Mr. Faull was back on guard. The noise in the room thickened and intensified. The individual voices blended into an indecipherable clamor. Jeremy turned towards him for a moment as if to say something, then went back to stuffing himself at the big table.

"Ting! Ting! Ting! Ting!"

The sharp sound punctured the wall of noise, at first barely audible and then sharp and clear as the voices drained away like water down the plug hole. It was Steph holding a glass aloft and tapping it with a spoon. Next to him stood DD, recently re-coiffed, and ready to wrap up the proceedings.

"Thank you, Steph. Out of chaos comes order."

She looked around, surveying the mess of food and disheveled bodies. "I know you are all excited. I know you are enjoying this feast; my goodness, some of you boys must be feeling sick." She looked at Jeremy who was on the far side of Steph, cream and icing on his face, in his hair, and dusting most of his dark school pullover.

"I don't intend to talk for long ..." But she did. For the next ten minutes or so the cast were regaled with high and low lights from the past few months, with particular attention focused on her part in converting this rough libretto into something that gleamed. As she spoke on, Steph adopted poses of exaggerated interest that provided a visual accompaniment to the laborious detail she wallowed in.

"When I first saw the material I had to work with ..."

"Sometimes the real drama happens behind the scenes ..."

"As for the shenanigans on the mystical island of Motutapu ..."

The room was filled with knowing looks and exaggerated embarrassment.

"I can only compare my dilemma with that of Prospero from Shakespeare's The Tempest, burying our collective transgressions full fathom five ..."

"Now our revels all are ended, so finally, on behalf of myself and Mr. Willis who would have loved to be here with us tonight but has been detained on urgent business ..."

At this moment, Steph seemed to become aware of something. His jaw dropped and his hands came up and hovered around his face. A moment later his wild eyes hunted for Devon.

Meanwhile, his little entourage, still reading his impromptu mimes, all scanned the room, hands on brow as if this was a "searching for Devon" exercise from Theatre Sports.

Dianna's speech ended with everyone thronging in search mode and the noise once again rising to a dense hubbub. By the time Steph located Devon, he was almost frantic.

"What's happened?" Steph asked.

"Farty knows but he's not saying anything, that's why he's on guard here I think. There's a cop car in the driveway ..."

He watched as Steph talked desperately to Mr. Faull. Mr. Simmonds appeared in the doorway, said something to Steph, and then led him away. After this, Devon felt ill. He couldn't eat, or talk, or do anything but worry. He knew now that the ship he had been sailing on all this time was not just doomed, it was already heading straight to the bottom. Then it all ended. The girls were herded together, the boys sent home or back to Marsden House.

Mr. Faull held Devon back until everyone else had left and then led him to the duty room. Mr. Simmonds was waiting in his office.

"Something's happened, Santos, and I believe you're part of it."

EIGHTEEN

He was taken to the headmaster's office. There he was questioned by three men: the headmaster, the school lawyer, and a detective from the youth section of the Newmarket police station. He was asked about money, about the drugs, about whether he had been given vodka by Mr. Willis. About his relationship with Steph and the role he had played in the tormenting of Briggs. He was even asked if he had anything to say about the theft of Mr. Simmonds's money box the previous term.

At first Devon offered full and detailed answers as best he could so that no one else was incriminated, but as the cross-examination began he was exposed. First he was told his story was "inconsistent", and then later, as they grew more impatient, this changed to "liar".

He looked at the clock in the cabinet opposite. It was nearly one-thirty a.m. He was so tired by now, that it was difficult to remember what he had said earlier. Finally the policeman read back his earlier statement slowly and deliberately, pointing out "things just didn't add up".

Devon knew he was beaten. He knew he couldn't hold out for much longer. Silence was his last defense. He folded his arms and stared straight ahead. He refused to answer any questions at all, even mundane ones like, "Would you like some water?" Or, "Would you like to go to bed?"

He could see their frustration mounting. They were tiring too. All he had to do was to stay quiet.

The headmaster began his last gambit. "I have one request for you now and I would like you to think about it, hard and long. Remember in the Bible, John 8, 'the truth will set you free'. You can stay silent, protecting the guilty, the people who have damaged this school and hurt the people in it, or you can speak up."

Devon stared at his feet.

"Speak up and you can stay with us, be one of us, and keep everything you have worked so hard to achieve. Silence will mean that you will leave on Monday for the last time and you will have nothing. All we can do is give you back to your people and say we tried, but it was no good. What do you say to that?"

For a while the only noise was the ticking of the clock. Devon felt the eyes of the three men boring into him. He was sure that in a moment he was going to scream and then the headmaster made a "brushing away" gesture and a noise like the release of steam. The interview was over.

That night, Devon was to sleep in the sick bay: a bleak little room up on the top floor. He was taken to the pens briefly to get his pajamas and a book but he was escorted by Mr. Henderson, the tutor from England. The few boys remaining in pens were fast asleep and all Steph's clothes lay out neatly organised on the bed, as if he might come back at any moment. Where was he? When would he be brought back to the house?

Back in the sick bay, Devon was locked in. He peered out the tiny window above the toilet. Even if he could fit through, the drop to a concrete path below was thirty feet. He wasn't going anywhere. The bed was hard, and had a waterproof sheet that crackled each time he moved. It was impossible to sleep.

He lay there for hours, replaying the events of the last few weeks, going over the details. He had been around Barwell's during crises before, but this was different. Every noise, every stirring in the corridor outside, made him sit up. This surely must be Steph, returned from some prolonged interrogation, triumphant once again. Steph was much too clever to get nailed for this, Devon was certain of that.

The following day was Sunday. He could hear the boys moving around in the corridor. At about nine o'clock there was the sound of a key in the lock. Mr. Henderson, the tutor who had locked him in the previous night, appeared in the doorway.

"You awake, mate?" His English accent was faintly reassuring.

Devon just nodded.

"That's the spirit. Here's your breakfast. You're going to have to stay here a bit longer until all this has been sorted. Okay? Come on through, Jem."

He stepped back and Devon was surprised to see Steph's understudy Jeremy with a tray of breakfast stuff. As he lay the tray on the table next to the bed he appeared to be mouthing something. A single word. Devon had no idea what it was, but it gave him hope.

An hour or so later, Mr. Faull appeared in the door way.

"Come with me now, Devon. It's time."

Devon shook his head.

"Actually Devon, I'm not suggesting. You will come, and you'll come now."

They strode vigorously around the perimeter of the school. The sky was a heavy roof of thick, grey rain cloud and there was not a breath of wind. There were a few people about: some boys practicing place kicks on the rugby field, and farther on, a couple of neighborhood kids doing something behind the gym, who scattered as Faull and Devon approached.

As they neared the chapel it finally began to drizzle.

"Well, look at that, how handy, a chapel that just happened to be here when we needed shelter from the storm."

"I wouldn't call this a storm," said Devon, the effort of speech almost too much for him.

"Oh, but it is, Devon, and you're slap bang in the middle of it."

"Here it comes," thought Devon, "poor old Farty is going to reach out and save my soul."

The interior of the chapel was gloomy and distinctly chilly compared to the air outside. They sat side by side in a pew near the back and said nothing. Slowly Devon's eyes adjusted and he could see flowers on the altar from the morning's service. It occurred to him that he had slept through Sunday chapel. What was that about? Why had no one woken him? Maybe he was already gone, like poor Steph.

After a while, Mr. Faull chuckled. The noise rang out in the quiet space with all the stridency of breaking crockery. Mr. Faull turned to face him with a sort of stupid smile on his face. "I just remembered something that happened to me in this very chapel years ago."

He waited for encouragement to continue, but Devon gave none.

"I was in the choir of Barwell's, like you, but we were a very different sort of outfit in those days. The music teacher was called Mr. Healy and he ruled with a cane and a hymn book. For minor offences, like poor timing or singing out of key, he would sail into our ranks and crack the offending boy on the head with an old edition of Hymns Ancient and Modern." He turned to Devon with a benign grin. "A book we all knew weighed more than two pounds in the hard back edition."

He paused again, waiting for some sign of interest.

"He wasn't the most coordinated of men, Mr. Healy, so often he whacked the wrong head or ended up hitting the tuneless boy on the side of the face. It might seem a bit barbaric to you, but we put up with it."

Pause.

"Do you know why we put up with it?"

"I've no idea," said Devon.

"We put up with it because every fourth Sunday there was a combined service with the girls from Saint Leonard's. You see, Devon, boys were the same then as they are now, and we did the same things."

Devon immediately thought of the things that he and Steph had got up to with Willie and wondered how much Farty had been told.

"Anyway, at the Easter service one year there was a tall Rarotongan girl in the opposite choir stalls. I felt myself overcome by powerful emotions."

Devon and Mr. Faull exchanged looks.

"I wrote a brief note to her during the service on one of the blank pages at the back of my hymn book, and carefully tore it out during the sermon. Towards the end of the service the two choirs combined on the steps facing the congregation for 'Gaudeamus igitur' and I took my chances and passed my note to this girl. What do you think of that?"

"Pretty extreme."

"Sarcasm isn't called for. It was a harmless sort of thing. Wouldn't even raise an eyebrow these days but it was quite out of line, in those times. We were all held back afterwards by Mr. Healy. This usually meant he was going to praise our efforts or give us a few tips. The girls were asked to leave with their teacher, and then Healy stared at me and went white with rage."

Mr. Faull adopted a theatrical voice beginning with little more than a whisper and ending with a roar: "How dare I use the sacred duty of choir for such a carnal purpose? What sort of person would rip a page from a hymn book? Did I have no care for how Barwell's was going to be viewed by the young ladies of Saint Leonard's? Was this a meat market?"

"I don't get that last one."

"Never mind. Next thing, without any warning whatsoever, he had me bend over one of the front pews and he gave me six on the arse. He was furious. It was a crazy rage, no sense in it. He capped it off by having me gated over Easter so I couldn't go home for the hols like the other boys. Do you think that was fair, Devon?"

Devon shook his head wearily, eager for this talk to be wrapped up.

"Neither did I. So I was mooching around the school for a few days, sweeping the driveway and clearing leaves from the bike shed guttering, thinking it was the end of the world when the groundsman, Bill Tucker, came up to me." He changed to a more personal tone. "We were all a bit scared of Bill Tucker because he was an old jail bird and there were rumors that he'd murdered his wife."

Devon was mute.

"Anyway, he came up to me and said this."

Mr. Faull put on some species of English accent unplaceable to Devon.

"Look 'ere lad, I know wot's 'appened, wot's bin did and wot's bin hid. But know this my boy, things like this 'appen to everyone and all ye can do is rise above it. Rise above it, lad."

"What does that mean?"

"It means this isn't a perfect world, there isn't perfect justice, so all you can do is make the most of things. Otherwise you'll roam the world with some great chip on your shoulder. That's been my philosophy ever since. Seize the moment, try to get some pleasure from little things. The things that happen which seem so unfair ... well, maybe they aren't. Sometimes you get nailed for something you never did but other times, maybe you got away with things and no one caught up with you."

They waited for a while after this. Devon knew that this was his cue to open up to Farty and for the two of them to hug and become "mates". But he wouldn't. He was crying out for comfort, for some act of tenderness, but he couldn't do it. It would be crossing the line. Joining "them". Selling out.

"Do you have anything to say, Devon? You're to give up everything, rather than just tell the truth?"

Devon had so much to say, but none of it to this man. Nothing now.

"No one can help you if you don't help yourself. You'd rather throw it all away?" One last desperate attempt.

Devon knew only silence could save him.

Farty sighed and shook his head then the two of them headed back to the main part of the school.

The two of them sat in the outer room. He could hear the muffled sounds of talk in the headmaster's office but it was impossible to work out who it was or what was being said. Next to him Mr. Faull pretended to read some boring-looking education newspaper.

After about ten minutes the big door swung open. Mr. Simmonds stood on the threshold, talking to the headmaster in the body of the office.

"Come through now, Santos, please."

Devon walked through and stood next to one of the big chairs which faced the headmaster's mighty desk. The shiny expanse of polished wood was clear except for a few sheets of paper which the headmaster was busily covering with his angry cursive scrawl. Next to the desk was the man who had been identified as the school lawyer. He looked over Devon with a practiced eye and then handed the headmaster a few pages of typed paper. The head suddenly ceased writing and looked up.

"Santos! I'm not going to exhume every sordid detail of what you've been involved in. I think we have quite enough for our purposes. Mr. Hammond here has prepared a statement I would like you to sign. Do this and it will be an end to the matter."

He passed the paper across to Devon.

"Pick it up. Read it. Then sign it."

Devon picked it up and skimmed the contents. It was a confession to being a party to the supply of drugs (cannabis, ecstasy and GBH) and alcohol (vodka) to other students. It identified "Mr. Willis, recently employed as music master" and another unnamed boy who was the victim of "drink spiking". There was no mention of Steph. When he looked up they were all staring at him.

"What we are looking for here is damage control. Looking at what can be saved. Do you think you can be saved, Santos?"

Devon said nothing and placed the paper carefully on the desk.

"I know what you're thinking, Santos!" the headmaster barked.

Devon was startled back into the moment.

"You're thinking, 'How can I do this and keep my honor? How can I avoid being seen as an informer?' But I tell you, this is not the time for that. The damage is done. All we can hope to achieve now is to purge all the poison from our system. This is a chance to be part of the cure, or part of the poison. Now sign it."

Devon shrugged and looked out the window.

"This is a simple decision: sign it and stay, or, if you refuse to sign, then I am afraid you have to go."

A long minute slid by, then the mood changed to brisk and businesslike.

"I'm not prepared to waste any more time on you. What you have been involved in is a cancer to a school like ours. The only remedy is to cut it out, and that's what we're doing."

There was another period of tense silence. Devon sat absolutely still, barely breathing. Finally the headmaster snapped. When he spoke this time he was shouting.

"We've given you everything we have to offer and you've squandered it on drugs and perversion. All we can do now is give you back to your people. Maybe they can do something with you."

The headmaster looked up at Mr. Faull.

"He will be kept away from the others until we can organize his return. Get him out of here."

NINETEEN

Back in the sick bay his things had all been gathered up in his bag and left by the bed. He tipped everything onto the floor and looked at it. On top of the pile of things was his old Bible. It lay there accusingly. "The truth will set you free." He knew there was no bluffing this time. He was gone. Heading back to Whareiti. Back to Ra. Back to the whole suffocating monotony that the old life represented. But this time it would be different. He would no longer be the "boy of promise" or "the boy who'd save the tribe". Now he would be "the boy who had failed". The one who had lost the scholarship. He could join the other deadbeats and pretend their life was all there was. This was the hand dealt him. He grabbed the Bible and threw it out of the tiny window over the toilet.

The afternoon rolled slowly on into evening. The duty tutors poked their heads through the doorway every hour or so and, as it was beginning to grow dark, Jeremy was escorted in carrying a tray. Macaroni cheese, standard Sunday night fare. Devon peered at him to see if there would be some repeat of the mimed message, but this time he was too closely monitored for that.

Some hours later, Devon had almost dropped off to sleep when he heard something being slid under the door. He turned on the light. It was a phone. He quickly crossed the room and listened at the door but there was no sound outside. He picked up the mobile. It was one of the supermarket jobs that were so common at school. It could be anyone's. He wondered who he was meant to be ringing. There was no one. Maybe it was a gift.

Some hours later Devon was awoken by a buzzing noise. It was the vibration of the phone in silent mode. He looked at his watch. It was after two a.m.

"Hello?"

"Hello, Devon."

"Steph?"

"Of course it's Steph. Who'd you think it was?"

"You sound different. It's the middle of the night."

"Really? It's not even midnight here."

"Where are you ringing from?"

"The airport."

"Auckland airport?"

"No, Melbourne. Tullamarine."

"Oh. That's why it's not so late for you?"

"You're a sharp one."

"Hey, man, I'm half asleep."

"Look, Devon I haven't got much time. I nicked my father's phone during the flight and he's at the airline counter trying to organize a search."

"God you're devious …"

"Flattery will get you nowhere. What's happening your end?"

"I've been expelled. Back to Whareiti tomorrow."

"Where are you now?"

"I'm stuck in this prison called the 'Sick Bay'. They're frightened I'm going to run away. I'm being given back to, in the headmaster's words, 'your people."

"Your people! That's a good one. How did you get the phone then?"

"Someone slid it under the door a few hours ago."

"That was my man Jeremy."

"I guessed, actually."

There was a pause.

"So what's happening to you?"

"Geelong Grammar. Prince Charles's old school. Just outside Melbourne. Nothing but the best for Steph."

"Doesn't sound too bad."

"Gulag Grammar? I loathe it. I never picked my father to do a thing like this. Just goes to show, doesn't it, behind every liberal, there's a Stalin panting to get out."

His tone changed. "Devon, I did everything I could to stop you from copping any flak. At one stage I had all these different groups having a go at me, one after the other, all trying to find out what happened. They had a crime but they had no evidence. They needed a confession. Wanted me to dob in Willie, but I wouldn't. They wanted your head on a plate, too."

"Yeah, I bet."

"I never cracked, Devon. I didn't cry. They really wanted me to. 'Show some remorse, Steph, that's all we need.'" His tone changed to one of outrage. "That was my father saying this, for God's sake, the guy on my side."

"Yeah?" Devon wasn't that surprised.

"'Do a deal: give him up, stop him from ruining other innocent parties like yourself'. That was the cops. They wanted a pederast for the courts. 'Think of your father's reputation. Think of the school. Don't you care?' That was the headmaster. They were relentless but I never broke down. I never cracked. And I kept you out of it."

Devon felt a flush of admiration for Steph's toughness.

"In the end, the deal was done by my father. 'Get Steph well clear and his report card will be unblemished.' Something of that order.

Hypocrites that they are."

"I never knew what happened. I never knew how much they knew. I guessed you hadn't given anyone up," Devon said.

"I didn't want you hurt." Steph paused, and then continued as if feeling his way through difficult emotions. "No matter what else happened, that was not going to be on my conscience. I know that you wouldn't have done half that stuff ... if it hadn't been for me. I feel I screwed everything up for you ... ruined your chances. I know how far you'd come ..."

"Stop it."

"What?"

"Stop feeling sorry for me. I always had a choice. I don't regret anything."

"True?"

"Sure."

"Non, je ne regrette rien. Just like Willis?"

"Oui."

"We never had a chance to get our stories straight before I was, as they say, from Barwell's womb untimely ripped."

"I know," Devon said wistfully, "We never had time for anything."

For a while there was silence.

"When am I going to see you?" Devon asked.

There was another long pause and then Steph came back with a quieter, more serious tone. "I'd like to say soon, or even one day in the distant future, but I've no control over what happens to me. I've traded that much away. Lost it. Everything's stacked against us, Devon. We broke through for a while ... learned what freedom was. It's like we found the window open, climbed out and lived in the real world for a spell ..."

"It was amazing. I knew it couldn't last."

"... and then we were spotted. The window was welded shut and we were locked in again. I can't believe that I'm never going to know that feeling again, or at least not until I'm so old it won't matter." He paused for a moment, then added, "Because I'll be too old to do anything with it."

"Fucken dismal outlook, man."

"It is fucken dismal. I am not going to show it any other way."

"Life's a bitch and then you die?"

"Something like that … but let's hope it's better expressed."

"That's the old Steph, pretentious as ever."

"Someone's got to maintain the standard." He broke into an accent. "It sho' ain't gonna be yo'all. You sound like a country boy."

There was a gap between them, like a departing ship, getting wider by the moment. Devon stared into the void, lost for words. When he eventually spoke he was shocked by the finality of his words and the weakness of his voice.

"I guess this is the point where you say, 'Have a good life.'"

"Is it? Okay, Devon, have a good life."

"Back at ya."

The words resonated in Devon's head. They were just the standard kiss-off but somehow they were true. His life lay before him. He thought of the time, all those years ago, when Ra had put that challenging choice into his head. Had demanded that Devon be the one to decide whether to stay in Whareiti or to plunge into the wine-dark sea of the unknown. He remembered his dream. The tipuna emerging from the darkness, row after row of them, their hands shivering and the whites of their eyes enlarged in pukana. Then the glint of an earring as Diego stepped forward to claim him as one of his own. From that moment, everything had been decided.

He woke early to the sound of bells ringing and boys hurrying off to perform their usual routines. He checked them off as he lay in bed. The wake-up call. The run. The shower. Breakfast. Dorm inspection. Assembly. Then the tutor Henderson appeared, carrying his breakfast.

"I'm sorry about what happened, Devon. You look after yourself, right?"

"Mr. Henderson, can you do me a favor?"

He shrugged. "Sure."

"Could you return this phone to Jeremy? I borrowed it a while back. Keep forgetting to return it. Tell him, thanks."

"No problem," he said, looking almost relieved, and then disappeared.

By the time Mr. Faull appeared Devon was ready to go. He was wearing his jeans and his HDT jacket. He left his uniform on the bed. Someone else could have it. He wasn't taking it with him, that was for sure.

Mr. Faull explained that the task had been given to him to drive Devon to the bus station. This would be Barwell's last contribution to his education: after this he was his grandfather's responsibility. They walked through the dining hall to where the staff parked their cars. Devon carried the same overnight bag he had used when he first came. It was lighter now, he thought.

The white Golf was parked in the lee of the dormitory roof. Mr. Faull popped the hatch for Devon's bag but he declined, preferring to keep it on his knees.

"Suit yourself, it's not a big car though," Mr. Faull said, avoiding all possibility of conflict.

He started the car then turned to Devon.

"This is it then: a sad day."

Devon said nothing, but tightened his grip on the handles of the bag.

"It's hard not to think of what might have been." Mr. Faull engaged reverse and slowly cleared the edge of the building. "But I really do believe that Barwell's has done all it could for you." He straightened up and nosed towards the gateway.

"From here on Devon, there won't be safety nets to catch you if you fall."

The traffic cleared and he swung left towards Newmarket.

"I do hope you have learned something from your experiences. Life's not complicated; it's just a series of choices between right and wrong."

They hadn't gone for more than half a mile when they came to a stop: the morning traffic was banked up ahead; there was some sort of road-works taking place. As they waited in the traffic, Devon unclipped his belt and turned to Mr. Faull.

"I've learned plenty, Mr. Faull, but it all comes down to this: there is freedom and then there is everything else."

He opened the door.

"And today I give away everything else, and I choose freedom."

He stepped out of the car.

"Libertad!" he yelled to the astonished face of his assistant housemaster.

As he closed the door, Devon leaned low to give Mr. Faull a parting wave and then headed back the way they had come. Like Diego, making his first strokes towards an unknown coastline, Devon felt a sudden lightness. The world was waiting for him, and now finally, he was getting closer, one step at a time.

ABOUT THE AUTHOR

Ted Dawe has worked over the years as an insurance clerk, store man, builder's laborer and fitter's mate, and flown hot air balloons over Hyde Park. He's also been a university student, world traveler, high school teacher, and English language teacher. His first novel, *Thunder Road*, won both the Young Adult Fiction section and the Best First Book award at the New Zealand Post Book Awards for Children & Young Adults and will be released by Polis Books. *Into The River* won the Margaret Mahy award, which is "presented annually to a person who has made an especially significant contribution to children's literature, publishing or literacy, and honours New Zealand's leading author for children."

Visit him online at TedDawe.com.

ACKNOWLEDGEMENTS

To Jane Ridall, without whom never a word would be written.

To Emma Neale, so much more than 'just an editor'.

To Penelope Todd, for proofing and taming that wild syntax.

To Ian McLeod and Alison McCallum for mopping up the widows and orphans.

To Barbara Larson, for ploughing through the 800 page early version.

To David (Nguyen Duc Minh), Jane and Rachel for the brilliant cover.

To Renee, for the layout and keying in.

To Oliver, for his smokin' website.

To all those came before, leaving their footprints on that windswept realm; my memory.